COVEN OF MAGIC

BOOK ONE

KRISTIN KOVA

There's a witch killer on the loose, and anyone could be next.

When I find the dead body of a young witch, I somehow become a suspect in her murder. No one cares that I'm innocent—I'm a fae-witch mixed species, and in sleepy Agedale Town, that's a crime in itself.

My only hope of exoneration is Gabi Pride, the newly appointed law enforcement of our supernatural town. The downside? She's my ex-girlfriend.

But proving my innocence is only the tip of the iceberg. If Gabi doesn't act fast, the killer will take another witch's life.

And next time it could be mine.

Fans of urban fantasy with mystery and slow burn LGBT romance will love Joy, a witch firmly out-of-her-depth; Gabi, a determined elven investigator; and their coven of misfit friends.

Buy Coven of Magic to start the supernatural adventure!

Previously published as *Fae Witch* under a different pen name.

Garnet, the healing stone

A clear, red stone that grounds spirit, Garnet can be used to encourage physical and emotional healing.

ONE
JOY

The word *naughty* was carved deep into the girl's cheek, bone-white skin peeling back to expose muscle and bone. Discarded in the sand beside her—and almost worse than the gruesome cut—was the girl's wand. It was slim and ebony and snapped into two pieces, with jagged splinters on the ends.

As soon as Joy Mackenzie registered what she was seeing—the wand, the blood, and the fact that the girl was actually a *corpse*—she skittered away with a cry, tripping over her boots and falling onto her ass on the grassy sand dune. Bile rose into her throat as she looked and *looked* at the girl, unable to tear her eyes away even as her stomach wrenched against her breakfast.

When she spotted the shape from across the beach, Joy presumed it was Old Josie, passed out on the beach again after one too many sherries. Not a dead girl with half her face carved off.

"Oh, god..."

Joy twisted aside as her stomach cramped, bile scorching her throat as she was violently sick into the sand.

Wiping her mouth on the sleeve of her coat and gagging as grains of sand clung to her lips, Joy looked across the beach to the blocky yellow hut of the nature reserve where she worked. It was hard sometimes to separate the structure from the sand dunes that cradled it, but a fat beam of sunlight caught the windows as Joy turned towards the building, like a divine figure sensed her desperation and sent help. But Joy was opening up the reserve today, and it was too early for even the most dedicated beach joggers to be out. There was nobody to help Joy, no one to tell her what to do about the girl rotting in the sand before her.

Clumsy, her eyes fixed on that yellow hut so they didn't return to the dead girl, Joy climbed to her feet, her stomach roiling again as her boots slipped on the sand. What she really wanted was to go home and bolt all her locks. But she couldn't leave the girl, the ... *body*, here. It wasn't right, and Joy had always tried to do the right thing, even if it was diffi-cult and she would probably be sick again.

On her feet, she fumbled in her pocket for her phone and took deep breaths to settle her stomach as she scrolled through her contacts to a number she hadn't used in years.

There hadn't been a murder in this town for as long as Joy had been alive. Back in the seventies, people were killed scarily often, usually the victims of inter-species fights, fae gang wars, or personal grudges—but then Clover Pride, one of the most powerful elves in the North, decreed herself Agedale's law enforcement, later joined by her husband, Bo. Clover had somehow earned respect from *every* species that lived in town, and, with her husband, they were as close as the community came to patrol, investigators, enforcers, and problem solvers all rolled into one.

But Clover Pride died years ago—Joy still remembered the shock and standstill all across Agedale as the news spread—and Bo had been injured on the job, forced to retire a year ago. Now, the closest they came to law enforcement was Head Witch Paulina, the leader of Agedale's only recognised coven, but she cared less about justice than having her every command followed. She was more a politician than a police officer. Joy had known the break-ins would start again, the inter-species spats, but ... *murder*?

With the word cut into the baby-faced teenager's cheek, so fresh and violent in Joy's mind even as she faced away, there was no chance this was an accident.

Joy pulled the collar of her coat—a fluffy, oversized grey thing—further up her neck and ducked against the salty wind as she held her phone to her ear.

"Hi, sorry, it's Joy—Joy Mackenzie. I didn't know who else I should call. I've found a ... there's a girl on the beach near my work, the reserve on the western edge, the yellow one with the solar panels on the roof, and there's—"

"Joy," said Bo Pride calmly. "Breathe. What do you mean there's a girl?"

"She's dead. I mean—I didn't check, I really should have, but I thought it was Josie at first, so I didn't even *think* to check her pulse, but there's ..." Joy took a breath, but it was little more than a scrape of air. How did she explain the word carved into the girl's cheek? Or the gore of half her face hanging off? "I think she's been murdered."

BY THE TIME HELP ARRIVED, Joy had moved a safe distance from the girl, and she had her arms wrapped around herself and her face buried in the sandy marabou of her coat. She couldn't stop shivering, both with the chill howling off the sea and the colder flame of her fear.

At first, Joy saw only one figure: the scarecrow-thin frame of Bo Pride, his dark hair tossed around by the wind and his hands shoved in the pockets of his brown leather jacket. But then the shadow split into two figures, the second in a long, black coat as familiar to Joy as breathing. Her heart leapt before it remembered everything that had happened and sank, her stomach twisting into an even more nauseated pretzel than it had been after seeing the dead witch.

Which was completely mad. She shouldn't feel sicker seeing a living woman than a dead one. And yet she was.

"You're back," Joy rasped when they were both close enough to hear each other. Her eyes appeared to be pinned to Gabriella Pride, refusing to move from her. Although Gabi took the opposite approach, her gaze fixed on the sea, her shoulders ramrod straight, and her lips pressed thin. Joy watched her take a slow breath and hold it before letting it out again, and as aloof as she seemed, Joy knew Gabi was as affected as she was.

"I'm back," Gabi confirmed, without even a hint of a smile. Her eyes drifted to the body across the beach, the witch's purple dress the single point of colour in the sand. "How long ago did you find her?"

Joy swallowed, a lump in her throat as she shrugged. She wanted to say it was because of the horror of the body, but the tears stabbing her eyes were purely because of the distance in Gabi's voice. "I don't know. A few minutes before I called your dad, I think."

At this, Bo—the former Pride—stepped closer and settled an arm across Joy's shoulders, surrounding her with the scent of tobacco and leather. "Let's go make you a cup of tea while Gabi works." It might have been awkward if they'd been strangers, but Joy knew Bo for years. He started angling her towards the primrose sanctuary, but a woman's nasally voice cut through the tiny bit of comfort that had begun to unwind inside Joy.

"Not quite so fast," the voice said. "I want to talk to the suspect."

Joy's shoulders slumped as she turned, all her energy seeming to drain from her as she met the narrowed gaze of Paulina Montgomery, the orange-haired, iron-willed Head Witch of their town. Leader of a coven Joy had been rejected from.

Paulina's status was embroidered in silver thread around the brim of her hat—a sophisticated style instead of the pointed hats of old—and the cuffs and hem of her cloak.

Not good enough for Paulina, for the only officially recognised coven in Agedale, Joy and a group of then-strangers had joined together out of desperation and loneliness to make their own coven. *The* coven, Paulina's coven, welcomed every witch in Agedale to join its twice weekly meetings, except if you were of mixed species, queer, transgender, nonconformist, or just didn't meet Paulina's ideal of the perfect witch. There were over two hundred witches in Agedale, and all but six were part of Paulina's coven. If Joy's dad had still been here, if he'd still been Head Witch, *everyone* would have been accepted. Not that he was a saint —far from it—but at least he wouldn't have kicked Joy out for being both fae and a witch, or Gus for living as male, or Maisie for being cursed into fox form.

Paulina was not a woman to be disrespected or crossed. In Paulina's eyes, Joy had done both simply by existing in the same town as her coven. By being a witch with a fae mother. Or maybe by being the daughter of Todd Mackenzie, her lifelong rival. Or maybe by being pansexual.

Joy was so busy being bitter about her exclusion that it

took a while for Paulina's words to catch up to her. "Suspect?" she gasped, her heart kicking faster in her chest.

"You found the body. For all we know, you killed him." Joy opened her mouth to tell Paulina it was a girl who'd been killed, but she snapped it shut when Paulina's eyes narrowed to slits at the audacity of her considering talking. "Call your boss—you won't be in today." Not giving Joy a single chance to argue, Paulina looked past her to Gabi, emerging from the tent she'd put up while Joy had been talking to Bo. "*Finally*. I want answers. Why's there a dead man on my beach?"

"Girl," Gabi corrected absently. Joy recognised the busy calculation in her eyes, and knew her mind was whirring, making clever connections like she always had.

Bo squeezed Joy's arm and whispered, "Don't worry. She can't lock you up without evidence. Gabi won't let her, and neither will I."

But Paulina was Head Witch—the woman who *ran* Agedale. Everyone knew Paulina could do whatever she wanted without consequences. Joy felt even sicker than before.

She let her eyes wander, and a shock went through her as her eyes accidentally met Gabi's, those same dark brown eyes she'd spent most of her teenage years staring into. Joy froze, her limbs forgetting they were in the middle of trembling.

Gabi Pride stood mere *footsteps* from her, in the same coat as ever but with disposable gloves on her hands. She looked exactly the same as she had six years ago, her straight black hair tied back, her skin pale, and her dark eyes intent. If Joy's voice hadn't dried up, a cry might have fallen out of her mouth. Gabi was back. Really back.

But Gabi wouldn't be happy to see Joy. Her heart shrivelled into a tight ball as she remembered the last time they spoke. She could hear the words of their argument as if it had happened yesterday, not years ago.

"You got everything you need?" Paulina asked Gabi.

"Not even close," Gabi replied in the deep, velvet voice that crushed something deep down in Joy. She sounded *exactly* the same. The same as she had all those times she whispered *I love you*. The same as the last day Joy heard her voice, with grief over her mum an ever-tightening noose around Joy's neck and acid spitting from her in the form of words. Hateful, meaningless words.

"Pride," Paulina barked, turning to Bo. "You take *her* in for questioning while this one gets the evidence."

Joy hunched her shoulders at the hatred in Paulina's voice, but Bo just hugged her tighter, ignoring the pointed look the Head Witch gave to his hand on Joy's arm.

"Not my job," Bo replied with what was probably too wide a smile for the scene on the beach. "Sorry, Paulina. Retired, remember?"

Paulina huffed, her face turning blotchy red. "Fine. Stay here and babysit her instead." She pointed a pudgy finger at Gabi. "Don't go easy on her. This one's got psychopath written all over her. You know what they say about quiet ones, and with her *parentage*..."

Fury coursed through Joy, momentarily erasing everything else. "What about my *parentage?*" she asked before she could stop herself. "You think because I'm a witch and a fae, I'm automatically a murderer?"

"No one thinks that," Gabi spoke before Paulina could. Her voice was soft, calming. So were her eyes when Joy met them. It somehow made her feel worse, to know Gabi didn't *entirely* hate her, not enough to obliterate any sympathy anyway. "But I'd have to interview you no matter what, since you found the body." She flicked a look at Paulina, defiance in the gesture. "You can go now. I've got it covered. And before you warn me to be impartial in my questioning, I'd like to remind you that I've spent the past six years in highly specialised police training. I've had the dubious pleasure of handling three murder cases already."

Paulina's eyes narrowed, her nostrils flaring at the insubordination. "One week, Pride. Remember that." She turned on her silver-heeled boots and trudged up the nearest sand dune, the bottom of her cloak dragging through the sand.

"Stay here with my dad until I'm done," Gabi said. Joy was too distracted by the sudden need to be sick again to realise she was talking to her. "Joy." Gabi's latex-gloved hand lifted as if to touch her but reconsidered; Joy caught it in her peripheral vision and the beach snapped back into focus. She managed to nod.

"Do you need to ... handcuff me?" She couldn't look at Gabi, her eyes instead on the little white tent covering the dead witch. Which wasn't any more reassuring than looking at Gabi.

Gabi sighed. It was such a familiar, frustrated sound that Joy couldn't help but be a little bit comforted. "No matter what Paulina says, you're not a suspect. You're a witness. So, no, I don't need to handcuff you." She paused, and added, "Just don't go anywhere."

It was an unnecessary thing to add—Gabi had known Joy since they were thirteen and was well aware of what a voracious rule-follower she was. She needed to be questioned, so she'd wait right here until Gabi was done and then answer all her questions. But...

"Are you..." she began, and then gulped to be met with Gabi's full attention, their gazes locked. "Are you the new..."

There wasn't really a word for what Bo and Clover had been.

"The new Pride?" Gabi's mouth twitched. "Yeah."

Your mum would be happy, Joy didn't dare say. Joy had never known Gabi's mum, not like she knew Bo, but Gabi had told her again and again how Clover wanted Gabi to follow in her footsteps and keep things safe and orderly in Agedale. Joy swallowed the words and nodded.

So Gabi would be questioning her—would be, no matter what she said, looking at Joy for any signs she'd killed this girl.

Joy pressed her trembling hands against her thighs and waited for her interrogation as Gabi disappeared back into the white tent.

TWO

GABI

One week, *Pride*.

As if Gabi didn't already know. As if passing this trial period with flying colours wasn't the most important thing she'd ever done. And it was fucking *typical* that she encountered a murder on her second day on the job.

She was tempted to heave a sigh and roll her eyes to the heavens, but she had a job to do, and complaining wouldn't get it done any faster. Besides, her dad was watching her, and Joy was pretending not to, but she was watching Gabi even closer.

Gods—Joy Mackenzie. Gabi's only love, the girl who still held her heart in a vice-like grip. She just *had* to be here on this beach, a witness in only the third call Gabi had responded to since yesterday, the first two being the theft of a rare porcelain ornament in an ongoing feud between elderly neighbours and—the icing on her first day cake— public indecency from a man Gabi wished she'd seen a whole lot less of last night.

As Pride, everything was her responsibility, but she

hadn't thought she'd be dealing with *this* on her second day. Or on her two hundredth. Agedale was a typically sleepy seaside town. Yet inside the white tent Gabi had erected, a girl lay murdered, no older than sixteen. She was caucasian, dark haired, with blue, now-empty eyes, with the word 'naughty' cut deep enough into her cheek to show muscle and sinew, and a deep gash from her throat to her stomach. Wand snapped, no phone or purse in sight. Taken, Gabi assumed, and the wand snapped to send a message. It would have been easy to assume this was an elf or fae murderer, a species motivated murder, but Gabi learned that not always the most obvious theories were true.

Gabi's original plan after finishing her field training had been to work for Liverpool's police and climb her way up to detective—not to become what amounted to a sheriff in her hometown. But this was no different to what she'd been trained for and what she'd expected to face in a big city. It was the fact of it being in *Agedale*, where Gabi had grown up playing on this strip of beach, safe in the knowledge that nothing really bad could happen, that threw her.

Now she was responsible for keeping everyone safe. And someone out there had killed a teenage girl.

Gabi took off her coat, zipped a clean forensic suit over her shirt and jeans, and examined the body, just standing there for long minutes on end and letting her mind process what it was seeing, making connections and jotting down the details. It had been impossible, in the beginning, faced with her first dead body, to look at the victim and not be sick, to not want to cry or run away or scream at the world.

It wasn't much easier now, if she was being honest. This was a person—a *person*, killed. Gabi had never been naïve enough to think murders never happened, but knowing and looking down at it were two different things. Her stomach had clenched into a nauseous knot the minute she pulled back the tent flaps and looked at the girl, her round cheeks, her big, unseeing eyes. Even the smell of decay—slight enough to tell Gabi the girl hadn't been dead for longer than a few hours—couldn't distract from the twist in her heart, the sickness steadily filling her.

She'd called her dad after that first murder scene and begged him to tell her it got easier to look at a corpse and not see a person, to stop the wrench of her gut and the pressure behind her eyes. He'd told her the day it got easy was the day she stopped being a good detective.

Which meant no, it did not get better. But it was easier to do what needed to be done when Gabi didn't think of her as *the girl*. In front of her now was a *body*. If Gabi relaxed her tight grip on the leash around her thoughts, she'd fall down a slippery slope, her inner voice telling her this was her fault. She'd been Pride for one whole day, and someone was dead on her watch. A kid.

The sound of Gabi's camera shutter was as loud as a gunshot in the silence that had filled the tent, blocking out the sound of the ocean and seagulls crying. Or maybe the rush of quiet had filled Gabi. She'd fucked up after one day. She'd *failed*. The thought did not leave, even as she finished her examinations and collected what bits of evidence hadn't been blown away by the wind or washed out by the sea, sketching notes for herself in her fresh notebook.

The heavy feeling over the body didn't help, either. As an elf, Gabi had environmental magic—and even though Gabi's magic only worked sporadically, her senses were faultless. Now, they were telling her something cruel had happened to this girl. Something had *tainted* her before she'd been killed. Gabi always sensed people, be it homely or concerned, ditzy or conceited. Gabi *always* got a sense about someone from the way they affected their environment. The way this body was affecting the environment ... her death had not been painless.

When it came to moving the body, getting it into the body bag, Gabi's senses flared and she locked her limbs on instinct, hand twitching towards the telescopic baton at her waist beneath the protective plastic suit. It felt like she'd inhaled chemicals, astringent and biting. Her nose burned, but more than that her *senses* burned. Something about the body was ... wrong. She'd known that already, sensed it through her power, but ... there was witchcraft or magic here. It wasn't a surprise since the girl had been a witch herself—the broken wand was evidence of that, as was the absence of either subtly (fae) or sharply (elves) pointed ears —but Gabi's senses were one hundred percent sure. This victim had been touched by something supernatural. Killed by power if Gabi's suspicions were right, not by a knife or brute strength, despite the cut on her cheek and the bruising around her neck.

But Gabi needed someone with stronger senses—and a more reliable magic—to confirm that. She'd always relied more on her mind and logic than her elven magic. Hence her very human career path.

Heaving a sigh as she braced for company again, Gabi pulled the tent flap aside and whistled, summoning her dad. "Help me with this body bag, would you?"

She scanned the beach while Bo made his way closer to the tent, alert for anyone watching—it wouldn't have been the first time a killer returned to oversee an investigation— but the beach was empty of anyone but Gabi, her dad, and Joy.

So far.

Gossip would spread. In Agedale, it always did.

Bo made a show of sighing, but he dutifully picked up one end of the bag and helped her carry the body outside. He had an overly grouchy look on his face, and Gabi smirked, waiting for whatever he was going to say.

"Do you know what retired means, Gabriella? Re-*ti*-red." He dragged the word out.

Gabi made a *hmm* sound, pretending to ponder it. "I've heard it means you laze around the house, available for assisting bright, young daughters in carrying bodies to their cars." Truth be told, it meant his leg—injured chasing down a teenage fae thief in the night—wouldn't stand his weight for long periods at a time, which in turn meant he couldn't be running after thieves and criminals whenever the need arose. And despite his insistence that he could stay on to fill out the necessary paperwork required of a Pride, Paulina had not so gently insisted he step down. Couldn't have her law enforcement sullied by a disabled man.

Gabi *hated* that bitch.

Bo tried to scowl at her reply and failed, laughing brightly, creases forming around his brown eyes—the same shade as hers. It was probably a bad time to laugh, given they were carrying a corpse and sliding it into the back of Gabi's car—she'd put plastic covers over the entire backseat in preparation—but she laughed too, needing the release from the stiff tension in her body and the sharp warning from her senses.

"Smartass," he said when Gabi had arranged the body on the back seat. "No idea where you get that from."

Gabi snorted, slamming the door to her black Ford Mondeo. "Old Josie tells me I'm just like my dad in his youth." She turned to look at him but caught sight of the figure on the beach instead, her arms wrapped around herself. Gabi's smile slid off her face.

Right.

Joy.

Questioning.

"Jesus, I don't know how to do this," she admitted, her chest pulling tight as she unzipped her plastic suit.

Until she'd seen Joy, Gabi hadn't realised she'd expected her to be the same. But of course, Joy was different, her hair longer and a different style—but the same vivid pink it had been years before. She'd even grown taller, though still nowhere near as tall as Gabi, and she dressed differently. Jeans and a mystical T-shirt instead of a long, swishy dress. Still the same bright pink furry coat though; that'd never change.

Gabi had hoped, in the quietest, smallest corner of her mind as she drove home yesterday, that maybe they'd see each other, and everything would be as it had been. But Joy was a different person, and Gabi hurt Joy in a way they'd never recover from—even if it had been an accident.

Any chance of friendship, or more, had died the same day Joy's mum passed away.

Her dad touched her elbow, and Gabi startled out of the memory. "Just be fair and thorough. You can do nothing more."

"Paulina's already out for Joy's blood." Gabi tried not to show how deeply that troubled her. Joy wasn't a murderer— she was kind and gentle and she worked in a sanctuary for near-extinct *birds* for gods' sakes. She did needlepoint and made handmade necklaces strung with sea glass in her spare time. She volunteered at every charity fundraiser and helped every little old lady across the street without prompting or promise of reward. Joy knew all her neighbours by name, spoke to them for minutes on end about their nephews in Australia and their latest brochure of

Witch Knitting Weekly, and she did it with genuine enthusiasm. Joy Mackenzie was not a fucking killer. And Gabi would be damned if she let Paulina set her up for the crime.

Bo didn't reply. He knew the way of Agedale better than anyone. As Pride, Gabi was responsible for enforcing laws and handing out justice, but she didn't have any true power. At the end of the day, Paulina was head witch; *she* was in charge of the town, and Gabi answered to her. Her shiny new car—or rather her pre-owned rust bucket—was courtesy of Paulina and she'd only been given it so she could get from crime scene to crime scene. Her kit and bag of tools were the same. If Gabi failed this trial, she'd have to pay back every last penny.

The thumbnail-sized golden sun badge on her collar and the ID in her wallet, too, could easily be revoked. She was at the head witch's mercy, and she knew it. So did her dad.

If Gabi screwed up, the job would probably go to Big Phil, the aptly named witch and groundskeeper of Agedale High who'd tried to intimidate the town into staying honest since Gabi's dad had retired—and failed. Thefts, attacks, brawls, home disturbances, and (of course) public indecency, had been alarmingly frequent under Big Phil's rule. Gabi suspected he only took the position to get free pints at the Tipsy Witch.

Gabi looked at her dad, his lined face and knowing eyes. "Fair and thorough," she echoed.

With a lot more effort and bravery than it should have required, Gabi set off back to the beach, to finish her observations of the scene, and to bring Joy in for questioning.

Fuck, this was gonna be hard. She could feel the ghost of their relationship breathing down her neck with every step she took.

THREE
JOY

I t took four hours for Gabi to finish collecting evidence and taking notes but now she and Joy were here, the door opening in front of them. The house looked the same. Narrow and tall and completely unremarkable from the outside, but inside it held so many memories. Joy walked through every glimmer of the past as she followed Gabi down the narrow, brown-wallpapered hall, past doors that Joy knew opened onto a sitting room used for informal occasions, a records room full of paper boxes overflowing with files, and into the room tucked beside the kitchen—the room Bo Pride always questioned suspects in.

Joy's heart raced, her palms pricking with sweat. Back on the beach, the sea had soothed her, keeping the frantic, falling-apart pieces inside of her steady through her fae nature, her connection with the sea. As much as Joy rarely called on the fae part of her, she'd been grateful for the tide, for the *shh* of the water that calmed her racing heart. Unlike a full-blooded fae, she didn't have wings or sharply pointed ears, but she always felt safer near the sea. Now, away from the water, her heart thumped in her chest, and fear shivered through her, gripping her throat tight. A witch had been killed—*killed*.

Joy couldn't get the image of the girl out of her head.

Gabi sat in one of the stiff leather chairs in the interview room, her notebook on her lap and her phone set to record, and Joy timidly took the chair opposite her, little tremors moving through her hands. Her eyes darted around the room, from the door to the small window to the placid art on the walls that was meant to be soothing, along with the pale blue decor. She reminded herself she wasn't nervous because she had anything to be guilty of. It was being in this house, being near Gabi, and what she'd seen on that beach. All of those things were out of the ordinary. One on its own she could weather, but all of them at once? She was crumbling.

Joy needed everything to be normal, *routine*. It was how she'd survived since her mum's death, how she'd got out of bed and gone to work day after day, how she was able to face the people of Agedale who had known her mum, who mentioned her *every* time they saw Joy. Routine was how Joy kept going, moving steadily away from that black hole in her past. It had been trying to swallow her ever since that morning she'd crept back into her house after a night spent on the beach, the morning she'd found her mum cold and still in her bed.

She died in her sleep; she'd *died* while Joy had been lying in the sand kissing Gabi, plotting the stars with their fingertips. While they'd been cuddling and laughing, Joy's mum had been *dying*.

"I need to ask you some questions," Gabi said now, facing Joy head on, her tanned face grave but her brown eyes sympathetic.

Joy could only look at Gabi's shoulder, too aware of

everything that had happened in those days after her mum's death to look her in the eye. The guilt was suffocating, *sickening*. What she'd said...

"I know," Joy said, nodding and trying to keep her voice even, perfectly neutral. She wanted this to be over so she could get to work, get back to *normal*, and forget this whole thing had ever happened. A girl killed; Gabi back home for the first time since she left for university when she was eighteen—and never came back for six years.

Joy had been thoughtless and callous the last time they'd spoken. She'd wanted space, time to mourn. She'd wanted Gabi to leave her alone for a few days. Not for a *year*, and definitely not for *six*.

Gabi sighed slowly through her nose, fiddling with her notebook, and Joy wondered if she was remembering everything that had happened too, everything they'd said—every word was here with them, hanging from the rafters like cobwebs left for dust. "Alright," she said finally, her expression focussed. "Start at the beginning—you were going into work? Tell me everything that you saw."

THERE WAS HARDLY anything for Joy to tell but the interview still took an hour, with Gabi firing question after question at Joy. Gabi seemed ... different. She'd always been serious and intent but there was a honed focus to her now, a confidence Joy tried for and always seemed to miss. Gabi seemed happy in herself, confident of her role and her job, and if Joy hadn't been so consumed with the need to leave, to get out into the sea-blown air where she could *breathe*, she might have been overcome with envy.

Her hands were shaking fully by the time they finished,

and Joy shoved them into her coat pockets, following Gabi back through the dim hallway to the front door. Automatically, her body on autopilot, she hopped over the board that creaked wildly, and she refused to dwell on the familiarity of the Pride House.

She couldn't let the past seep into the present when Gabi had so clearly moved on with her life. But she couldn't seem to stop the memories rising up, like hungry sea monsters smelling blood.

"I'm sorry," Gabi said abruptly, hovering on the threshold as Joy took a few steps onto the street outside, the cold already seeping into her bones through the fake fur of her coat. For a second, Joy thought she was apologising for all the bitter history between them, and she opened her mouth to say she was too, but Gabi went on, "For having to bring you in like this. I wouldn't—" She bit off whatever she'd been about to say, her expression going eerily hard, a stranger staring out through her dark eyes. "Paulina. Nice to see you again."

Her tone communicated that it was anything but nice.

Joy turned, hugging her arms around herself as dread opened like a pit under her feet, her body tumbling in. Paulina was storming down the road from the high street, coming straight from Town Hall, Joy guessed. When the large woman was close enough, she flapped her hand at both Joy and Gabi, the crisp paper in her grip crumpling.

"Joy Mackenzie," she said in a triumphant voice. "I have a warrant for your arrest. Pride, do the honours."

Joy's heart crashed to her boots. "What—" she started, but she was suddenly too breathless to finish. Arrested? Joy had never been arrested in her life. She'd never committed a *crime*, unless you looked really deep into her internet history and found the one time she'd torrented an episode of

Gilmore Girls (before she'd suffered a bout of guilt and deleted the episode without watching it.)

Joy had never ... and now she ... *arrested?*

"Excuse me?" Gabi demanded in a cold, steely voice. Joy didn't dare look at her fully, but she saw Gabi from the corner of her eye: she stormed down the path, her long coat flaring out behind her and her black ponytail trailing like a whip on the wind. "On what grounds? I *just* finished questioning her. What evidence do you have that I don't?"

"What I have," Paulina replied coolly, adjusting her pointed hat on her red head, "is a witness who saw a woman matching this witch's description half an hour before Mackenzie called in the body."

Every time Paulina said Joy's surname, more and more derision oozed through. Joy couldn't stop shaking, each word falling like a nail in her coffin. She wanted to defend herself, but she couldn't get her mouth to open.

She wished Bo hadn't gone home and left Gabi to interview her, wished he was here—he was the only person, other than Joy's absent dad, who'd ever been allowed to stand up to Paulina. If Paulina told Gabi to arrest Joy ... she'd have to. Joy's next breath let out a pathetic whimper.

"Well," Paulina snapped, flapping her doughy hand. "Get on with it."

Joy peered up long enough to see Gabi reading the arrest warrant, her mouth set in a hard line. She handed it back and took a pair of handcuffs from one of her coat pockets with a growl of a sigh. Joy startled at the sight of them, another cry tumbling from her without her permission.

She flinched, screaming at herself to fight, to draw her wand, to say something to defend herself, as the cold shock of the metal met her wrists, the warm touch of Gabi's fingers as she efficiently locked Joy's hands in front of her body just as unbearable.

The spelled metal cuffs rattled as Joy trembled, her eyes fixing on Gabi, pleading. But all Gabi did was dispassionately rattle off Joy's rights.

Everything Joy had said, everything she'd shouted and spat at her the last time they spoke ... she didn't *deserve* to have Gabi still on her side—but if she just handed Joy over to be locked up in the Town Hall's damp, rotting cells ... Joy was going to break. Her heart would crack in two, her composure would shatter to pieces, and the tears stinging her eyes would come pouring out.

"You still have no evidence," Gabi told Paulina in a neutral tone, her fingers lingering on Joy's wrists a moment too long. Joy clung to the moment, taking comfort in it that Gabi probably didn't intend to give. "I assume it's my job to find it before forty-eight hours are up?"

"It's your job to find it," Paulina agreed, a sour twist to her mouth as she looked at Joy. "But I can hold Mackenzie for as long as I want. You're playing by human rules, Pride. You need to remember that Agedale's a witches' town."

Gabi said nothing to that, and Joy desperately scanned her expression. Gabi's whole face was studiously normal. Flat. Joy *knew* that look—it meant Gabi was feeling too much at once. It meant she was *angry*. At Joy. Because she thought—she thought Joy killed that girl.

Joy's bottom lip caved in, wobbling. She wanted Bo, she wanted her mum back, but mostly she wanted her coven. They'd get her out of this ... right?

"Well," Gabi said finally, "I'd better get to work." Her eyes flitted to Joy and held her gaze, but Joy couldn't read anything in those dull, brown eyes. "I'll be around to see you tomorrow morning for follow-up questions."

Joy's breath caught—Gabi thought she was ... she really believed Joy was guilty.

Joy was so numbed by that realisation, by being *arrested for murder,* that she'd been bundled up the high street and down the road to the ruins of Town Hall before she realised. People were watching, whispering, as Paulina led Joy, hand-cuffed, up the still-intact stone stairs and through the ancient columns that led to the restored lobby. Even though Gabi had argued it was her job to transport a prisoner to the cells, Paulina had grabbed Joy and hauled her off person-ally, enjoying every moment, especially whenever Joy stumbled.

Joy caught the eye of Old Josie, a woman Joy had always considered a friend, and her tears finally spilled over. The grey-haired woman tutted, and Joy's chest crumpled, thinking the sound was directed at her until Josie spat, in her usual acidic way, "What a way to treat that poor girl. As if she hasn't been through enough with Charity's passing." One of Josie's friends murmured her agreement, but Paulina barked, "Away with the lot of you. This is none of your business."

"Joy?"

Joy twisted her head, knowing that voice. Neil Ivers, her neighbour and her mum's best friend—her friend too, in that way of next door neighbours who knew everything about each other. She saw the shell-shocked expression on his face change to outrage, but then she was shoved past the marble columns and into the lobby.

Town Hall staff watched with open mouths as Paulina roughly guided Joy across the marble floor, past the towering statues of head witches past—the founders of Agedale from the fifteen hundreds. Joy tried not to hyper-ventilate as Paulina huffed, leading her to a heavy door that led away from the restored section of the building to darkness and decay, to the cells that lurked below.

Joy knew this place inside out, had run wild through both the restored halls and the eroded ruins as a girl when her dad was Head Witch. But she'd never been through this door. She'd never fumbled her way handcuffed down the dark steps on the other side, water trickling down the rough stone around her.

Her childhood playground had become a tomb, and the saltwater and magic smell of the building was no longer a comfort. It was a reminder of all the spells wrapped around the town hall, keeping her locked down here.

She could have tried to fight, but she'd have lost. Paulina was Head Witch for a reason: she was the most powerful.

Joy didn't have anyone outside waiting for her to get home, worrying when she was late and then absent altogether. She had friends, she had her coven who were her new family, but they all had their own homes, their separate lives. Her mum was gone, her dad lost, and the rest of her family ... Joy knew very little about them.

But at least Neil knew—he might be able to find her coven, let them know Joy was in trouble. And she had Gabi and Bo, although with what Gabi had said about finding evidence ... she *didn't* have Gabi. Not at all. Not in any way.

Paulina shoved Joy down the last few steps, the temperature dropping the lower they got, until Joy was shaking because of cold as well as terror. Would she ever be released? Paulina had always been out to get her family, ever since the coven voted her dad as Head Witch instead of her years ago. And even though he ran and she got the position in the end, she still glared at Joy and her mum, still hissed about them, still turned the main coven against them until Joy was forced to form her own—something without precedent in Agedale.

Now, Paulina brimmed with victory and satisfaction. Joy could see it in her eyes when they finally came face to face with the ancient cells. The metal had been set with sea magic; when Joy stepped into that cell, every bit of magic she possessed would be stripped from her.

Joy's heart sped up at the thought, her whole body chilling, but she never thought Paulina would hold out her hand and demand, "Your wand, Mackenzie."

"No," Joy breathed. She'd never once surrendered her wand—not *ever*. It hadn't been out of her sight for even a moment since she trawled the cave along the seafront for a piece of amethyst large enough. Her wand was narrow, twice the length of her hand, and glittered like heaven was trapped inside it, alternately lilac, gold, and starlight white. It was part of Joy, as a witch's wand was part of any witch.

To hand it over ...

"Your *wand*, Mackenzie." Paulina crowded closer to Joy, so close Joy could make out the tiny hairs on her cheek, the freckle on the edge of her nose, the seething hatred in her eyes. "I won't ask again. Don't make me take it from you."

Joy's hand shook wildly as she slipped it into the inside pocket of her coat, handsewn specifically to hold her wand close to her heart. She could fight Paulina ... but she didn't dare. And maybe it made her a coward, but she was too afraid to fight.

She held on tight to the crystal, hesitating the whole way as she lifted it out, inch by inch. Paulina snatched it from Joy before she could prepare herself for the wrench of handing it over, and a sob crashed up her chest and out of her mouth. To see Paulina tuck that wand into a pocket in her cloak, *Joy's* wand...

It was nothing after that to be shoved into the cell, to hear the metal clang as she was locked inside and to then feel the zip of magic as Paulina tipped three drops of a potion over the lock.

The Head Witch walked back up the slope, a spring in her step.

Joy curled her shaking body up on the thin mattress on the floor. Sounds poured from her, cries and half broken words and pleas. She was alone. She had never been this alone before, not even when she'd ached with loneliness and prayed for her mum to come back. This was a new level of emptiness. And her normality, her careful, precise armour against that void of grief ... it had a crack right through the middle of it.

FOUR

GABI

G abi felt like a zombie the next morning as she threw her coat on and pulled her hair into a tight ponytail. She hadn't had a single hour sleep, not with going through her notes and the samples she'd collected, plus poring over Joy's statement and having to conduct a post mortem on the dead girl. Gabi hadn't found anything to suggest who had killed her. No blunt force trauma that required more strength than Joy possessed. No traces of DNA. No sign of a witch's curse.

At least Gabi had a time of death—sometime between seven and nine a.m.—courtesy of the flies swarming the body and the absence of salt water on her clothes; the witch had been killed after the tide went out.

What spoke the most to Gabi was simple: she could find no killing blow, she couldn't say definitively how the girl had died, beyond the posthumous carving on her face. Which meant there was magic at play like she first suspected, either fae or elven power or witch's magic. There were plenty of spells that didn't leave the taint of a curse, and they were more than capable of killing someone.

But even with magic responsible, what she found during the post mortem was ... strange.

The girl's torso was cut all the way down to her stomach, and her insides had been filled with rubbish. Old cat food tins and empty crisp packets—things the killer must have dug out of someone's bin.

Gabi had spent a long time going through that rubbish painstakingly for a clue to the person who had put it there, but there was nothing. So, she returned to the theory of magic.

Fae magic tended to drown or suffocate people, thanks to their connection to sea and storm, but there was still a chance the killer was fae. Or the nature-based elves could be responsible, Gabi's own people. Their magic was tied to the environment, and usually harmless, but on the spot, Gabi could come up with a handful of ways their power could be used to kill without leaving a mark. And witchcraft ... Gabi didn't truly understand all the ways it could be used. Their magic was limitless.

It brought her no closer to finding out how the girl had died, which brought her no closer to finding the killer. And all the while Joy was locked in a cell in Town Hall, relying on Gabi to prove her innocence—or guilt. But Gabi rolled her eyes at herself for even thinking that. No, no matter how much time had passed or how different Joy was, there was no way she'd kill anyone.

And even if she did, she wouldn't scoop out their innards and replace them with trash.

The wind that hit Gabi when she opened her front door woke her from the fugue of sleeplessness. She hefted her bag higher on her shoulder and headed up the road, walking with purpose towards the crumbling, elegant building of Town Hall at the end of the road, right on the sea's edge.

She had to shake off her uncertainty, had to appear a hundred percent confident or Paulina would pounce on Gabi's doubts, and then she'd never get this job. Her trial would fail, her future in Agedale dead. She could still find work in another town, but ... there was something about this place now that she was back. Agedale was calling to her—the rush of the sea, the obnoxious screams of the gulls, the salt and sand smell of it, and the distant spires of tents in the elven community.

It was home.

She wanted to *stay*—against all odds, despite running from this place when she was eighteen, she wanted to stay.

"I'm here to question Joy Mackenzie," Gabi told Paulina's pretty assistant when she crossed the unnatural lobby—intact and opulent but surrounded by ruins. Katrina, the woman's name tag read. A new addition to Agedale whom Gabi had never seen before. Blonde, pale, with brilliant blue eyes and a disarming smile. Gabi was not immune to her charm, but the spell didn't last long, the reason she was here cutting off any flirting before it could begin.

Katrina consulted her computer screen and flashed Gabi a smile. "Right, I can see you on the schedule. Would you like help finding the cells?"

"I'll be fine," Gabi replied with a tight smile. She'd been here with her dad a few times before she went to uni, back when he'd been showing her the ropes of his job, hoping she'd take the reins from him instead of going to Liverpool. "But thanks for the offer," she added genuinely.

Katrina smiled again, all perfect white teeth and glittering eyes, but Gabi struggled to smile back. She was remembering Joy yesterday, tears streaking down her face, blurring the freckle just above her mouth, an aberrant spot in a freckle-less face.

Gabi's heart clenched as she moved deeper into Town Hall. She fought back memories as they assaulted her, but she had no armour against them. She'd never really moved past them, never moved on the way her roommates at uni had tried to convince her to.

But they said that about first loves, she reminded herself, her usual refrain. First loves never left you. This was normal.

The air grew colder as she pulled the heavy door open, left unlocked just for her, and began to descend the damp, musty staircase. She knew the history of these cells, knew the famous names who'd occupied them over the years, knew the gruesome stories of what jailors had done to their prisoners. The idea of Joy down here, even if she *had* killed that girl on the beach ... Gabi moved faster, taking steps two at a time. She didn't think Joy was a killer, not if she was being honest with herself. But the things Joy had said the last time they spoke and the cruel, callous way she'd treated Gabi for months before that ... *that* girl might be cold enough to kill someone.

"Stop it," Gabi hissed at herself. "Joy didn't kill the witch and you damn well know it."

The girl Gabi saw yesterday, shaking from head to toe, whimpering, *that* girl couldn't hurt a fly.

Gabi didn't realise she was still expecting to see *that* Joy, the crying, shaking one, when she reached the bottom of the slope, peered into the nearest cell, and saw an unmoving ghost.

"Joy?" she breathed before she could remind herself to be professional.

Joy was sitting on a thin mattress, her knees pulled to her chest, her body only moving shallowly with every breath. Her open eyes, familiar chocolate brown, fringed with thick lashes, stared at nothing. Even as Gabi moved closer, her heart kicking into a gallop, Joy's eyes didn't track the movement, didn't focus on anything.

Gabi knelt, dread uncurling from the pit of her stomach. She didn't care about the dirt staining her trousers or the brackish water soaking the hem of her wool coat. What had they done to Joy? Scenarios flashed through Gabi's head, the cruelty of magic added to the cruelty of the human mind...

She shuddered as cold raced down her spine—but red hot rage filled her chest, and it took everything in her power not to race back up the stairs and slam her knuckles into Paulina's smug face.

"Joy," she whispered, watching her ex-girlfriend so closely. Her head was facing straight forward, her pink hair no longer the gentle, tamed waves it had been yesterday but a ratty, damp mess of strands thanks to water trickling down the wall behind her. She looked empty. Despite how their relationship had ended, despite the fierce ache and the razor-sharp anger Gabi still held onto, she was *terrified*. Utterly petrified that Joy had been broken beyond repair— and it was Gabi's fault. Why hadn't she fought Paulina more? Yes, she would have failed her trial by pissing off her boss, yes, she would have lost the job she needed to make her mum proud, but those things were trivial compared to seeing Joy like this. Compared to looking into her unseeing eyes and knowing her soul could be gone, she could be breathing but dead—in her mind, in her soul, where it really mattered.

"Joy," Gabi tried again, wrapping her fingers around the iron bars even as her elf nature flinched. *Please*, she didn't say. *Please don't be gone. I need to ... there's so much I should have said yesterday when I had the chance. I need to tell you that I'm sorry, that you were right, it was my fault you lost those last hours with your mum, that you never got the chance to say goodbye.*

The cell was small enough that Gabi could reach out, the tips of her fingers brushing the edge of Joy's knee, and it must have been enough for her to feel it because Joy moved an inch, just a shudder, but it was enough. She was still aware, still in there.

"Joy Mackenzie," Gabi went on, strength coming to her voice. The cold seeped into her body through her kneeling legs but she didn't care. "It's Gabriella Pride. It's Gabi. Remember? You saw me yesterday; I told you I'd come talk to you. Can you say something, love?"

Joy swallowed; Gabi tracked the movement like it was a miracle. "Gabi," Joy rasped, and finally, *finally* her eyes focussed on something. On the satchel at Gabi's side, thrown carelessly onto the floor.

"What did they do to you?" Gabi didn't mean to ask, but now that Joy was coming around, relief was turning to blind fury. She had no right to it, had no claim to Joy, but still it filled her like lava.

Joy opened and closed her pale hand, staring at it. Gabi expected a number of different things to come from Joy's mouth but not, "She took my wand."

The world stilled around Gabi for a moment before that rage came rushing back in. Her voice was calm when she asked, "She took your wand?"

Joy nodded, a tear trickling from the corner of her eye.

The one crime you never committed against a witch —*especially* to a fellow witch. And Paulina had taken Joy's wand. That *bitch*. "Come here," Gabi murmured. "Let me get a look at you."

With no reaction and no change in her expression, Joy

unfolded herself to her feet. When Gabi stood too, Joy leaned closer. There was a spell around the cell, Gabi could feel it, but she tested its boundaries by putting her hand through the bars again—and as she suspected, Paulina's foresight was shit, and the spell only forbade anything passing *out* of the cell.

"Can you ... can you get it back?" Joy asked, her voice so weak, her eyes finally daring to meet Gabi's. Gabi's anger lit on fire at the pain she found in Joy's chocolate eyes, etched into her pleading face.

"I'll try," she replied. She cupped Joy's chin, tilting her face so Gabi could inspect a scrape on her jaw—it looked a few days old, not inflicted by Paulina or her witches—and her eyes—slowly becoming more focussed. Gabi found she couldn't let go. She'd never wanted to; it was *Joy* who hadn't wanted Gabi. Gabi let her hand fall from Joy's cheek the moment Joy leaned into the touch, her heart tripping over itself. It had been *years*; she should have been *over* Joy. She was only going to get hurt again if she let herself get carried away.

"I'm sorry," Gabi said, and wasn't sure what she was apologising for—for the touch, for not stopping Paulina taking Joy's wand, for everything.

Joy's eyes fell shut; she leaned her face against the bars, as close as the spell would let her. It looked like she was breaking. And Gabi knew—she knew without asking, but she had to ask anyway.

"Joy. I'm going to ask you just once, and I need you to look at me." Joy's eyes fluttered open; worried, full of bleakness and suffering. Strands of damp pink hair clung to her cheeks, making her face look thinner. "Did you have anything to do with that girl's death?"

Joy's eyes widened with surprise, or shock, or something

sharper. She stumbled back and in a low, raw voice said, "No. I just ... I just found her."

Gabi nodded, relief easing her tense shoulders. "I had to ask, Joy."

Joy turned away to face the water trickling down the back of her cell, her shoulders hunched, and her arms wrapped around her middle. "I know. You thought I did it."

"No." Gabi waited until Joy turned and held her gaze. "I didn't. But I had to ask to be completely sure. I can tell when you're lying, Joy, so—" Too much, too close—too close to acknowledging their history, to admitting that they had friendship and love and grief and rage between them. "I'll find whoever killed that girl, Joy. You won't be here forever."

"Thanks," Joy rasped, dropping her gaze. It was nothing like the impassioned rant or the bubbly rambling or the bright laugh Gabi heard like an echo from the past.

She had to get out of here, the memories biting deeper. Maybe it was selfish of her to leave when Joy had to stay, but too many ghosts were between them.

Gabi found herself wordless, just watching the rise and fall of Joy's shoulder blades as she turned to the water again. She was still in her grey faux-fur coat, the fabric matted and soaked, and she was shivering. Gabi frowned, adding another task to her to-do list. When she came tomorrow—because she had to, she couldn't leave Joy alone down here no matter what had happened between them—she'd have her bag full of water, food, and the biggest, fluffiest blanket she could find.

She didn't know how to say goodbye, opening and closing her mouth so many times she lost count, so she just met Joy's gaze and turned, passing through the arch that led to the steps back aboveground. No physical locks—just witchcraft keeping unauthorised people out.

"I didn't mean it," Joy said in a panicked voice, just as Gabi reached the steps. Gabi turned, confusion pinching her eyes. Joy was pressed to the bars, her pale fingers wrapped around them, her expression desperate. "I didn't *mean* it, Gabi. What I said, after my mum ... I was angry and I just ... I lost control of my tongue. I didn't mean it. Any of it."

"Any of it," Gabi echoed, staring down at the wide stones that made up the floor, unable to hold Joy's gaze. "You didn't mean *any* of it."

Gabi had never been able to forget what Joy had confessed that day, when all Gabi wanted was to comfort her girlfriend and Joy locked her out. She'd wanted to hold Joy and tell her she was *sorry*. But Joy wouldn't let her in, wouldn't even *look* at her after she'd had to pull Joy out of her mum's bed—with her mum's body still between the sheets—and into her own room while Gabi's dad took Mrs Mackenzie away.

Joy had lashed out, Gabi knew—had known all these years that was why Joy had said what she did—but she thought she'd lashed out with the *truth*. Not with lies.

"You didn't mean it," she repeated, the disbelief wearing off. Anger rose in its place, and *outrage*, but one look at Joy, scared and suffering in the cell, and she couldn't hold onto it. Gabi's voice was hollow when she asked, "Then why did you *say* it?"

Joy shook her head, the slow trickle of tears becoming a fast stream. "I don't know."

Gabi had to turn away just to pull her thoughts together. She couldn't think about this now. She had a job to do, and that was more important. She couldn't ... she couldn't face this, not now or ever. "I have to go. I'll be back tomorrow."

"Gabi—"

Gabi took the steps at a fast clip, her chest cinched tight. Nothing had changed—she had to find whoever had killed that girl, she still had weeks of work to fit into hours.

Nothing had changed.

But that was a lie to herself, and she knew it.

FIVE
JOY

"Leave me alone, Gabi," Joy said in a dead voice, curling up tighter on the bed, clutching the teddy bear her mum had given her for her nineteenth birthday.

A sigh came through the door, sad but frustrated too. "I'm your girlfriend, Joy. Let me in. I just want—don't shut me out. Please."

Joy gripped the bear tighter, her mum's pale, lifeless face flashing behind her eyes. She couldn't stop seeing it, couldn't stop reliving that moment she'd snuck in after being out all night and realised the house was far too quiet—the moment she'd come upstairs and reluctantly opened her mum's bedroom door, part of her already knowing what she'd find.

"Don't shut you out?" Joy's laugh was callous and brittle, an alien sound even to her own ears. She had no control over it. "Why would I let you in? You kept me down on that beach, Gabi. You convinced me to sneak out and watch the stars while my mum was dying in her bed. I didn't get to say goodbye, or tell her I loved her one last time, or even hold her hand as she slipped away, and it's—all—your—fault!"

A pause, as Joy breathed erratically fast, tears scalding her cheeks. And then in a choked whisper, Gabi said, "I know."

"Leave me alone, Gabi. I don't want to see you again." The words were like piling pain on top of pain. She didn't know what she was saying—she didn't want Gabi to leave, not really. She didn't want to be alone. Except she did want to be alone, at the same time. She felt empty and too full of feeling, her mind both silent and roaring.

She wanted to be left alone for the rest of her life, and she wanted Gabi here holding her, even if her touch wouldn't mend the hole inside Joy, even if those two things were incongruous.

Gabi was quiet for a long time, her voice carefully stripped of any feeling when she asked, "Are you breaking up with me?"

Joy screwed her eyes shut, breathing impossibly fast, furious and bereft and desperate for solitude, for touch, for her mum's arms around her.

She didn't know why she said it, but there was a hole in her chest, a screaming howl inside her head, and she just wanted it gone. She wanted it all gone.

She wanted her mum back.

"I don't love you anymore," Joy choked out, her voice a whip cutting any and all ties between them, shears severing the threads that had linked every bit of their souls for years. Joy almost took it back, almost unsaid that heinous lie, but the pain inside her had found an outlet and it took full advantage of it. She kept speaking, poison falling from her tongue.

"I used to love you, but I haven't for a long time. I didn't know how to tell you." This last part was the worst deception, because it made everything she said more believable.

What was she doing?

"*Then why did you—*" Joy could hear Gabi take a deep, long breath. "*Why did you* stay *with me, Joy?*"

Joy squeezed her eyes shut, her fingers in fists around the teddy bear. The words sliced her tongue as she spoke them. "*There wasn't anyone else, and I didn't want to be alone.*"

Gabi's laugh mangled the silence. "*So, you stayed with me because I'm the only gay girl you know? Seriously, Joy?*"

"*Sorry,*" *Joy breathed, and meant it. She just wanted Gabi to go, to leave her alone for a while. She couldn't breathe, couldn't think with the roaring between her ears, and Gabi's presence only made Joy hurt more.*

Every time Gabi asked if she was okay, or if there was anything she needed, it was another reminder of where Joy had been when her mum died. Not here, not home where she should have been. She couldn't stand it.

"*So you don't love me,*" *Gabi clarified, her voice flat.*

Joy screwed her eyes shut and said the final word that would buy her silence and a reprieve from the crippling guilt.

"*No.*"

I just want silence, *she thought but couldn't find the words to say.* I just want this torn-apart thing in my chest to stop hurting.

"*You don't want me.*"

A tear wobbled at the bow of Joy's lip. "*No.*"

Silence, and the scuff of Gabi's shoes on the carpet—and then the front door slamming shut.

Joy curled up on her side and tucked her face down, inhaling the smell of her mum's shirt, and cried herself to sleep.

SIX
GABI

The last thing Gabi wanted was to get held up in the lobby of Town Hall—she needed to get home, organise her notes, organise her *life*, but there was a pile-up of spectators in the lobby, snooping as an angry young woman hissed and snarled at a mountainous security guard. Gabi elbowed her way around the gossipers and crossed the lobby, not caring one single bit about the drama until the mountain of a guard replied—in a voice several octaves higher than Gabi's judging mind had expected— "Paulina has given orders. No visitors in the cells."

Visitors. Gabi paused in surprise, and then resumed walking twice as quickly, the elegant statues of the town's founders blurring as she took the marble floor at speed. Gabi had been down to the cells—there was only one pris-oner. Which meant this was someone who cared about Joy.

Something like relief unknotted Gabi's heart, the fear that Joy had been on her own all this time, that Gabi had walked out and left Joy utterly alone.

The angry woman—Gabi put her about twenty—had black, poker-straight hair to her waist, a distractingly beautiful face if you forgave the sneering, murderous intent scrawled across it, strong eyebrows that promised at least one injury to the security man's person, and bony limbs wrapped in varying shades and textures of black. Tight jeans, heavy boots, leather jacket, and a vest artfully ripped down the middle of the band print. This was a species of person Gabi did not usually get close to—she looked to be the antithesis to Gabi's organised calm. This girl was chaos and fury and—and she was currently thrusting the tip of her black wood wand into the security guard's chin.

"Hey, now," Katrina, the pretty blonde receptionist, said, her face bleached with worry. "There's no need for that."

"Shut it, Yoga Bitch," the dark-haired witch spat. Gabi glanced at Katrina, who clearly knew the confrontational one at least in passing, but the pale witch just shook her head and sighed, returning to her desk.

"That's *it*," the guard snapped in his high voice, reaching into his back pocket—not for cuffs, Gabi knew, but an incapacitation spell.

"It's alright, Griswald," Gabi said coolly, drawing the man's attention as she approached. There was a moment of confusion when he looked at her, that first assumption of knowing her because she'd spoken his name turning to bewilderment because *he* didn't recognise *her*.

Yet.

If she passed Paulina's trial, everyone would know that she was the new Pride, Clover's heir. Then everyone would drop their problems at her front door. She'd be chased down the street because something or other needed fixing, or the infamous Daryl had cursed his neighbour again—not with magic but with dirty words, which in a small, seaside town was far worse. But for the moment, no one had figured out who Gabi was.

"I'll take over, if you don't mind," she went on, taking advantage of Griswald's slowness, and honestly wondering how he hadn't realised his name was printed on the tag clipped to his breast pocket. She supposed Paulina employed him for brawn, not cleverness. And Gabi was getting judgemental again—she heard her dad's voice warn her to be more forgiving, that as Pride she needed to make an effort to understand people, not just facts and figures. Maybe Griswald was a genius at carpentry or a talented artist or—Gabi gave up. Trying to understand people was hard under usual circumstances but impossible with Joy incarcerated.

"Excuse me, bitch—" the snarling woman began, but Gabi gave her a look that told her she was not fucking about.

"Either you come with me or Griswald here incapacitates you with the spell he's got in his hand."

Her eyes dropped to the guard's hand, in which was a paper sachet, easily ripped, its contents poised to hit the woman right in the chest where she'd inhale them without much choice. She swore, letting her wand drop. "Fine, I'll leave. But I'll be back every fucking day until you let me in, I swear to—"

Gabi huffed a pissed off sound. She really *wasn't* in the mood. "Only one person can approve that," she said shortly. "And Paulina's never going to approve you. There's no point shouting at poor Griswald, he's just the door guy."

"Thank you," Griswald exclaimed, and then paused, not sure if she'd insulted him.

Dark and Snarly opened her mouth to spew more poison but Gabi cut her off, hurt and anger boiling up in her after the conversation she'd just had with Joy and cutting her temper short. "Friend of Joy's, I assume?"

Eyes narrowed, eyebrows slashed further together, arms crossed over her leather jacket. The witch looked vaguely familiar, but Gabi couldn't put a finger on why. "What the fuck's it to you?"

"I'm the person who's going to get her out of that cell." Gabi clenched her jaw, ignoring the onlookers as they disbanded, bored. "Do you think you could deign to assist me in that? Or are you too busy wasting time Joy doesn't have spitting venom at guards?" It took everything in Gabi to not swear.

The woman's dark eyes narrowed dangerously; Gabi glared right back. "I'll help," she huffed eventually, her mouth in a thin line.

Gabi turned on her heel and left the toxic Town Hall behind her, feeling like she could breathe again when she was standing by the side of the road, inhaling the salt, earth, and sea, her sleek ponytail caught in the wind. Gabi waited for a break in traffic and jogged across the road, not waiting for Dark and Snarly to catch up. "I'm Gabriella Pride," she said when they were on the steep road down to Gabi's house—the Pride's house. Her dad lived across town in a nicer bungalow, but this shitty terrace house had always been home to them both if they were being honest. The bungalow was less home than their attempt at pretending they were normal, civilised folk.

"Victoriya Stone," the witch replied, putting her wand in an inner pocket of her jacket and looking less inclined to hex Gabi. "So you're the new Pride."

Gabi nodded, skirting a particularly determined grey cat who wanted to rub its tortoiseshell face on Gabi's jeans.

"For now. If I get on Paulina's bad side by the end of the week, you're stuck with Big Phil."

Victoriya made a sound in the back of her throat. "That guy's a wimp. He wouldn't even arm wrestle me."

Gabi gave her a measured look. "I wouldn't arm wrestle you either. I couldn't be sure I'd keep the arm."

Victoriya's eyebrows flicked up, surprised if Gabi was reading her right. Maybe a touch pleased at the assessment.

"Here," Gabi said, turning onto a bare stone path. She fished the old set of keys from her pocket and let herself into the building, taking off her stress like she'd removed a coat. This house had always been a safe place. Back when it had been her dad's place of work, she'd come to visit on evenings when he was busy, investigating or filing paperwork or fines. It felt natural that the place was hers now.

The house looked like every other terrace house on the street, but inside, the ground floor had been turned into an office, two interview rooms, and a tiny kitchen where Gabi made coffee in between working—she'd already gotten a lot of use out of the Tassimo. Upstairs, it was like any other house: two bedrooms and a bathroom, the front room looking out onto the quiet street and the others backing onto the bare yard of the butcher's behind the house. Thanks to its handy location—and an arrangement her dad made with Will the butcher years ago—Gabi had access to the old cooler building where meat used to hang. It had been cleared out and upgraded years ago and now served as their —her—morgue.

It was strange to think of all this as *hers*, and even stranger to be here without her dad. But the house was perfect for her job, and really, the position came with the assumption that the town would be able to find her—at all hours—at the house. It had come to be known as the Pride House

It was damn daunting to have to fill *his* boots as well as her mum Clover's. Doing a coroner's job? Fine. Photographing and collecting evidence? Second nature. Investigating? Thanks to her education, totally doable. But being a pillar of the community, someone they could rely on and turn to for every disaster? Gabi baulked.

Better to do a job she was sure she could actually do.

"Shut the door behind you," Gabi told Victoriya and marched right to the kitchen at the end of the hall. It was a squashed, tiny space barely big enough for the well-loved table and the cabinets along the walls, but this room took another portion of weight off her shoulders.

Here, Gabi felt capable, not small and insecure and alone. Here, she had her mum's experience and her dad's knowledge to help her, even if just in spirit—and if that didn't work, her dad was a phone call away.

"You're one of Joy's coven," Gabi said as Victoriya leant against the threshold. Not a question.

She wanted to change into her running clothes and pound the beachside path until she could think clearly again—until she could get the image of the dead girl from behind her eyes, until she could push out the memory of Joy staring into space. But she didn't have time for that. She'd just have to find a way to function while stressed, anxious, and mildly nauseated. But what was new there?

"I am," Victoriya confirmed. She prowled around the table to lean against the worktop next to the mug tree Gabi's mum made out of clay when Gabi was five. The townspeople had their own ways of repaying Gabi's parents—electric bills paid, money waved away when they did the weekly shop, casseroles upon casseroles left on the doorstep in the winter, quiches upon quiches in the summertime. Gabi had grown up with every day having the same initial excitement and mystery as Christmas morning, never knowing what would have been left for them overnight. One of those gifts had been a pottery class. Actually, a lot of them were classes at the community centre—as a child, Gabi had gone through sewing, pottery, painting, arts and crafts, knitting, and flower arranging. And those were just the ones she could remember.

She wondered if people would start leaving *her* casseroles and paying *her* bills for her; God knew the wage Paulina paid her was barely enough to scrape rent, electric, and water, let alone a TV licence or Wi-Fi. Her dad was still paying the bills on the place from the savings left from Mum's life insurance, but that wouldn't last forever. Gabi needed to pass this trial for more than one reason.

For more than ten.

She flicked on the kettle, trying to hide how frayed and stressed she was. "Here's the situation. Paulina is determined to prosecute Joy for murder for some innate personal reason, and all the while whoever actually killed a girl is out there. I need to find them, not only to get Paulina to hire me full time, but to free Joy. I could use help." A *lot* of help, but she didn't add that part. "Are you on board?"

God, let her agree to help.

"Obviously," Victoriya snapped, her dark eyes narrowed. "Joy's my friend. I'm not gonna let her rot in a fucking cell when she couldn't even hurt a puppy." She leaned towards Gabi, her gaze sharp. "Who's the girl though? The dead one?"

Gabi sighed. A missing persons report had been filed two days ago but Paulina hadn't bothered to pass it on to Gabi. Gabi only knew *now* because the girl's parents had gone to her dad, as most people did when Paulina was too busy to address their concerns.

She needed to visit her dad's old neighbourhood watch network and let them know to report to her. Once those nosey old people got hold of the news that she was the new Pride, it'd spread like witchfire. *That's a good thing,* she reminded herself, *you want people to approach you.*

Later—she'd deal with that later. For now, getting the witches to identify that wrong sense Gabi had picked up from the girl's body was more important.

"Agree to help," she said, "get your coven to help too, and I'll tell you everything I know."

"They'll help." Victoriya's anger was palpable, her jaw clenched. "You think we're going to sit back and let Joy stay in that place? Salma's probably at your dad's now, asking for help."

Gabi took a steadying breath, trying to brush off the memories that had filled every dark corner of her mind when Joy told her she'd lied. "How soon can you gather them?"

In answer, Victoriya began tapping at her phone, her sharp black nails scratching the touchscreen with every word.

SEVEN

JOY

"I've brought you some water," a sweet voice murmured an hour or so after Gabi had left. Joy lifted her head from the musty mattress in her cell to see a tall, blonde woman in her thirties push a bottle of water through the bars with her lacquered red fingernail.

"Thanks," Joy rasped, wary. This was Katrina, Paulina's assistant, the woman who'd sat on the front desk and watched as Paulina hauled Joy in. She was as bad as Paulina.

Or ... maybe she couldn't do anything to question Paulina. Maybe all she could do was this: little kindnesses when the Head Witch's back was turned.

Katrina smiled, her eyes a clear crystal blue that brimmed with sympathy. She was beautiful, but Joy didn't feel any reaction. Her heart still hadn't mended since her and Gabi's conversation. The only thing that kept her upright and not flopped back on the mattress, blocking out the world, was the water dripping down the back wall. Joy's fae nature tied her to water and allowed her to connect with it at any time, even if she wasn't fae enough to harness it. It was a talent leftover from the days when fae used to command huge, extravagant armadas, when even pirates were helpless to fight them when the fae set their sights on their ships.

The fae who lived on the cliffs of Agedale—in vast houses and lavish mansions, with private cliff paths and secret cave systems that let them access the water—could raise storms and thrash the seas whenever they wished, but Joy had only ever been able to do small magics: purify water, get rainwater on her coat to dry, help her kettle boil quicker. Her magic was diluted thanks to her human blood. Still, being near the sea could soothe her quicker than any hug or spoken reassurance, and even rainwater, soaked up from the sea as it was, had an effect.

The slow stream of water dripping down from some crack high above washed strength into her, kept her eyes dry and open, kept her from collapsing. It wasn't a big magic—it was the smallest kind, merely the natural power of the water—but here in this cold, merciless cell, it felt like the biggest bit of magic in the world. She had her hand behind her to prop her up, but also so every drop from the wall splashed her knuckles and soaked into her skin.

"Are you alright?" Katrina asked, leaning closer to the bars. "The way Paulina brought you in … that was unnecessary."

Joy bet she hadn't said that to her boss. But she appreciated Katrina saying it, nonetheless. "She thinks I killed that girl," Joy replied, not knowing why she was defending Paulina's treatment of her.

"Still." Katrina's smile fell. "You must be traumatised. I know I would be; stuck in here."

Joy dipped her chin but said nothing. Another raindrop

splashed onto the back of her hand, imbuing her with strength.

"I might be able to help," Katrina went on, her voice hushed as she came closer to the bars, so out of place in her crisp jacket and pencil skirt. So out of place with her compassion and care. How had this woman ended up as Paulina's assistant? They were as different as could be. "I'm a healer—that's what I specialise in. My bond is earth."

Joy nodded; her witch sister Salma was aligned with the same element. Joy, it went without saying, was aligned with water, and preferred to cast her spells with potions and—a newer method—with sea glass and crystals.

Witches could use countless methods to cast witchcraft, whether that was brewing a potion, speaking an incantation, writing sigils on paper, or even sketching them in the air with a wand like her friend Gus did. Joy cast most of her spells with her coven, her crystal wand gripped in hand. Without that wand, witch magic was impossible. And more importantly, without something to anchor her to her element, Joy would be put in danger of using raw witch-craft. And that could kill her in seconds. She needed crystals, needed that protective wall between the sheer power of magic and her vulnerable body.

But it was strange, witchcraft. Some witches went their whole lives working spells with their wands in one hand and a potion in the other, only to find out in their twilight years that their power was stronger when they looked into a flame or sat out in the moonlight. Joy's mum used to say that magic had a mind of its own and would reveal its secrets when it saw fit and not a moment sooner.

"You don't have to help," Joy murmured even as she climbed to her feet, her legs aching from being cramped in a too-small position all night. "I don't want to get you in trouble."

Katrina's smile turned soft; something about the woman gave Joy an older sister vibe, not quite motherly but halfway there. "Don't worry. What Paulina doesn't know won't hurt her." Katrina got out her wand, made of spindly ash wood and carved all over with scenes too intricate for Joy to make out, and reached her hand through the bars, past the enchantment Paulina had set to keep Joy locked in. Eager to be rid of all her aches, Joy held out her hand, reminded of the times Salma had taken her hand and woven a spell to ease a migraine or period pain. But the moment Katrina's hand touched Joy's, the woman flinched.

"What is *that*?" she hissed, her eyes flying wide to Joy's complete confusion. "What's that on your hand?"

"Oh." Joy realised her hand was still dripping water and shook it together off some of the droplets. "It's just rainwater. It's coming down the back wall there..." She trailed off at the look on Katrina's face; she looked like she'd been stung. "Sorry. I didn't know it'd be a problem, I forgot I even had water there."

Katrina recovered, waving a hand with a self-deprecating laugh, her smile still a bit wobbly. "Looks like my witchcraft doesn't like water. It felt strange, like an electric shock."

"Oh." Joy let her hand fall back to her side. There would be no easing of the aches in her legs or the crick in her neck, no gentle soothing of the pain in her chest. "Sorry, I didn't know it would..."

"It's fine." Katrina's next smile was as sunny as the ones before, her eyes sparkling like aquamarine. "I'll have to keep my magic away from yours. No problem. I should go before

Paulina notices I'm not at my desk. I'll bring you another drink later, see if I can get Paulina to give you some food."

At the reminder, Joy's stomach growled. She hadn't eaten anything for twenty-four hours. Paulina's treatment of prisoners was nowhere near legal, but she'd never be brought up on charges for it. Who would Joy even report it to? Gabi, who answered to Paulina and believed Joy killed that girl on the beach? No.

At the reminder, the pain in her chest became enough to engulf her whole body. Gabi thought she'd killed someone, and she hated her. As soon as Katrina was gone, Joy's face crumpled.

She folded herself back onto the mattress and pressed her face to her knees, tears breaking free of her eyes before she could stop them. Would she ever get out of here? Would Paulina ever bother to throw her scraps to eat, or would Joy starve to death? How long could a person go without eating? Joy didn't even know. She wished she'd asked Gabi to bring her food when she came back tomorrow morning.

If she ever came back.

She *hated* Joy. Truly, honestly hated her.

More tears ran down Joy's cheeks, her breathing a broken mess of gasps and hitches. For a long time, she sat there, reliving their break up, staring at nothing as the pain in her chest stabbed deeper. The worst thing was that she knew it was *her* fault, had known she'd messed up since the *second* she heard that Gabi had left town. But she'd still been buried deep in the grave of her loss, and she couldn't drag herself out of it long enough to apologise. If Joy was being honest with herself, even now she was never further than a few steps from that grave.

But she wasn't being honest.

EIGHT
GABI

Gabi opened the door with a new tension to her shoulders, masking her dread and expecting Paulina, and blinked in surprise at the three witches and one fox gathered on her doorstep. Joy's coven.

She tried not to let the sudden force of her relief show. They'd come.

Paulina had finally forwarded Gabi the missing persons report for a fifteen year old girl who matched the description of the victim. Her name was Freya Faulkner. Gabi had only had time to scan the brief details Paulina had sent—mostly notes on her family and their untrustworthiness in Paulina's opinion because of her aunt, Ingrid Faulkner, a human married to a witch—but it had driven home the necessity of Gabi's work. Not only to prove Joy's innocence, but to get justice for this girl. And with what Gabi had sensed on the beach, and on the body, she couldn't do it alone. She needed a witch to sense that astringent wrongness too, that chemical scent that had nothing to do with the usual butcher's shop smell of a murder scene.

"Thank you for coming so quickly," Gabi said, pressing

formality into her voice to cover the note of relief. If anyone had the same motivation to find Freya Faulkner's killer as her, it was these witches.

The tallest witch came forward, an elegant black woman in her late twenties with a close-cropped afro and ivy wound around her long white dress. She offered Gabi a strained smile and in a deep, rich voice said, "Thank you for trying to free our Joy."

Gabi just nodded, not sure how to respond. Joy was hers too, or at least she had been.

To the earth witch's side, a tanned guy in his twenties watched Gabi with tired eyes and wariness, his denim jacket battered and his brown hair a windblown mess. He looked as rumpled and exhausted as Gabi felt inside.

She looked from the black witch, to the only male, to the girl on his other side. She was younger than the others, teenaged, and about as different from them as they were from each other. The straight-backed black woman, the scruffy, slouching guy, and the curvy young girl with her hands clenched at her sides, her jeans ripped at the knees and her eyes bright with makeup and tears.

Her aqua vest had a sketchy rendition of the peace symbol on it but the red circles around the girl's eyes and her tear-bitten cheeks were anything but peaceful. Next to her blonde curls, the ends dyed blue, her red face was vivid. Gabi felt a twinge of guilt for asking her to come here and examine a body. It would be upsetting for anyone.

And the fox ... Gabi didn't know where to begin with this fourth stranger. But she was a girl, too, and older than Gabi according to the venomous witch waiting in the kitchen. Gabi had to remind herself to treat the fox like a witch instead of an animal. So she gave her a nod of greeting and let the fox trot down the hall, followed by the trio of odd witches. Gabi shut the door with a heavy sigh behind them, the piercing cry of a seagull making her want to cry out too, if only to release some of the maelstrom inside her.

Instead, she swallowed a breath and followed them into the kitchen where Victoria lurked like a particularly deadly reptile.

"First off," Gabi said, taking a spot against the wall near the kitchen door while the witches squashed around the table, the fox climbing up the jeans of the only male in their group to get onto the tabletop to watch Gabi. "Can you introduce yourselves? I'm Gabriella Pride, you might know my dad, Bo. I'm taking over his position." *Hoping* to take over, but she didn't feel like explaining her trial period. There was no other option than success; she *couldn't* fail, not when it was about making her mum proud *and* freeing her ex-girlfriend from prison.

"Salma Nazari," the tall, black witch introduced herself with a mild smile, her energy grounded, calm. Not surprising for an earth witch—and the ivy around her waist was a dead giveaway of her magical alignment. Now that she'd said her name, Gabi vaguely remembered her as the art technician at school. In her late twenties, she was the eldest of the coven members. Which made her the unofficial Head Witch of the coven, not that Paulina would let anyone else claim the title in her town. God forbid.

"I'm Gus," the guy mumbled, tracing an old scar in the table where it veined off into more scratches, evidence of Gabi's childhood boredom. He waved a hand, lacklustre. "This is my sister, Maisie." Gabi looked at the big girl with blue in her hair, but it was the fox that yipped. And if Gabi wasn't mistaken, there was amusement in those black, beastly eyes.

"Are your senses the same as a regular fox's?" Gabi

asked, her mind cataloguing the next few tasks she needed to do. Still, she didn't miss those black eyes narrowing.

"That face means she's thinking about biting you," Gus clarified, scratching his jaw and smirking a little.

Gabi suppressed the urge to sigh, forcing herself to explain *why* she'd asked the question. "The smell is going to be bad enough for *us* when we go to the morgue. If your senses are more heightened than ours, especially your sense of smell, you might be better off waiting out here. You might not be able to sense any magic over the smell."

Maisie blinked, and then with deliberate slowness, shook her red-orange head.

"Alright," Gabi said, happy to move on. From what Victoriya had told her, Maisie was a witch able to transform her shape, but she'd shifted too many times in a short space of time and been stuck as a red fox for the past two years. Gabi pitied her, but she didn't have time for anything other than clinical observation. Too much weight rested on her shoulders.

"I want to see her."

Gabi turned to the youngest coven member and was startled to find tears silently sliding down her red cheeks. The witch gripped a pendant at her neck, her knuckles white, but her blue eyes when they met Gabi's were strong —hard. She swallowed and said, "My ... my cousin Freya went missing last night just after tea, and—I'm not stupid. Victoriya texts us to come see if we can sense who killed a girl you found this morning on the beach—" She pushed back her shoulders, her chest rising and falling fast under her peace shirt. "I want to see her."

Silence—utter silence among the witches.

"I don't know if that's—" Gabi began.

"You didn't tell us," Salma breathed, more worried than

accusatory. In a rush, she pushed out of her chair and wrapped her arms around her coven member, their heads touching. "You should have said something, Eilidh."

Eilidh. Ay-lee. The name clicked—Eilidh Faulkner. She'd been mentioned in Paulina's file, the daughter of the witch male and human woman.

Gabi sighed, closing her eyes for a long blink. She had to do the right thing, no matter how bad she felt for the girl, no matter how much of a bitch it made her. "I'm sorry. I can't let you near her. Not until I've finished..." *Examining her* sounded too cold.

"Right." Eilidh scrubbed tears off her face, her mouth set in a firm line. She sat stiffly, her jaw clenched so hard it might break, Salam's arms wrapped around her from behind. "Fine, whatever, I get it."

Maisie uncurled herself from the middle of the table and pressed her snout against Eilidh's face, making a low, mournful sound.

"I know, Mais," Eilidh murmured, her voice thick with emotion. Gabi wanted to look away, uncomfortable with their emotion, their familial intimacy.

"You two stay here," Gabi said, rising and ready to be done with this. "Gus, Victoriya, Salma." She met their eyes one by one and prayed this worked. She needed a lead, a hint, a direction. "Let's get this over with, and then you can..." She meant to say *do what was more important*, spend time comforting their coven member, their friend, but she didn't know how to word it without sounding heartless and cold.

She turned on her heel and led them back into the hallway to the external door at the far back. "The morgue's through the garden," she explained without looking back.

Garden was possibly not the best word for it, as it

implied grass. The outside space was a weed-infested square of paving stones with a cinder block shed interrupting the fence between the Pride House and the butcher's opposite. The shed didn't look like much from the outside, but it was better than the equipment Gabi had used in training. She stopped in front of the door and faced the three witches, Salma anxious but composed, Gus slouchy and terrified, and Victoriya ramrod straight and scowling, likely to cover up her unease.

"You don't have to look at the body," Gabi told them. "Earlier, when I first found her, I sensed something wrong around her with my environmental magic. Something sharp and chemical, like nothing I've felt before. I want to know three things—if you sense it too, if you recognise it, and if you can sense the presence of a witch, fae, or elf near Freya. Anything you can tell me will help."

"Help you get Joy out?" Gus confirmed, flicking brown hair out of his face, his eyes wide fixed on the morgue door. "Or help you send her down?"

Gabi stilled.

Everything inside her shut off; she couldn't explain it. Her fears, right there in the open, thrown back at her. What if she found something and Paulina took it to mean that Joy had committed the murder? What if Gabi failed so monumentally that Joy lost the rest of her life, her existence spent locked away?

She met Gus's eyes—scared and distrusting—but didn't know what to say.

Victoriya made a sound in the back of her throat, kicking a shrub with a heavy black boot. "Do you idiots never listen when Joy speaks? Or maybe it's just me she Skypes when she wants girl talk." She snorted. "Pride here is Joy's ex. And judging by how wound tight she is, she still has feelings for Joy." Victoriya's sharp eyes met Gabi's, wry and knowing. "Am I wrong?"

"Joy is my ex-girlfriend," Gabi admitted. And suddenly, as if they'd been handed to her, she found the right words. She met Gus's assessing stare and said, "I'm not going to help Paulina frame Joy for this. I'm not gonna let anyone suffer for this crime except the murderer who committed it. I need your help—to free Joy. Do I have it?"

The wariness left Gus gradually. "Of course," he said, shrugging and plaintive. "She's my best friend."

Victoriya raised an eyebrow, her leather jacket creaking as she spun towards him. "Rude."

"One of," Gus clarified, a smirk in the corner of his mouth, giving life to his face for the first time. "She's *one of* my best friends, of which I have more than one."

Victoriya didn't look at him, her nose in the air, sulking. Gabi almost smiled but all at once the gravity of their situation came back to her. Urgency crushed her chest like an anvil. "Ready?"

They nodded.

Gabi unlocked the morgue door, leading the three witches into the icy room. When everyone was inside, she clicked on her tape recorder and rolled Freya's drawer from inside the refrigerator—but left the sheet covering her body. Gabi wasn't surprised to find everyone hovering right by the door, even Victoriya's face pale. Salma was the first to venture a step nearer, a long minute later, but only with her strand of ivy wrapped around her hand like a touchstone, a comfort blanket.

"It feels green," Salma said, a distracted, faraway look on her face. "And black."

"Old," Victoriya added. Gabi didn't know what to make of *green and black and old.*

"Life," Gus said, his eyes distant, unfocused. "Or death maybe. An arcane witch?"

The only non-elemental witch known to exist, or at least the only one Gabi knew of. Unlike witches bonded to the elements, arcane witches were bound to the dead—to spirits and bones and dying things. Originally elemental, their magic changed when they witnessed a death by witchcraft or committed the dark act themselves. There were two in Agedale that Gabi knew of, and unlike the arcane witches in scary bedtime stories, they used animal bones and dying plants to work their witchcraft. But that might explain what Gabi had sensed on Freya's body...

"No," Victoriya and Salma said together, effectively ruling out that theory.

"What then?" Gus asked with a huff, crossing his arms over his scrawny chest. "Because this is freaking me out, guys."

Victoriya took the last few steps at a determined rush, standing as close to the body as Gabi was. Her beautiful face was so stark that she looked like a different person. "This bitch is old. We shouldn't mess with her."

"Her?" Gabi latched onto the detail, watching Victoriya like a hawk. "Are you sure?"

"Yes," the witches answered at once. It was disconcerting, but Gabi supposed that was what came of being a small, close-knit coven. You knew each other as well as you knew yourself.

"You said she was old. How old?" Gabi pressed. "Is she elderly? Can you tell me her ethnicity, her appearance?"

"It's only a sense," Salma explained in a low, smooth voice. "We can sense it's a woman, that she's old—older than a human life—but we can't *see* her. She's ... she's angry and patient and fair."

"None of it makes sense," Victoriya agreed at a hiss.

"Kind," Gus added, scratching the back of his neck. He was still a few paces back, his head turned down. "She's nice to some people but ... does this to others."

"*Kind*, Gus?" Victoriya asked with a snarl. Her eyes were glued to the hump of the girl's body. "*Seriously?*"

"No, I get that sense too," Salma said, calm enough to soothe even Gabi's temper. Her eyes were closed, her face in a mask of contemplation.

"Why?" Gabi asked, careful to keep her tone from demanding. It was amazing that they could give her this much information. She told herself to be thankful. "Can you sense why she killed—"

"She was angry with her," Salma said in a voice so deep it was a rumble. "Freya had done something wrong."

"She'd been bad," Gus whispered, then shuddered. "We shouldn't be able to sense that."

"Thank you," Gabi said in a voice as level as she could make it. Her body had broken out in chills all over, hairs standing on end even after the gruesome things she'd seen over the course of training. "That's enough. We can go now."

"*Wait.*"

Gabi startled. The voice was a snarl—and it came from Victoriya, right beside her.

A charge of shock ran through Gabi when her eyes fell on the witch's fingers, snaked under the grey-blue covering and wrapped around Freya's dead wrist.

"Victoriya!" Gus shouted in alarm, reaching for his coven member, but Gabi caught Gus's hand before he could touch Victoriya. Her eyes were fixed on the witch's fingers, interlocked with the dead girl's. She wasn't thinking about contamination or evidence or anything she *should* have been thinking about. She was thinking about Regina Stone, who was psychometric, and who Victoriya was a younger copy of.

That's why Victoriya looked familiar at the Town Hall —Gabi had seen the witch's mum every day at the hospital when her own mother had been a patient. Back when they thought there was a chance she'd live.

If Victoriya was even a fraction as talented as Regina, she could point Gabi right to the killer. Joy could be freed before sunset.

"I can't see who killed her," Victoriya muttered, her mouth twisted. "But I *can* see ... red fingernails. Manicured maybe. Something dark. Blood? A vial of it? No. A small bottle. Freya is folding her hands around it and smiling, thanking someone. But it's not what she thinks it is. It's a sleeping tonic, not a study boost spell."

Gabi opened her mouth to thank Victoriya for the details, but a shout came out instead as Victoriya swooned and fell. A shadow moved in the corner of Gabi's vision to catch Victoriya. As the shadow resolved into Gus, Gabi's stomach turned over. She'd known there'd be a price to be paid for freeing Joy, but she assumed *she'd* be the one to pay it, not someone else.

A large brown dog came bounding out of nowhere, growling low in its throat, its tail tucked between its legs as it nosed Victoriya's limp form. When she didn't respond, the dog whined, pressing its face into Victoriya's hair.

There really shouldn't have been a dog in the morgue, but Gabi wasn't sure if this dog was actually a witch, so she made an exception.

"Has she done this before?" she asked Salma as the woman hovered near her coven members, worry etched deep in her face. She'd appeared almost calm in the kitchen before, but now she was anything but, chewing her lip and helping Gus, who was struggling to hold up Victoriya's weight.

"Not that I know of," she replied absently.

Gabi nodded, dredging her memory for what to do when someone fainted. She had no idea and made a mental note to research it later. When Joy was freed and the true killer caught, anyway. "We should take her out of the cold."

"Get off," a voice snarled, and Gabi exhaled in relief as Victoriya wrenched herself out of Gus's hands and found her balance after swaying a few times. "Whoever touches me next gets their hands chewed off."

Gabi blinked at the threat and eyed the dog who'd begun licking Victoriya's face in long swipes. "Tiny, *off*," Victoriya snapped, but she curled a hand in the dog's fur despite her venom, comforting the animal. Gabi blinked, and realised the giant dog was a *familiar*.

Salma and Gus moved back, giving her space, but Gabi hesitated near Victoriya. Her stomach was in knots, guilt tasting like bile in her throat. She was responsible for Victoriya passing out. Her fault. "How do you feel?" she asked, bracing for injury as she leant closer to the witch.

Victoriya acted like Gabi hadn't spoken, glaring around at the morgue. "Why is this place as cold as the goddamn arctic?"

Gabi debated explaining, but she suspected Victoriya would set the dog on her if Gabi put her in a worse mood. She headed instead to the door, hoping the others would follow her example and a bit shocked when they did. Her mind was occupied, turning over everything the witches told her. It wasn't much, but it did narrow the suspects down to well-presented women. Female, manicured nails. Had they confirmed the killer was a witch or not?

Victoriya's fainting had put a ripple in Gabi's memory but at least she'd had her tape recorder on.

"Stop fussing, *grandma*," Victoriya snarled at Gus, but Gabi could sense there was no viciousness behind it. "Shit—Gus. Ignore that, I'm being a dick. Blame it on the psychometry—"

"Victoriya," Gus cut her off, rolling his eyes. "Chill. I know you didn't mean anything by it."

"Still makes me a dick, even if I didn't mean it." Victoriya looked ... ashamed. Gabi watched their interaction, confused and interested. She tried not to let her shock show when Victoriya grabbed Gus's arm roughly, dragged him to her, and hugged him in what looked to be a sharp, painful grip. It only lasted a few seconds, but it told Gabi a lot; as snarly as Victoriya was, that acid hid a true and loyal heart.

They four of them—plus Tiny—convened in the small kitchen with the others, squashing in around the table Eilidh and Maisie occupied along with a half-demolished tin of biscuits and a cup of green tea. Gabi had expected them to clear out after their job was done, but it appeared they were staying, at least for a while. She put on the kettle and got out five more cups, and then hesitated.

She eyed the fox, who eyed her back. Water? Tea? The fox rolled her eyes.

"Who wants—" Gabi began, opening the coffee canister and the bread box filled with various boxes of tea.

"Coffee," Victoriya demanded, dropping into the chair beside Eilidh and rapping the girl on the head.

"I'm fine," Eilidh mumbled but Victoriya looked sceptical. "Can I have tea, Gabriella? Or—should I call you Pride? Is it rude to call you Gabriella?" Eilidh's red-rimmed eyes fixed nervously on Gabi, her round face red and tear-stained but her eyes somewhat less haunted than before. Whatever Maisie had done, the fox seemed to be a comfort.

"You can call me Gabi," she said after a moment, her heart pounding in anticipation of rejection. This was Joy's coven, Joy's family. Surely, they'd shun any hint at familiarity with the woman who'd hurt Joy and then fled after Joy hurt her back. "What tea do you want, Eilidh?"

Eilidh hauled herself out of her seat and came over, trying a smile that didn't quite warm her eyes. "What have you got? I just had green tea last time because it was all I could find." She peered into the bread bin cluttered with boxes in various colours and brands, and said so quietly that only Gabi could hear, she asked, "How is she? Joy? I should have asked before, but with Freya..." Eilidh swallowed the words, and then filled her lungs with shuddering air and pressed on. Gabi was struck with sudden admiration for her bravery; she certainly hadn't been as strong when her mum died. "You're worried, right? So, it must be bad? Is she ... is Joy okay?" Eilidh's bright blue eyes met Gabi's, bleak and full of dread.

Gabi bit the inside of her lip and bought herself a moment by pouring boiling water over the tea bag Eilidh selected—peppermint and green tea. "Paulina took her wand," she replied in a voice so quiet she hoped to hide her fury.

Eilidh's eyes widened. Filled with rage. "She—how? How is that legal?"

"Paulina doesn't care about legal." Gabi became aware of her lip curling back and straightened her expression, stirring Victoriya's coffee next, then making her own extra strong. Eilidh put a regular tea bag in one cup and an apple and cinnamon bag in another, and Gabi wondered if she needed the normal act of making tea to steady her the same way Gabi did.

"Can you get something to her?" Eilidh whispered, fire and retribution in her eyes. Her hand was white-knuckles on the mug handle, and it occurred to Gabi that Eilidh had never once asked if Joy was guilty. She knew for a fact she was innocent.

"I'm going to try." Gabi stared at the mugs, trying in vain to burn away the image of Joy in the cell, weak and terrified, her skin translucent and red around her eyes. "Tomorrow morning."

Eilidh nodded, her blonde and blue hair swaying. "I've got a key for her house. Could you take her a bag of crystals? Just a small one? If she doesn't have her wand ... she'll need them."

Gabi smiled, as warm as she could make it. "If there's anything else she might need, bring that too. I don't know if I'll be able to get them to her, or if they'll be confiscated, but I'll try. The way she's been treated, you're right, it's not legal."

Eilidh looked at her, endless depths of emotion in those grieving blue eyes. "We're gonna help. You get that, right? Not just this one time, with ... with sensing whoever killed ... her. But until Joy's out, until she's free. We're gonna help you, whatever you need."

Gabi nodded, wordless. Her throat was dangerously close to closing up, so she began depositing the cups on the table in the hopes of scattering the choked emotion.

"So, what's next?" Victoriya asked, looking right at Gabi, seeming to echo Eilidh's statement of cooperation and assistance.

Gabi swirled the contents of her cup and took a long drink of bittersweet coffee. "I need to go over my notes and photos from yesterday again." She shouldn't be telling them any of her process but if this meant getting Joy out... "If you all intend to help with this, you need to be officially listed as consultants. There are forms to fill out."

"Whatever you need," Salma agreed in her rich voice, her ivy still wrapped around her hand even as she lifted her mug to her full lips. "And I was thinking, if you had any evidence from the killer ... we could try a locator spell."

Gabi shook her head helplessly. This was useless—all of it. But the coven were helping, and the more help Gabi had, the quicker she could work. She took a breath, held it, and let it out slowly until she wasn't blinded by pessimism. "There's nothing for you to get a trace on, Salma. For now, just—"

Gabi stopped dead. She'd noticed something in the morgue, while Victoriya wrapped her hand around the dead girl's wrist. Her mind had been processing it all this time, ticking away in the background while she was focussed on Victoriya fainting and Joy's incarceration.

Freya had *blood* under her fingernails. A sure sign she'd scratched her killer. It would take days for the lab to get back any sort of DNA match but with those nails ... if Joy had killed her, she would have scratches somewhere on her body.

Hope—this was a glint of hope.

Gabi's breath stuck in her throat; her heart raced so fast she went dizzy. She didn't bother explaining her revelation to the witches; she just shot out of the kitchen, coffee still in hand, and raced into the morgue she'd forgotten to lock.

There was Freya, the sheet pulled back over her arm, and there, when Gabi leaned close, was the blood and skin cells. How she'd missed this before she didn't know, except stress and lack of sleep and the shock and absolute pain of seeing Joy again had muddied her clarity. It didn't matter; she'd seen it now and that was what was important.

She put her coffee on a table at the side, breathing quickly, and jumped out of her skin when the witches—all five of them, the fox included—poured into the icy room. Salma's arm was around Eilidh, but the young witch wore an expression of defiance and hope, of all things.

"What—" Gus began but Salma shushed him.

"Let her work," she murmured quietly, and they gave Gabi space.

Little tremors ran through her hands, adrenaline pumping through her veins and Gabi flicked through the folder of photos she'd printed that morning before going to see Joy. There, a close up of Freya's right palm. She must have been blind to have missed the blood before, but she reminded herself it didn't matter.

"I need everyone to leave," she announced without turning. "I have to write a report, and then I have to conduct a physical examination."

"What's going on?" Eilidh asked in a strained voice. Hopeful but trying to repress it.

"Eilidh," Salma said, soft but stern. "Let's leave her to it. Gabriella, your dad has my number. Please call if you find anything."

Gabi nodded, already pushing them out of the front door of the Pride House so she could get her laptop to type up her rapid thoughts.

NINE
JOY

J oy startled out of a too-short sleep at the sound of an argument getting closer, voices growing louder, angrier. Her body ached everywhere, her nerves frayed to tatters. She kept her knees close to her chest, bound her arms around them, and strained her ears.

"I'm perfectly capable of doing my job," spat a voice Joy knew well.

Gabi.

She sat up straighter on the damp mattress, her eyes pinned on the stone archway, tremors moving through her body. Even the drips of water couldn't calm her now. Was this it? The end? Would she be taken to trial, condemned, and executed?

"That remains to be seen," replied a gravelly voice. Paulina. Joy pressed both hands over her mouth to trap a whimper. She should fight. She could try to run, at least, couldn't she?

But would she make it past both Paulina and Gabi and up the long stone staircase?

Joy's stomach crashed when the two figures appeared

from the dark arch, Paulina's face set in anger as she neared the cells and her red hair frizzy from the damp.

"Get your clothes off," she spat, flicking a frustrated look at Joy, the muscles in her jaw all clenched.

"What?" Joy's breath caught at the words, at the look of seething hatred Paulina threw her way. Not even the bars of the cell could protect her from that hate.

But her clothes—she couldn't do it. The Head Witch has taken everything else from her, but not this, not her modesty.

"*Now*, Mackenzie. I won't tell you again." From the depths of her black cloak, Paulina removed her wand, a stumpy hazel wood, smooth and unadorned.

Shaking so hard her teeth rattled, Joy looked to Gabi for reassurance, but there was such fury in Gabi's dark eyes that Joy found no comfort there. Her breath shattered and Joy realised too late that it was the beginnings of a sob, the sound ripping free into the echoing cells.

Neither Gabi nor Paulina spoke.

"Why are you doing this?" she tried to ask, her breath scraping. She couldn't take her eyes off the threat of the wand aimed between the bars.

"It's a physical examination," Gabi said—calmer now. Something doused her fury. Joy shook harder, but slowly got to her feet. "I just need to take some photos, check you for cuts and scratches. It won't take long."

"You can't make those kinds of promises," Paulina disagreed, her hand white on her wand. "It'll take as long as it takes. Mackenzie, I'm sure I told you to remove your clothes. *Quickly*, before my patience wears out."

"You hired me to do a job, Paulina," Gabi replied coldly. "Let me do it."

As Joy's hands shook on the buttons of her coat, Gabi

took out a camera and fixed a flash onto the top of it. Joy's whole body trembled. She didn't want to take her clothes off, and especially not in front of someone else.

But she didn't want to be hexed or cursed, either.

"Unlock the cell," Gabi ordered Paulina—*ordered* her. The shock of that allowed Joy to slip the damp fur off her shoulders and take hold of the hem of her top underneath. In one rough movement, and before she could really think about it, Joy ripped the purple cotton off her body and over her head. She clutched it hard in her fingers, not letting it fall to the floor like she had her coat, a flimsy safety blanket.

She flinched hard at the squeal of the cell bars swinging to admit Gabi.

"Look at me," Gabi said calmly, drawing Joy's focus. "Just me. Okay?"

Joy tried to take a breath, but her lungs wouldn't fill even a fraction. Her chest tingled, itchy awareness of Paulina seeing her nakedness and the prick of the cold cell combining until it felt like needles pricking her arms, her chest. She refused to take off her jeans and didn't even reach for the button.

"I need you to hold out your arms." Gabi looked Joy in the eye—steady, gentle. Joy forced her locked fingers to surrender the top, a cry slipping free as it fell, and she held out her trembling arms while Gabi took photos from different angles. Joy's gaze flinched past Gabi's bent head as Paulina moved closer, scowling at Joy's hands, and all at once she wanted to take them back, cover her body, and be sick. "Turn them over," Gabi instructed, and then, "Eyes on me, Joy."

With effort, Joy dragged her eyes back to Gabi, the camera held up to her face as she photographed Joy's palms, the inside of her elbow, and her forearms. "Alright," she said, lowering the camera for a moment. "Now I'm going to take photos of your chest and stomach. Keep your arms by your side."

Joy struggled to move her arms, locked as they now were. Her chest rose and fell fast with panicked breaths, her stomach forming knots on knots. She couldn't keep her eyes on Gabi, had to squeeze them closed as the shutter closed fast, one photo after another of Joy's body, her skin, the pearlescent bra she'd picked out what felt like a year ago, thinking it was cute and apt because it had little birds embroidered over the cups and Joy was recording numbers of endangered birds that day.

"Turn around, Joy."

She did, her mind stuck on that morning. She hadn't even got into work. She hadn't called her boss to tell him she had to miss today—she'd completely forgotten—and now no one would have recorded those important numbers—

"Done," Gabi said, and Joy's breath fell out of her mouth all at once. Her eyes opened slowly, wanting to stay soldered shut. Gabi had bent to retrieve Joy's clothes and now held out her top, which Joy quickly hurried to yank over her head. She was still frozen cold, still shaking violently, but she felt less like she'd been cut open and laid bare for all to see. She felt the tiniest bit better too when Gabi hung the camera around her neck and helped bundle Joy into her fluffy pink coat, even if it was wet and cold.

"Satisfied?" Gabi demanded, and it took a slow moment for Joy to realise she was speaking to Paulina. Not her —*Paulina*. "No cuts, no bruises, no scratches. And yet Freya has skin under her nails and defensive wounds on her hands."

Joy dared a glimpse at Paulina, but only because Gabi had placed herself between them. The Head Witch's face turned a mottled dark red, and she looked like she'd swallowed a sour sweet, but she did something very strange. She looked at Joy and said, "You're free to go, Mackenzie. Pride, fill out the necessary paperwork."

And then she stormed off up the ramp.

Joy didn't understand the words for a long while and couldn't begin to even process their meaning.

Free to go...

Joy could leave? She could go home?

Her breath hitched, the only warning, and then Joy collapsed into wretched, gasping tears. Her knees weakened, sending her to the floor, but arms wrapped around her, deceptively strong and muscular, and the lens of a camera was digging into Joy's stomach, the embrace an awkward comfort.

The touch ... it unlocked something in Joy, and her hands scrabbled for purchase on Gabi's wooden coat, clinging to her for dear life—for dear freedom.

"Is it—is it real?" she asked, her voice thick and clumsy. "Can I—"

"You can go home," Gabi replied, guessing her thoughts. Her hand slid down Joy's matted hair, just once, but it calmed Joy enough for her to get hold of herself and stem the flow of her sobs.

"Thank you," she rasped, moving away a step and rubbing her face dry on her sleeve.

But Gabi shook her head hard, that furious expression returning to her face. "You should *never* have been here in the first place." Her eyes were dark, that same bottomless black they'd been when she'd arrived with Paulina. "Come on. You don't need to stay here any longer."

Joy was still struggling to process her liberation, but she

quickly followed Gabi out of the cell, as if lingering would leave her trapped there another day.

She braced for witchcraft to slam into her, keeping her captive, as they headed for the archway. When it didn't, Joy exhaled a shuddering breath and let her feet spirit her up the ramp and into the light, fresh air of the lobby.

She didn't believe it, even as Gabi got a set of papers from the friendly receptionist, even as Joy filled in her details and, with utterly numb fingers, signed her name. Even as she stepped tentatively past the columns on the front door and into the fresh air, it took a long moment for it to hit her. She'd thought she'd be locked down there for the rest of her life.

But she was free.

TEN

GABI

Four weeks before Gabi left for uni—three weeks before she and Joy broke up—Joy had given her a cross of rowan branches, bound by purple thread in the middle. It was supposed to be for protection, but Gabi hadn't known that when she'd taken a fancy to it. Then, it had hung in Joy's bedroom window over a plant of basil and a garland of some other herb. Now, Gabi watched Joy's eyes slide to it in the Law House's hallway, her stare lingering as she realised Gabi had not only kept it but brought it to her new home.

She couldn't possibly know Gabi had taken it to the flat she'd shared with three other students in Liverpool, unwilling and unable to throw it out. But Gabi still felt like her feelings were laid bare as Joy passed through the hallway and into the kitchen.

Joy was shaking, and all Gabi could do was sit with her at the table, emptied of every comforting thing she might have said, instead full of rage and cold and protectiveness. She was breathing hard; she had to get herself under control, but she didn't know how.

"Are you alright?" Joy asked finally, breaking the tense silence that hung over the shabby kitchen table. Gabi met her earnest brown eyes and everything inside her softened.

Not now, she hissed at her own heart. *Not when she can see every emotion on my face.*

"Am *I* alright?" Gabi couldn't quite contain her bitter laugh. "Joy, you were just locked up in a damp, horrid cell and—*your wand,*" she realised with alarm. "Paulina didn't give it back."

Gabi shot to her feet, her mind jumping from one thought to the next. "I'll go back to the town hall and get it—"

"No!" Joy's breathing came quicker, harsher, her face paling. She reached her hand out, seemed to remember their history, and drew it back. "Please don't—don't leave me alone. I don't want to be—"

True and absolute *fury* speared Gabi. She was going to murder Paulina for that panicked look in Joy's eye alone. Never mind everything else she'd done.

Gabi checked her rage as she walked around the table, stuffing it down where Joy wouldn't see it. Ignoring every bit of logic that reminded her they weren't friends anymore, she pulled Joy from her chair and bound her into a tight hug.

Safe—Joy wasn't locked away at the mercy of Paulina fucking Montgomery. She was safe.

"I'm not going anywhere," Gabi vowed, her hands flexing against Joy's back. And no matter what history was between them, no matter what hurt and painful words still hung in the air, Gabi wasn't leaving Joy's side for a fucking second.

"If this was any other town," she said, simply because she needed to fill the silence and she had so many thoughts in her head, they were clamouring to get out, "I could file charges against Paulina for how she treated you. You have rights, even as a murder suspect. But here..."

"I know," Joy mumbled against Gabi's shoulder. "It's okay."

"It's not. It's fundamentally *not* okay. Just because we're supernatural doesn't mean we should be stuck in the past." Gabi was breathing hard, worked up again.

"Fundamentally," Joy repeated. It sounded like she was smiling. Why the hell was she smiling? "I'd forgotten how you talked."

"Oh," Gabi said lamely.

Joy wasn't smiling anymore. "I'm sorry, Gabi."

"Joy, you don't have to be—"

"You just got me out of jail, made Paulina let me go, and you—you *believed* me, you didn't think I'd hurt that girl and —" She took a raspy breath. "I hurt you, those things I said, I was so cruel and heartless and you still—you still got me out and I—"

Gabi's arms tightened around her. She didn't want to let Joy go but there was the reminder again, the reality of the mess between them. Joy wasn't Gabi's to hold.

"You don't have to be sorry," Gabi murmured finally, discarding every other response. Her eyes were stinging, her heart thumping fast. She still loved Joy. God, even *years* hadn't dimmed the sheer force of emotion. Even now, Gabi loved her.

"Ugh," Joy said, putting space between them, glancing awkwardly away as she plucked at her damp-stained clothes. "I need to shower."

Gabi's mouth flickered into a hesitant smile. She leaned against the worktop for stability. "I wasn't going to mention it but ... your hair's kind of ... brown."

Joy laughed, a bright sound out of nowhere. Her eyes lit up, her whole face softening, and Gabi's heart thumped, helplessly fallen.

"Is it alright if I—I meant, can I use yours? I don't want to go all the way home to—"

"It's fine," Gabi said, gentling her voice. "Take as long as you need; you know where the bathroom is."

Joy turned to the hallway, but she hesitated. In a rush of movement, she caught Gabi's hand, sending Gabi's heart rate skyrocketing. Joy had always been warm where Gabi was cold and even now, her hand was hot.

"Thank you," Joy breathed, her solemn brown eyes holding Gabi's gaze. She wasn't thanking her for the shower.

Gabi nodded, her throat tight. Touching—Joy was *touching* her. Every thought fell out of Gabi's head as her focus narrowed to that point of contact. And then before Gabi could do anything more than stare at her, Joy was out in the hall, trudging wearily up the stairs.

"Your coven will be here soon," Gabi called up the staircase. She'd texted her dad to call Salma as soon as they left Town Hall. "I'll let them into the kitchen if you're still in the shower."

"Thank you." Joy's reply was ... small.

She shut the bathroom door, but Gabi knew she was crying. She wished she could go up there, bundle Joy into her arms and hold her all night, but Gabi wasn't sixteen anymore. Things had changed, *years* had passed.

She was relieved when an animal scream sounded at the front door, a high, panicked shrieking that quietened only when Victoriya snarled, "For fuck's sake, Maisie," and hammered on the door with her fist.

The coven was here.

ELEVEN

JOY

Joy waited under the spray of hot water for her tears to stop. She could still see the cell around her, feel the chill air on her skin, the trickle of water over her hand. Part of her was stuck in the moment when Paulina forced her to remove her coat and the top underneath.

Joy shuddered hard enough to rattle her bones, her head pressed to the cool tile of Gabi's shower and shoulders jumping with suppressed sobs.

She couldn't get her body to still, couldn't make the tears dry up, so she just waited for it to burn itself out. It finally did, what felt like hours later, and left her hollow chested. She wished the spray from the shower was rainwater, wished for that cool calming influence on her fae senses, even if it only soothed for a moment and didn't fix the root of her fears.

Only the thought of Gabi and her coven convinced Joy to drag herself from beneath the water. Numb, she stepped out of the shower.

She flinched, crying out when an orange blur threw itself at her and wound around her ankles. She reached automatically for her missing wand but let out a rough sigh when Maisie let out a familiar high keen.

Joy couldn't tell if her fox-bound friend was chastising Joy or apologising for scaring her. Joy grabbed a well-worn soft blue towel from the rack on the wall and wound it around her body before she fell to her knees on the rug.

Maisie burrowed close, the cold point of her nose leaving a wet streak on Joy's neck, and Joy held on tight to her friend. Only then did the grip on her chest start to ease.

"Sorry," Joy said but wasn't sure why.

Maisie made a noise in the back of her throat and nudged Joy's shoulder hard enough to bruise.

"Right," Joy murmured, laughing. "Don't apologise. Sorry." She thumped her head. "That came out by accident, I didn't mean to."

"Joy," Salma called from outside the bathroom door. "I've got your wand and your bag from the town hall. Do you want it in there with you?"

"Can I—" Maisie nudged Joy when she stopped, her face hot and eyes burning, close to crying again. "Can I have some clothes? I don't want to put these back on."

Every moment of wearing them would remind her of the cell and reinforce that it hadn't just been a bad dream. She'd really been locked up for witchicide.

"Of course," Salma replied, her velvety voice comforting even through the door. "I'll go find you some."

Joy felt closer to falling apart with every second she sat there, staring at the multicoloured tiles of the bathroom floor, but then Salma was back, nudging the door open just wide enough to slide Joy a bundle of fabric. Maisie kept close to Joy as she stood, shaking again, and struggled to get her legs into the soft jogging bottoms, fumbling her unsteady arms into the long sleeved T-shirt and hoodie. It was only when Joy was dressed, the top clinging to her generous curves, that she realised they were *Gabi's* clothes. They smelled exactly like her—peppermint and freshly printed pages. Joy's bottom lip wobbled, foretelling more sobs.

Maisie nudged Joy's leg, making a quiet sound—a question.

"I'm alright," Joy replied in a thick voice. She didn't want Maisie to worry; she didn't want *any* of them to worry.

Joy wished she could convince her face to pretend everything was normal, but that was too much to ask. At the very least, she could stop hiding in this bathroom.

Her fingers on the handle, Joy took a deep breath and held it in her lungs long enough to steady herself. It was a trick she'd learned from Gabi when they were much younger.

The minute Joy stepped foot in the kitchen downstairs, she found her fingers locked around the bulbous end of her amethyst wand. Her coven launched forward and bundled her into a hug, a mess of limbs and worry and love. They were all talking at once, and it threatened to overwhelm Joy's eardrums, but a tiny smile tugged at her lips.

Gabi hung back but Joy could feel her eyes on her.

"I'm going to *murder* that bitch Paulina," Victoriya snarled, holding her silver lighter in white-knuckled fingers as if she'd call up witch-fire right this moment. But she didn't let go of Joy for a second.

"Thanks," Joy rasped, crying again but for a good reason.

"I might even condone it," Salma said, rubbing Joy's back, her earthy scent overwhelming Joy's senses.

Gus and Eilidh held her tight enough to bruise, close

enough that the turquoise ends of Eilidh's hair ended up in Joy's mouth, and even that was absurdly comforting.

Joy pulled back enough to wipe her eyes. "Thank you."

She might recover. From being locked away, from being wandless, from seeing a dead girl. As long as she had her coven, she thought she might recover. But there was a new fear there, telling her Paulina would find another reason to make Gabi arrest her, another reason to lock Joy in that cell again and *for good* this time.

She shuddered and looked at Gabi. "I want to ... I want to help you find the person who killed that girl."

"No," Gabi shot down without even considering it. Her oval face had shuttered, her brown eyes blank, but Joy knew there was emotion underneath it, just well hidden.

"If she—" Joy swallowed the lump in her throat, extricated herself from the group hug, and tried to pull herself back together. "Paulina will find a way to send me back there—"

"She will *not*," Gabi cut her off, and there was sudden fire in her eyes, strangling her voice.

Joy blinked, and this time she wasn't sure why she was going to cry. "*Please*. I can't—I can't do *nothing*."

Gabi gave Joy a long, searching look. After a prolonged moment, she sighed and crossed her arms across her tight white shirt. "Alright," she agreed. "You can help."

"And the rest of us?" Gus asked, scratching the back of his head and rumpling his dark hair. "Are we still part of the team?"

Gabi closed her eyes, just longer than a blink. "You're putting yourself in Paulina's sights. You have to know that. She wants Joy convicted of this crime for some unfathomable reason—if you help me find the actual killer, she'll know your names. She'll *remember* you."

And that was never a good thing when it came to Paulina.

"You think she doesn't know us already?" Victoriya's remark was bitter—but she was right. She raised a sharp eyebrow, somehow managing to look dangerous in tight exercise pants and a vest so low-cut at the sides Joy could see her bra. She'd clearly come here straight from teaching her dance class, or maybe even ran out and left her students there. Joy felt another part of her soften with affection.

Victoriya went on fiercely, "We all applied to be part of her coven, and she told us to fuck off. Joy's mum is fae, Eilidh's is human, and Paulina's a prejudiced piece of shit when it comes to species. She doesn't want her witches *contaminated*."

Gabi went still. "She didn't say that."

"She did," Joy sighed, running her thumb over the familiar crystal of her wand. "She said that about me—and Gus."

Gus snorted. "Oh yeah, she *hates* me." Not that he was her biggest fan either, since she was one of the most transphobic people in this town.

Gabi shook her dark head, her jaw clenched. Her shoulders rose and fell with a hard breath. "I fucking *hate* that woman."

Joy blinked. Gabi hadn't sworn much when they were younger. Now, apparently, she swore freely and with relish.

Sadness threatened to crush Joy at the thought of everything she'd missed, but there was curiosity there too, the desire to learn what was new about her oldest friend.

"We all do," Salma agreed, twisting a rope of ivy around her wrist, the movement absent. "She's offended each and every one of us in some way. The words she's used to describe my mother..." She snapped a leaf off the stem.

Gus sighed. His eyes were bleak, enhancing his uncommonly rumpled look, his jeans well-worn and his shirt—emblazoned with the logo of some metal band—wrinkled and unironed. Gus might not have had the best things, or have lived in the best house, but he always took the time with his appearance. Joy's heart ached when she realised he was probably too busy worrying over her.

"Look, Pride," he said, "we've all got our reasons to do this. It doesn't matter if Paulina gets her knickers in a twist. We're used to it. She already thinks we're dangerous because we're different."

"I can't believe you're talking about her underwear," Victoriya snarked, pretending to gag.

"I know." Gus faked a shudder. I'm so brave."

Joy almost laughed.

"She shouldn't get away with shit like this," Gabi seethed through gritted teeth.

"Who's going to stop her?"

Joy jumped at Eilidh's voice. She sounded ... different. Weaker, like she'd been the one in the cells instead. Joy reached out and threaded her fingers with her friend's, squeezing reassuringly.

Gabi didn't reply because Eilidh was right; Paulina sat at the very top of Agedale's hierarchy. Only the most powerful fae and the elven elders would challenge her, and Joy had neither of those on their side.

Silence settled over them, a swiftly closing net that made Joy's chest tight. It was a reminder that Paulina could turn up at any moment and throw Joy back in jail, no matter what evidence Gabi had to prove she wasn't a murderer.

"So, what's first, boss?" Gus asked, slouching into a seat at the table.

Gabi sighed, rubbing the bridge of her nose. "First, I

need silence to concentrate, which means you all need to leave." She lifted her eyes to Joy's face, her gaze so gentle it hurt. Her voice softened, too. "Unless you want to stay. I can rig some tripwires around the house with my magic if you'd feel safer here."

Joy opened her mouth to shoot down the offer but ... she would feel better with someone else's magic around the house. And she wasn't sure she wanted to go home yet. It was so close to the beach.

So she swallowed her pride and nodded. "If that's alright. I don't want to get in the way though—"

"Joy," Gabi stopped her and smiled—*smiled*. "It's fine. You're always welcome."

Joy's heart gave a fatalistic thud; she dropped her eyes before Gabi could read all the feelings she still kept inside her.

"*Wow*." Gus drew out the word. "Here I was thinking I'd come over to protect you. You, me and Mais would have a sleepover, maybe watch some scary films, Netflix and chill."

Joy's face heated. She rolled her eyes and reached across Eilidh to shove Gus's shoulder. "Shut up. I'm not 'chilling' with anyone."

Gus sighed, dramatic to the very last. "I thought you'd finally admit your all-consuming passion for me. I know it burns with the force of a thousand suns."

Even Eilidh laughed at his over-dramatics, though the sound was subdued. Joy held her hand tighter, worry spiking, but Eilidh avoided her gaze. Joy studied her more closely as Gus and Victoriya began to bicker.

Eilidh's hands were clean, her clothes smudge-free, and it was so strange to see her without a single bit of charcoal staining her—evidence of hours spent in her makeshift studio in her garden shed—that Joy wanted to question her. But there was something about the way Eilidh held her chin up, her expression tight, that made Joy hesitant to push.

Instead, her eyes drifted of their own accord to Gabi. Part of her still couldn't believe she was back, after all this time. Gabi looked up at that same moment, sensing Joy's attention, and her stomach flipped. It was like she was thirteen again and seeing her for the first time. It was like she was sixteen and head over heels in love.

"So, how did you two lovesick morons break up?" Victoriya asked abruptly.

Joy's whole body stiffened. She could no longer meet Gabi's eyes.

G abi nearly choked.

"Emphasis on the love*sick*," Victoriya went on, "because this shit is nauseous."

"It's *nauseating*, technically," Gus corrected at the same time Salma gasped, "*Victoriya!*"

With a frown, she added, "I'm so sorry, Gabriella."

Gabi waved a hand, feeling more awkward than she'd felt in the entirety of her life. She wanted to fall into bed and block out the past few days, or burn them out of her memory completely on the rowing machine upstairs, but neither were viable. One, there was only one bed and Joy needed it more, and two, there was so fucking much Gabi needed to do and even standing here, keeping an eye on Joy as she was, she was still conscious of the time slipping away. The witch-killer moving freely through the town.

"Seriously, though," Victoriya pressed, green eyes bright with vicious curiosity.

Gabi sighed and repressed the urge to massage her tired eyes; Victoriya wasn't going to drop this.

Gabi suddenly wished she was somewhere else, *anywhere* else. She didn't want to relive that day she'd stood outside Joy's bedroom door, her heart breaking clean in two when Joy said she'd fallen out of love with her. But it had been a lie, if Gabi believed what Joy had told her yesterday. Which she did. Even when the truth hurt, she knew it when she heard it.

A lie had kept her away all these years, even when she could have—and *should* have—come back on weekends and holidays to visit her dad. To visit other family members she'd neglected, too.

"Victoriya hasn't been house-trained yet," Gus very seriously told Gabi, ducking a sharp elbow from his friend. "We haven't managed to teach her a single manner, let alone mann*ers,* plural."

Victoriya just arched a dark eyebrow, looking from Gabi to Joy and back again. If Gabi ever needed a suspect interrogated, she'd found the perfect candidate to do it. "Well?"

"Stop hassling them *right* this minute," Salma hissed, clipping Victoriya's ear.

"It was ... stupid," Joy murmured before Gabi could formulate a response, something that would both satisfy the witch and not reveal anything personal.

Gabi gripped the counter behind her tightly at Joy's words. A stone had dropped in her stomach; Gabi's body had gone perfectly still.

"I was..." Joy twisted her pale fingers together under her too-long sleeves. Gabi was acutely conscious, had been since the moment Joy had come back down, of Joy wearing her clothes. Fae were the territorial, instinct-driven species, but even as an elf Gabi was not unaffected by the idea of her scent being all over Joy again.

"It was just after my mum died, and I wasn't ... *me*. I

was angry," Joy said in a lowered voice. Gabi wanted to hug her, the impulse so strong she had to take a deep breath to fight it off. "I said some things I didn't mean, and I should have apologised, but by that point we'd already ... drifted."

Gabi had already moved to Liverpool, she meant.

Gabi felt like all her insides had crumpled. She couldn't stop herself, the urge to comfort Joy so severe she had to reach out and lay her hand on Joy's arm, just for a second. Joy's eyes flashed with an unidentifiable emotion as she looked at Gabi's fingers, curled around her forearm, and right when Gabi was about to snatch her hand back, Joy smiled.

Her heart pounding, Gabi leaned close enough to whisper without being overheard, "I'm sorry too. And I forgive you."

Joy's answering smile lit up her whole face. For a split second, the girl who was terrified and burdened because of the past two days faded—at least until Victoriya spoke.

"Well, shit," Victoriya murmured, flicking her lighter open and shut, open and shut. "That's fucking tragic."

Eilidh, who'd been so silent Gabi had almost forgotten she was there, pushed back from the table, dropped her hand from where it clutched her necklace—a bird's talon and several grey and white feathers—and bound Joy up in a big hug, her mess of blonde and blue curls falling on Joy's shoulder.

Gabi startled when Eilidh released Joy and immediately drew *Gabi* into a hug that smelled of mint and lemon. She stiffened but let the witch hug her despite her own discomfort.

"If you want me to get Theodore to peck Victoriya, I can make that happen," Eilidh offered as she stepped back, her eyes bloodshot up close. Gabi wondered how long she'd known her cousin was dead, the hallmarks of a sleepless night written all over her. Gabi would have to speak to her about Freya soon, but not now.

"Theodore?" Gabi murmured. Had she missed a coven member? She'd assumed they were all here.

In answer Eilidh pointed at the cupboard behind her, squashed on the top of which was a snow-white sea gull. Gabi startled; how long had it been sitting there?

"He's my familiar," Eilidh explained, trying her best to smile.

Gabi realised, all at once, that no one had told Joy the body on the beach belonged to Eilidh's cousin. Was it intentional? Did their worry for Joy prevent them from troubling her more? Gabi understood the urge to coddle her but if the coven left without illuminating Joy, *Gabi* would have to tell her. Joy would find out tomorrow anyway, and Gabi wasn't stupid enough to think Joy would get a good night's sleep as long as she didn't know the girl's identity—not when Joy had spent the past two nights locked in the dark, cold quiet of a jail cell.

Anger rose with a vengeance at the reminder of Joy's suffering, but Gabi reminded herself she had no right to those feelings.

Eilidh blinked at Gabi with hollow blue eyes. Had she noticed Gabi's thoughts racing, her mind spinning?

"Victoriya's a bit mean," Eilidh whispered, "but you'll get used to her. And she doesn't mean any of it. Not seriously."

Gabi nodded, not sure how to reply. Eilidh spoke as if Gabi would be spending a lot of time with the coven. She definitely had to *consult* them since she needed their help, but she wouldn't be *hanging out* with them. Still, she made herself murmur, "Good to know."

Salma let out a grand sigh and stood from the table, her grey dress rippling down to her feet along with a few stray leaves from the plants wound around her. "We should be leaving. We've troubled Gabriella quite enough."

"It's fine," Gabi rushed to say.

Victoriya opened her mouth—but Salma grabbed her jacket and hauled her out of the chair, cutting off her words. Victoriya grinned. She loved it, loved winding them up. The only way to beat a girl like that was to ignore her. Gabi filed that away for later.

Salma let go of Victoriya's jacket and pointed her firmly towards the door. "We're leaving. *You* can go wait on the doorstep. Gus, put that back. Maisie, you're not keeping that scarf. Eilidh, dear, I'll drive you home."

Gabi wasn't very surprised to see that Maisie had curled up on a scarf Gabi had left on a chair, or to find Gus spinning an acid-green spatula around his fingers so fast it blurred. They were hard work, this coven, Gabi thought, and felt a bit sorry for Salma, who was either their mother or their keeper.

"And me?" Joy asked in a quiet voice.

"You," Salma said, patting Joy's cheek with a gentle brown hand gleaming with gold rings. Definitely mother, not keeper. "Stay here and get some sleep. And try not to worry; it won't change anything."

Joy sighed, her mouth twisting into the smile-frown Gabi recognised as meaning she was nervous.

"You'll be fine," Salma reassured. "Gus, for the last time, put that back."

Gus reluctantly put the spatula back in the yellow mug of utensils. As soon as he stood, Maisie yipped and followed him, sparing a backward glance for the scarf that was apparently very comfortable. All at once, Salma herded everyone but Joy out of the house, calling goodbye as she went.

The door shut with a slam, and Gabi fought not to tense. This felt very different to being alone with Joy in her cell.

"Joy," Gabi started, meaning to apologise. For what happened six years ago, for this awkward tension between them now, for having to be cold and distant earlier when she was taking photos to prove Joy was innocent. But she slammed her mouth shut. How—*how* did she put all her feelings into words?

Before she could even attempt it, Joy blurted, "I still love you."

Gabi blinked.

She swore her heart stopped its anxious beat.

Joy still what? She loved who? *Gabi?*

"Holy shit," Gabi whispered without truly meaning to.

"Oh, God," Joy breathed, her eyes so wide, so panicked. She backed up across the kitchen and bumped into the door. "Um. I meant to apologise for everything I said to you all those years ago. I didn't mean to—I'm going to—*bye.*"

Joy *ran*, speeding into the hall and up the stairs.

Gabi heard the bathroom door shut and took an unconscious step, her mouth working around silent words. Joy's words repeated again and again in her mind as she tried to find a different meaning. There was no way Joy could still love her, not after arguments and years and miles had wedged so much space between them.

And what did that *mean*? Was Gabi supposed to do something, *say* something? She pulled her hair, ragging it from its neat ponytail, and let out a loud groan of frustration.

Should she pretend she felt nothing for Joy, or tell her

she still had feelings, too? She didn't know if it was love, because how *could* it still be love after they'd changed so much and lived through such different things? They weren't the same two girls.

But her heart was still racing and thumping and there wasn't much arguing with it.

THIRTEEN
JOY

Oh, *God*. Why had Joy said that? She shut the bathroom door and slid down the inside of it, ignoring her many aches as they flared up. Why couldn't she have acted like a normal person and had a normal conversation instead of blurting out that she loved Gabi?

Well—because she was still wound so tight, she was close to snapping, and she was terrified and jumpy and emotional after everything that had happened. But how was she supposed to face Gabi now?

Joy flashed back to being inside that cell, the cold and damp not the worst of her conditions, but rather the waiting, the fearing, and the space to *think* and fill her mind with terrors. She couldn't go back there. She couldn't do it again. But how was she supposed to work with Gabi now she'd blurted out her feelings?

Joy pulled her knees to her chest and thumped her forehead against them.

It took ten minutes for the mortification to wear off. She needed to text Eilidh and Gus and the others, and make sure they all got home alright. Huffing, trying to banish those words from her head—*I still love you*—she patted the pocket of her borrowed hoodie for her phone.

"Oh, no," she breathed, pausing her search. "Ohhhhh, no."

Joy's amethyst wand was tucked into the waistband of her pants, but she vaguely remembered putting her phone down on the kitchen table.

"Please, no," she groaned, squeezing her eyes shut as if it could block out the past twenty minutes.

But she could picture it now, the pink casing winking at her from her memory, sitting right next to the pot of tea on the table. Joy warred with herself, but the need to check her friends' safety won out in the end.

Groaning and berating herself the whole way, Joy pulled herself to her feet, cracked open the door, and tiptoed back downstairs.

She could do this. She'd just pretend she'd never said ... what she'd said. Easy. No problem. She could do this.

It was too much to hope that Gabi would have gone up to her room; no, she was pacing the kitchen floor. Joy tried to duck in and out, but Gabi was too observant for that.

Her clever brown eyes swung to Joy, and she froze, phone in hand.

"I—" Joy started, but it was too awkward, and she didn't know what to say. She held up the pink phone she'd snatched from the table, not looking directly at Gabi. "Sorry. I'm gonna—go to sleep. Like Salma said."

Ughh, shut up, Joy. Stop making this nightmare of a day worse.

She backed up slowly, unable to even look in Gabi's direction, let alone meet her gaze. Her heart pounded, pushing embarrassment into every inch of her just in case there remained a dark corner that *wasn't* utterly mortified.

"Joy," Gabi sighed. "You don't need to be..."

But Joy took another few steps. "I'm going up to sleep. No problem. No worries."

Yup, she definitely needed both those statements. This was going *so* well.

"Take the bed in my room."

"But you—" Joy met Gabi's eyes without thinking, a frown creasing her brow.

"I'm fine on the couch. I won't get much sleep anyway; I only need a few hours. I'll be fine." Looking closely, Joy thought Gabi looked exhausted. She should be sleeping more. Joy hesitated to accept her bed.

"Joy," Gabi said in a voice so soft it was barely there, making Joy swallow hard. "We should talk."

Joy shook her flaming face. "We can forget what I said, it's alright, really. I was—I was under duress. The dead girl and—being locked up—Paulina—seeing you—it was a lot to take and—"

She dared a mortified look at Gabi and found her —smiling.

"Under duress?" Gabi asked, the side of her mouth curled up. Joy's heart did a stupid little jump; she told it to stop that immediately.

When Gabi laughed, it was like being in the past. It was like no time passed at all. Joy rooted herself firmly to the spot on the linoleum to stop her traitor legs from rushing across the small distance. She wanted to throw herself into Gabi's arms, but they weren't together, this wasn't high school, and Joy had embarrassed herself enough tonight.

"I should go to bed," Joy repeated for the umpteenth time, walking backwards. Oh god, did that sound like an invitation? She really hoped not. Even if it *was* Gabi's bed and she didn't really *need* an invitation to use it and—

"I still," Gabi said quickly. "I have—certain feelings. For you."

Joy stopped walking, her heart missing its next beat. "You have what?"

"Certain feelings," Gabi repeated, closely examining a scratch in the table's surface. "For you."

Joy felt a laugh rise, and wondered if she was hysterical as she choked it down. After today, she wouldn't have been so surprised. "What does that mean?"

"It means I have certain feelings for you." Gabi shifted her weight, shoving her hands into her pockets, her shoulders rounded.

Ooookay.

Joy neared a step against her better judgement. "Is that why you kept the rowan cross?"

Gabi nodded.

Joy was making her uncomfortable.

"Alright," she said after a moment. Maybe they needed to get all of this out in the open. "We'll talk."

She hoped she'd get through the conversation without blurting out anything else.

FOURTEEN

GABI

When Gabi drew her coat around herself the next afternoon, her body aching from the magic she'd used to set up a magical warning system around the Law House, she was surprised to find she wasn't nervous about going to Joy's house later. She was due to meet the coven when she'd finished work—well, when her official work hours were over. She never actually *finished*. They'd agreed to gather everyone together to discuss how the witches might assist Gabi in finding the killer, which *should* have made Gabi nervous, or at least reluctant to share space with the chaotic coven again. But instead, she had an extra bounce in her step and couldn't quite keep the smile off her face.

The day passed in a blur of activity, Gabi's favourite type of day. The kind that kept her moving, kept her mind occupied, and kept her too busy to let a single worry of failure into her head.

She went from house to house, questioning Eilidh and the other friends and family of Freya Faulkner with confidence and sympathy—something Gabi struggled with on an average day. She hadn't fully found the balance of sounding capable enough to be respected but sympathetic enough to coax people into talking.

Afterwards, her mood stayed buoyant even as she went door to door near the beach, where someone might have noticed something suspicious. It was a long shot, but she put up a board asking for people to come forward if they'd seen anything the morning of the murder. By the end of the day, Gabi's business card wallet was empty, and she'd accomplished nothing, but at least she'd tried.

The only thing nagging at her was that she hadn't had enough time to interview the witness Paulina had conjured, the one who saw someone who looked like Joy on the beach that morning.

It was five o'clock by the time Gabi got home, the sky dark already at this time of year as she heated up a microwave meal. Piling her bag, notebook, tablet, and ever-demanding paperwork on the table, Gabi allowed herself five minutes of stillness and quiet. Five minutes of inactivity to eat her food and begin to unspool the tension in her body, before she made herself a strong coffee and, tapping her fingers on the table in indecision, made a video call to one of her professors from university.

She'd only been in his class for eight weeks, a night course she attended to keep her communicative skills up to date—to help her come across as anything but a cold-hearted bitch, a reputation she'd earned after a few months on campus. Coming across as a detached, unaffected cop was fine when intimidating suspects but witnesses ... not so much. The problem was Gabi preferred all her emotion to be on the inside, far down where no one could see it, not written across her face.

But through the class she'd met Rick Ali, whose main

passion was criminal profiling. With a case like Gabi's current one, she could use some light shed on the sort of person who carved the word *naughty* into a teenage girl's face and stuffed her insides with rubbish. Short of knowing the killer was female and about Joy's height—if Paulina's witness could be believed—Gabi knew fuck all. She needed to narrow down the suspects, especially since Agedale was seventy percent female.

"Gabriella," Rick greeted when he accepted the call. His eyes crinkled at the edges, a smile spreading across his brown face. "I heard you got offered a job."

"Trial," Gabi corrected, sitting straighter and trying not to let her frustration show. "It's nothing guaranteed yet. And about that trial..."

"This isn't a social call then," he said knowingly. "What kind of criminal are you searching for?"

Gabi curled her hands around the base of the chair where he couldn't see. "A killer. And not a regular one."

Rick pushed his glasses up his nose and leaned closer to the screen. "How much can you tell me?"

"Without getting in shit with my superior? I don't know. She's ... strict." That was definitely *not* the word, but Gabi would prefer, but she had to at least *try* and stay professional. She took a breath and sat straighter. "The victim is a teenage girl, not involved in anything criminal from what I can tell, just a regular girl. Argues with her parents, sneaks out to see her boyfriend, goes shopping with her friends." To the two shops in Agedale that sold something other than food and spell ingredients—options were limited. Gabi learned all this from questioning Freya's family today. "And yet her body turned up on a beach with the word *naughty* carved into her cheek, and her body was cut open and filled with empty crisp packets and cans and take-away containers."

Ordinary household rubbish. Gabi wasn't sure if that was supposed to mean something. Was it a metaphor for the girl being trash? An anti-witch agenda perhaps?

Rick blinked, processing the information. "The killer wants you to delve into her secrets—the victim's. That much is clear. Do you have anything on the killer?"

"Just a gender. Female. And she has painted fingernails if that helps."

Rick tapped his lip, thinking. "To carve a label like that ... it's strange she didn't write what the girl's actual crime was. That she'd classify her as naughty, leave that message for the world to see, but not tell the world what the girl had done..."

"What are you thinking?"

Rick sighed. "That this girl may not be the last. Your killer is angry—and righteous. She's passing judgement, maybe sees it as her duty to pass that judgement for one reason or another—maybe she's cleansing the girl in death, maybe purifying the world by ridding it of this 'naughty' girl. If that *is* the case, she could easily find others that don't meet her standards."

"That doesn't help me." Gabi pushed back the urge to sigh. "I need to know what I'm looking for."

"Someone hiding in plain sight." Rick removed his glasses to rub his eyes, reminding Gabi of the fact he'd probably been teaching all day only to come home and have her throw this on him. "She'd need to be around people, somewhere she can keep an eye on them, watch them for signs of being 'naughty'. You can rule out loners and people who keep to themselves."

"So, she'd be involved in everything?" Every gossiper in

Agedale ran through Gabi's head, but there were too many of those to narrow down.

"She'd certainly be involved in most things. And she'd be watching people closely—keep an eye out for that."

"So, in other words, this doesn't help me."

Rick sighed. "With what you've given me, this is the best I can do. I'm sorry, Gabriella."

Gabi shook her head. "No, I'm sorry. I shouldn't have bothered you with this, it's not your job."

"I told you to come to me if you needed help. This qualifies."

Gabi smiled despite herself. "Thank you."

Rick shrugged, a smile teasing his face. "No problem. Call me again if you find more information, I might be able to narrow down your pool of suspects."

"I'll do that."

Gabi ended the call, drawing in a long breath and letting the information absorb. The chances were she'd already met the killer. She could have spoken to her today while she walked down the high street—if Rick was right that she'd want to be involved, she'd have heard Gabi was asking questions and come to see for herself.

Gabi flipped open her notebook, running down the list of names, but no obvious suspect jumped out. She'd have to dig deeper into every one of these people.

Tomorrow, after she interviewed Paulina's miraculous witness. Right now, she had a coven meeting to get to, and she was already late.

FIFTEEN
JOY

From the outside, Agedale might seem like any other town in England. It was the size of a village but awarded town status in the seventies because of the rarity of a purely supernatural community. Quaint, narrow terraces filled the centre, with tidy pavements and window boxes on every sill, and each door was painted a bright jewel tone. Among them were shops with thoughtful window displays, a bakery with woven baskets of biscuits and pasties, and a pharmacy with a dish of clean water outside for passing dogs. There were larger houses for the wealthy closer to the sea, with big driveways and expensive cars, vast herb gardens, and even an ice sculpture maintained by a natural witch with an affinity for water.

And right at the end, Joy's house. Closest to the sea, the small stone house had been painted a rich sky blue. An earth witch's garden sat at its front—blooming roses, fat sunflowers, delicate bluebells—and in a narrow strip down the side of the house, a bed of rosemary and bettony and foxglove lived. In the back garden, almost visible, a variety of trees grew, each one possessing a different magic quality, used in wands and love spells and charms for good health and protection.

Joy stood on her front step with her wand in hand, breathing in the scents of the sea and the smells of all those flowers and herbs vying for space in her garden. She fixed her stare on the sloping road, scanning every pair of headlights that swung over the top before inevitably turning off before they came close.

Gabi was late, and Joy was worried.

She wrapped her arms around her middle, her heart sinking with every minute that passed without Gabi's appearance, and the urge to walk into the centre of town and search for her was growing. She didn't want to—didn't want to go *anywhere* alone—but her paranoia and jumpy fear had shifted to fear for Gabi, and somehow this was worse.

All Joy wanted for days was for everything to settle back to normal, for coven life to get her through the week, but right now Joy couldn't think of anything she wanted more than to see the headlights of Gabi's car make their way down the road to Joy's house.

Today was a bad day. Unwilling to let her week be unsettled any more, Joy had gone into work. She'd opened up the conservation centre fine and had been okay recording the numbers of three kinds of bird. But she'd flinched at the sudden rush of the sea, and when she'd set out to check on two rogue familiars who'd let themselves loose in the sandy grasses, she fell apart.

When her shoes crunched through the sand, it hit her that no matter how hard she tried nothing would go back to normal. Not ever.

A girl was dead, Gabi was home, and Paulina...

It had started with a weight on Joy's chest, like an

elephant crushing her ribs, and before she'd realised it was even sneaking up on her, Joy couldn't breathe. She'd been on the phone to Salma for a full half hour before she could draw a breath, and think straight, and function again. Even with her wand gripped so tight in her fist, she was terrified to lose it again, to have it *taken*.

It was a different kind of feeling now, but the gut-deep sense of being out of control and powerless was the same.

When the road stayed dark, Joy turned to head inside, to rally her coven and go out looking for Gabi. But a glint of light drew her eye, and her heart skipped when headlights swung down the road at the top. The crunch of tires on sandy tarmac had never sounded so good.

Holding her breath, Joy prayed the car kept coming—and when it did, when it stopped outside Joy's house and Gabi stepped out, Joy couldn't stop her feet from racing down the gravel driveway.

She threw her arms around Gabi before she knew what was happening, stumbling until Gabi's arms came around her instantly, solid across her back. Joy's shakiness paused, even if only for a moment.

"Hey," Gabi murmured, trying to pull back, but Joy's arms were thoroughly locked. "What's wrong?"

"You're late." Joy put all her effort into getting her arms to release Gabi. *Not your girlfriend, not yours, not anymore.* But the clamour of heartbeats in her chest and the swoop in her gut, not to mention the urge to hug Gabi again and never let go ... those were damning. Joy *wanted* Gabi to be hers again.

But it was never going to happen. No matter what Gabi said about having *certain feelings* for Joy—those were remnants and echoes. Joy had shattered any chance at a relationship between them years ago.

She swallowed and made herself step back, muttering, "Sorry. I shouldn't have..."

"Joy." Gabi caught her arm before she could put more than a foot between them, her brown eyes gentle with concern. "You're allowed to hug me."

Joy shook her head, flinging pink strands into her face. She shouldn't be allowed, not after the way she'd hurt Gabi.

"Let's go inside. Everyone's probably wondering where I went."

"Or Maisie's keeping an eye on you from that bush there and Victoriya's watching you from the window." There was a smile in Gabi's voice that made Joy's heart beat hard. But Gabi was right about her friends—two eyes glowed from a yarrow shrub and above, Victoriya's scarecrow figure loomed in the window.

"Get out of there," Joy huffed to Maisie, shaking her head. "If you inhale enough of that, you'll put a love spell on yourself."

Maisie chuffed but slunk out of the flowers. Joy watched her closely for wobbly walking and dazed eyes—yarrow was a powerful ingredient of any love spell, strong enough that sitting in it for prolonged minutes could put you into a trance-like state—but Maisie trotted into the house like all was well.

Joy paused on the threshold, not looking directly at Gabi but speaking to her. "Are you alright?"

"I'm fine, Joy." Gabi rubbed the back of her dark head, and adjusted her automatic response to, "I'm just tired."

Joy felt suddenly bad for dragging her to a coven meeting. "We won't be long. Just tell us what we can do to help, and we'll do it."

"I know." Gabi touched Joy's elbow, and awareness of

that heat and contact, even through layers of clothes, made Joy's skin erupt into buzzing.

She couldn't help meeting Gabi's eyes and found them fixed intently on her. Under the porch light, Gabi looked tired but determined.

"Are you sleeping?" Joy asked before she could stop herself. She was so used to fussing over her coven that it came naturally.

Gabi squeezed Joy's elbow before letting go, a smile in the corner of her mouth. "You don't have to worry about me."

Joy went exceptionally still when Gabi's thumb traced beneath her eye, the calloused pad scraping delicate skin. She couldn't explain why, but this felt like the first time Gabi had ever touched her. She didn't dare move and was terrified to shatter the moment. "How are *you* sleeping? Did you sleep last night?"

They'd stayed up talking, and Gabi had done something utterly miraculous: she made Joy forget about Paulina and Freya and the cell for a little while. She made Joy feel *safe*.

"Four hours," Joy replied. "I think that's good."

Gabi again brushed Joy's cheekbone with her thumb but then dropped her hand, her eyes flickering as the moment passed. Like Gabi just remembered they were broken up the way Joy kept doing.

Her whole body in turmoil, Joy headed inside, trying to hide how she felt.

The scent of old houses and musk and the valerian tonic she'd made last night greeted them as they stepped into the hallway, wiping their shoes on the door mat. Victoriya had given the mat to Joy last Christmas; it had a black cat at the side of bold black words declaring *pussy is a sexist insult*.

Joy saw Gabi notice the doormat, her mouth curling with a deeper smile.

"Victoriya," Joy offered by way of explanation. Not that she disagreed with the mat's sentiment.

"Finally," Gus groaned, poking his shaggy, brunette head around the kitchen door. "I've got an idea how we can help."

Gabi's eyes swept the hall, the rooms branching off from it, and the well-worn stairs that led to the bedrooms and bathroom, taking in all the details that had changed—and everything that had stayed the same.

Joy watched her shoulders drop in relief, and desperately wished she could know what was going through Gabi's head.

"Alright," Joy said, shutting the door behind them, feeling better for that barrier between her and the dark world outside. "What's your big idea, Gus?"

SIXTEEN

GABI

Despite the fact the coven had come together so Gabi could tell them what she needed, last night they ended up telling *her* what they were going to do. Gabi didn't argue—what did she know about witchcraft, after all? All she understood was they would gather the ingredients to glimpse a *scene*, but not how that scene would narrow down a suspect pool. It was a name Gabi was most interested in—if the coven could uncover the killer's identity, she could have them arrested and locked up *tonight*. Anticipation wormed through her stomach even as she tried to quell the hope.

Until she heard from Joy later, she had work to do, and she needed a clear head.

Freya's funeral had been this morning, a mere twenty-four hours after she'd released the body. Witch burials were quick—Gabi remembered that from Joy's mum's death. Memories had pelted her like stones when she attended Freya's funeral, her attention travelling over everyone in attendance. But there's been no one out of place but Gabi, the rest of Freya's family. It was a long shot, but it wouldn't have been the first time a killer attended their victim's funeral.

Gabi sat in her car now, settling herself into a better headspace. She'd read over the statement the witness—a male witch called Abram Charles—had given to Paulina, and she already knew where she wanted to focus her questioning. More importantly, she wanted to know if he was in Paulina's back pocket.

Being a witch meant he *knew* Paulina, even if she wasn't the type of head witch to take an interest in her coven's personal lives, unlike the previous head witch— Todd Mackenzie, Joy's dad.

Gabi tightened her black ponytail and stepped onto the street, slamming the car door behind her. She locked away her personal reasons for wanting this case shut, pushed back the part of her that was furious this man was responsible for locking Joy in a freezing, damp cell at the mercy of Paulina. The way Joy looked the night before, suffering and traumatised from her incarceration but so strong...

Gabi had to physically shake herself to bring focus back, but when she knocked on the door, that all fell away. Cool professionalism settled over her, squaring her shoulders, lifting her head.

"Abram Charles?" she asked briskly when he opened the door. He was a slight, balding mixed-race man in a battered brown suit and slippers. "I'm Gabriella Pride. I'd like to ask you a few questions about the morning of the second of December. Can I come in?"

"Um," the man replied, his hand tight around the side of the door. He looked from Gabi to the rowan cross hanging over her head, and reluctantly opened the door to let her through. Gabi took notice of three other crosses before she entered the hall and was swamped in a heavy, herbal scent.

She didn't know much about witchcraft, but she knew those crosses were for one thing alone: protection. What was this man so afraid of?

"I told Paulina everything I know," Abram said without prompting, leading Gabi into a musty front room occupied by large bookshelves and old, dark furniture. A pot of tea sat cooling on a well-loved coffee table, perfuming the air with spices and witchcraft like Joy's house had when her mum, Charity, had been alive.

"It's just a routine call," Gabi said to put Abram's mind at ease. His eyes flicked around the room, alighting on her but not for long, his fingers twisted into a knot in front of him. "I want to check some details, if you don't mind."

It didn't matter if he did mind, but this was a trick she'd learned in her communication classes. Offer them the illusion that they're in charge.

"That's okay," Abram replied, though his nervous tone suggested he was anything but okay. His brown eyes flicked to the window, then back to Gabi.

"You were on the beach at five-fifteen, you said in your statement. Is that correct?"

Abram nodded his shaved head, twisting his fingers together until the knuckles turned pale. "That's right."

Gabi got a notebook from her bag and flipped it open in case she needed to take notes. "Can I ask why you were out so early?"

"Oh, I—I was walking my dog."

"Your dog?" Gabi kept her face blank, but internally she catalogued the tidiness of the house, the lack of hair on the sofas, the absence of pet beds, toys, and general signs of a canine living in a house. Even Joy's house was covered in fur, and some corners of her furniture had been gnawed on thanks to Victoriya's pack.

"Yes," Abram said quickly, breathlessly. "He's out with my sister right now, she walks him in the afternoon you see; she gets lonely."

Gabi gave him a bland smile and jotted down her suspicions. "Can you tell me about the person you saw on the beach? I know you told Paulina, but I want to make sure I have the details right."

"Yes, yes, of course." Abram reached for a cup of tea that must have been cold and choked it down. "Well, it was still quite dark, so I didn't see her face, but she was definitely a woman. Quite tall but not overly so, not too thin, long hair—I can't say what colour. I watched her walk from the end of Beach Road down towards the east end, but I didn't think anything of it until I heard you'd found that poor girl. Like I told Paulina, she looked young, twenties maybe, and she was wearing those tight trousers girls are wearing these days." *Leggings*, Gabi translated, taking note of everything. "And this big, fur coat."

"Fur coat," Gabi repeated, tapping her pen on paper.

"Yes. I definitely remember that."

Gabi smiled and got to her feet. "Thank you, Mr. Charles. That's all the questions I have for you today."

"Oh, that's—you're done? Good, good, happy to be of service."

Gabi drank in every detail of his house and him before she left. Definitely no dog, and he didn't strike her as an early morning jogger, either. He was scared, that much was obvious, and Gabi didn't want to jump to conclusions—that was a surefire way to kill her career—but she couldn't dodge the hunch that he was scared of his head witch. Paulina was too involved in this shit.

Abram Charles had just added what might seem like killer testimony against Joy—out of nowhere. This fur coat detail was miraculous—and new. He hadn't mentioned it in his first statement, which meant either time was doing its usual warp on a person's memory, *or* he'd been fed that particular detail.

Funny how that had come out *after* Paulina saw Joy curled up in a fur coat in the cell she'd shoved her into.

She needed to verify Abram's story, find his sister and this imaginary dog, and then put pressure on him to tell the truth. But she couldn't ignore the urge to tail Paulina for the rest of the morning.

Gabi climbed back into her car, slammed the door behind her, and realised she was smiling. She shouldn't have been—but she was.

THE AFTERNOON WAS A WRITE-OFF. After watching Paulina for hours and witnessing nothing suspicious, Gabi headed back along Beach Road into town, and staked a table in the bakery that possessed a godsend of a coffee machine. Gabi downed a double-shot americano and went over the post mortem on her tablet, typing up her thoughts on Abram Charles while she had the time.

Maybe she'd have a few hours to *finally* get started on moulding Freya's last days in a linear order instead of the patchy timeline she had now. It'd help if the businesses in Agedale had CCTV, but thanks to boundary spells, they didn't need them to catch thieves, so Gabi was left with the accounts of friends and family to figure out how Freya had come into contact with the woman who killed her.

She ordered another coffee and a trio of shortbread biscuits shaped like Santa when a shadow fell over her and the chair opposite squeaked back. Gabi raised an eyebrow, not in the mood to be bothered, but she removed the ire from her expression when she saw it was her dad.

In his mid-forties with thick black hair, rich amber skin, and a mischievous twinkle in his eyes, Bo Pride was still as handsome as he'd been as a young man. As Gabi was *constantly* reminded by the appreciative eyes that slid over him. His injury and retirement had not diminished his ability to charm a woman with a single look. Gabi rolled her eyes and ignored him, returning her attention to the tablet until Lilian, her favourite baker-barista, brought over her americano and biscuits. One was promptly snatched up, her dad crunching through it.

Still typing, Gabi said, "I know you were taught manners, but you seem to have forgotten them."

She watched her dad brush crumbs off his coat from the corner of her eye. "Pot," he said. "Kettle. Black."

Gabi pursed her mouth, but he was always able to draw a smile out of her. "What are you doing out, anyway?"

With a flourish, Bo produced an envelope from his breast pocket.

Her full name inked in elegant green on gold paper, a flourish on the ends of each letter. Gabi scrunched up her face, ignoring it even as her stomach turned over.

She didn't want to read it, didn't want to hear the newest apology, the latest plea for her to talk to him, to let him explain. Gabi was too hurt to even entertain it, and she'd inherited the fierce grudge-holding of her mother's side. She wasn't forgiving and forgetting any time in the next five years.

"You'll have to reply to him at some point," her dad said with a knowing look. "Give him a break, Gabi, it's been years. And I know you miss him."

She said nothing, just glared at the report on her tablet.

Bo sighed, shitting in the wooden café chair. "Should I put this with the others?"

"Put it in the fire," Gabi hissed under her breath.

Her dad sighed but he let the subject drop, nodding at her tablet. "What've you got?"

"What I've got is confidential and not accessible to the general public." Gabi gave him the same cool look he'd given her all those years he'd had her job.

She tried not to grin with the satisfaction of it.

Bo shook his dark head, his smiling eyes curved into crescents. "Sometimes I think you turned out too much like me."

"That's why you like me so much," Gabi pointed out, claiming a biscuit before he could snatch another.

Bo crossed his arms on the table and leaned closer, lowering his voice. "How did it go last night? *And* the night before? Are you still refusing to tell me if you talked to Joy?"

Gabi took a long drink to figure out how to respond, the ice coffee sliding smooth over her tongue. She'd become addicted to iced americano in Liverpool and drank gallons of it even in winter.

"It went fine," she said finally,

"Fine," Bo repeated incredulously. "*Gabi.* How did it go? Was it that bad?"

She shook her head, dark hair whipping her face. "The coven told me something useful about the killer. Not much, hardly anything really, but it's more than I had. And Joy told me she still loves me," she tacked on at the end, as if she hadn't been obsessing over it.

"And that's bad?" Her dad peered at her, eyes less smiling. "Shall I assume you *didn't* tell her you still love her?"

Gabi already wished she'd never said anything. She demolished the biscuit with restless fingers for something to do, annoyed when she got crumbs on her tablet. "It's fine. It's all just..."

"Fine?" her dad guessed, watching her sadly.

She let out a sound between a sigh and a growl, and jumped when her dad covered her hand with his warm palm, squeezing.

His joking nature was replaced by fatherly concern. "If you love her, you need to be brave, Gabi. *Tell* her. If she still loves you, there's a chance at a future there. *Do not* let that go just because you're scared."

"I'm not scared," she lied. "I told her ... some things."

It had been timid and vague, and she'd been holding back but *still*, it counted.

Her dad just squeezed her hand again. "Come by the house later. I'll make sure there's a decent meal waiting for you."

"Alright," she agreed because she was already a little tired of toaster waffles and pot noodles. "Thanks, Dad."

Bo braced his hands on the table and rose, eyes landing on her hand, drumming on the table top. "No more coffee."

"I'm fine."

Bo smirked, gripping the table as he came around to hug her shoulders—all he could really get to with Gabi sitting down. "Is that the only word in your vocabulary today?"

She scowled and nudged him away—lightly, aware that he wasn't steady on his feet. "Now that's just impolite."

"Where do you think you got your mad skills from?" His grin was rakish. "I've been training you since birth. I'm your sensei in all things sarcastic and cutting."

Her brows drew together as she gave him a look severely questioning his sanity. "Senseis are Japanese. We're Chinese," she said dryly.

He pretended to wipe a tear, grabbing the stick he'd

hooked on the back of his chair. "So blunt, so sarcastic. The protégée's going to surpass the master."

Gabi rolled her eyes, but she was grinning.

"No more coffee," he ordered, stealing another hug. "And eat more than a biscuit for your lunch."

"It would have been *two* biscuits, but a thief stole my other one," she drawled, ignoring thoughts of that green envelope circling her mind, waiting to pounce.

"Weird, that," he said, fighting a smile. "How's the heater working in the Law House? There's a knack to it. You have to jiggle the little—"

"Dad."

"*Someone* has to make sure you're taking care of yourself, and if you won't talk to Joy—"

Gabi pointed at the door, her expression flat with exasperation, her chest warm with love.

Bo snorted and shuffled out of the exit, looking far from apologetic about the biscuit theft.

SEVENTEEN

JOY

An ache had stuck behind Joy's rib cage and refused to move. She hadn't quite realised the heartache of losing Gabi had faded until it returned in full, stabbing force. She needed to move past it. Had to find a way. Gabi would have made a move last night if she still wanted Joy, right?

Joy sighed and put a small copper pot on her stove, heating water to stew herbs in. A quick emotional-pain tonic should take the edge off.

She'd decorated her house for Christmas, hoping it would boost her mood, but even with garlands and wreaths and poinsettia strung from the low ceilings and the staircase bannister, she still felt achy and despondent.

At least the house had the earthy, floral scent she loved so much about Christmas. It would be even better when she tied cinnamon sticks onto the tree. Not that she'd gotten around to buying a tree yet. She'd *meant* to get one the day she found Freya on the beach, but well ... all of that happened.

Joy finished hanging a wreath of evergreens on her front door, managing it one-handed thanks to her unwillingness to let go of her wand for more than a second. Wind swirled around her, like it worked for Paulina and was trying to take it from her, and she tightened her grip until her joints ached.

She stepped back to admire her handiwork—intentionally off-centre as her mum's had been every year—when a hand touched her shoulder.

Her breath clogged in her throat, and she spun on instinct, wand raised and her left hand ducking into her cardigan pocket where she now kept a protection spell. She'd ripped into the paper sachet before she recognised the kind receptionist from the town hall. She relaxed, letting out a low breath.

Katrina's eyes lingered on the sachet and Joy could have sworn something flickered in her eyes, probably sadness or sympathy. It was all Joy saw lately. Well, that and suspicion from witches who didn't know her—but knew she was a murder suspect.

"Oh," Joy laughed breathily. "Sorry. I'm a bit jumpy. There's a murderer loose, so..."

And I'm terrified your boss will imprison me again.

Katrina smiled and shrugged off Joy's apology, her long blonde hair bouncing. "No need to apologise. I was just finishing up a run and I saw you. I thought I'd come and ask how you were doing."

"I'm alright," Joy replied, trying to smile even as her heart kept racing and the panic remained. "Better now I'm home."

Katrina nodded and that was definitely sympathy in her eyes. "I'm sorry about the way Paulina treated you. I asked her to be kinder but ... you've lived here longer than me, you must know what she's like."

"Yeah," Joy agreed, noticing that despite Katrina's accent, she'd picked up their contractions and the ebb and flow of the local accent, too.

Katrina's eyes flicked to the sachet in Joy's hand again before drifting to the sun gilding the beach in pure gold. "I should go, or I'll miss my pilates class. I'm glad you're doing better."

"Have fun," Joy said, not knowing if that was the right sentiment for someone swapping jogging for pilates. She supposed it explained the lithe figure Katrina usually hid beneath flouncy blouses and long skirts. To Joy, exercise was a little too much effort, hence her wobbly belly and big thighs.

"See you later," she said, smiling a bit easier. It was surprising how much seeing a friendly face eased her nerves.

Katrina waved and jogged off.

Even though Joy's jumpy fear had calmed, her chest still ached viciously. Rubbing at the spot over her pained heart, Joy admired her wreath one final time and went inside. She triple checked the door was locked before she plopped into a chair at the kitchen table, inhaling the fresh, woodsy scent of her home.

Still thinking about Paulina's assistant, Joy washed a pain tonic down with a cup of green tea and a lemon biscuit. It was better than thinking about what might happen if the spells she and her coven were going to cast tonight didn't work.

If they didn't find the person who'd actually killed the girl, Joy knew it wouldn't be long before Paulina found another witness to incriminate her, or a piece of magically conjured evidence.

Sighing, Joy finished her tea and started spell prep. Her coven wouldn't arrive for another hour, but at least she'd be busy. At least the sounds of her knife on the wooden block and the bubble of boiling water on the stove were normal. She needed normal now more than ever.

EIGHTEEN

GABI

Freya was the most wholesome, harmless girl in the whole damn town. Gabi wouldn't have been surprised if she was a Brownie or delivered cakes to the elderly or voluntarily ran marathons for charity. After interviewing every family member she could get her hands on, Gabi was stuck on what Joy's coven had said when they sensed the power on the girl's body. Freya had been *bad*, had done something wrong.

Hence after a morning of following up minor reports—a public disturbance with emphasis on the *pub*, and a bright pink front door whose elderly neighbour wanted Gabi to 'get rid of' because it was 'an absolute eyesore'—Gabi now waited in traffic at the end of the workday to visit the steep terrace house where Freya's best friend lived.

If Freya *had* been less than innocent, it would be her friends—not her family—who'd tell Gabi, intentionally or otherwise.

Her heart beat a little faster, her blood pumping with useless excitement. The chance that she could uncover a snippet of information to unlock the whole case, however scant that chance was, was hard to fight. She parked outside a brown terrace house with every Christmas decoration imaginable flashing cheerfully from the face of it and took a breath.

When Gabi rapped on the door, a frizzy haired teenage girl in a glitzy skirt and top swung it open, an intent expression on her dark face.

"Finally," she declared, ushering Gabi inside.

She tried to hide her surprise at the unexpected greeting as she was led into a living room decorated as wildly as the outside, the air spiced with cinnamon.

"I've been waiting for you all day," the girl said in a rush. "I heard you went to see Freya's mum and dad."

"I did," Gabi confirmed, struggling to adjust to this vivacious personality. After a moment, she realised it wasn't excitement jolting through the girl. It was manic energy. Gabi wondered where her parents were; given the time of day, they were likely still at work. "Skye Dawson?"

Skye nodded, a blur of movement that made her dark curls ruffle. "It has to be Brent," she blurted out.

Gabi wrote down the name, raising an eyebrow for Skye to continue.

"They were arguing, and they'd *never* argued before, so how could we know what he's capable of when he's angry? You hear it on true crime podcasts all the time—guys get angry, and they're so sweet that you'd never expect it but that doesn't make it less real. It was probably an accident, but you never know—"

"Skye," Gabi interrupted, then remembered to soften her tone. "Who's Brent?"

"Freya's boyfriend. Macon Brent." Gabi made another note. "They'd been seeing each other for four months, which is—it's kind of a while, you know?"

Gabi nodded, glad Skye had slowed her speech slightly so she could keep up. "That must have been a serious relationship."

"Yeah, exactly. He seemed nice. I mean, he's been hanging around with us ever since he and Freya got together and he doesn't even swear, but you just can't know someone."

"What were they arguing about?" Gabi asked, watching Skye glare, presumably at her memory of Macon Brent's face.

Skye exhaled a rough breath, pinning a heavy look on Gabi. "Don't tell anyone this, okay? No one knows except me and Brent."

"Okay," Gabi lied, her pen hovering over paper.

"She cheated on him." Skye's brown eyes were wide— she looked eager to speak to someone about it. "It was Scott, you know that spotty guy from year eleven?"

No, Gabi did not know Scott, that spotty guy from year eleven. "You said Macon knew Freya had cheated?"

"Yeah. She told him. What an idiot! She actually *told him*. I mean, they got back together after going on a break, and they *seemed* alright for a few days. But you just can't tell with the quiet ones, can you?" She leaned towards Gabi, the look she gave her conspiratorial. "You know what they say."

Gabi nodded, hoping she appeared thoughtful and not rude as she scratched down the important points in her notebook. "I know what you mean."

Beware the quiet ones.

"Oh God," Skye blurted suddenly, flapping her hand expressively. "*Please* don't tell her mum and dad. I wasn't meant to tell anyone. *Please*. I don't want them to think she's a slut."

Because that was the worst crime a woman could commit, Gabi thought sourly. She took a breath, thinking of a way to keep Skye talking without lying. "I won't tell them unless I need to."

"Thank you." Without warning, Skye burst into tears—full, ugly sobs. "I miss her. Already. That's stupid, right? It's only been a few days."

"No," Gabi disagreed, her voice naturally gentle. She put down her pen.

She knew how quickly missing someone could creep up on you; her mum's face flashed behind her eyes.

"That's not stupid at all, Skye." She handed a tissue to the girl, feeling like a bitch for dragging her through this. But if Gabi failed to get an important piece of information, a killer could go uncaught. At some point down the line, they could kill again. Gabi was always conscious of that possibility.

Skye sniffled, tissue pressed to her nose. "Thanks."

Gabi smiled in acknowledgment, and asked in as gentle a voice as she could muster, "Is there anything else that stood out in the past few weeks?

Skye blew her nose. "Not really. Freya was just ... normal."

"You spent a lot of time with her?"

"Yeah." Skye shrugged, brushing away an errant tear. "Less than normal because of the food drive."

"The food drive?"

"At town hall. They were asking for tins of food and stuff. Freya was there all weekend helping out."

Gabi wrote that down. She hadn't been far off in her earlier profiling. The girl was a saint. Well, except for the cheating.

"Alright," she said, getting to her feet and tucking her notebook away. "Thank you for speaking to me."

Skye blew her nose again, sniffling. "Just ... arrest him, okay?"

"I'll find whoever hurt your friend." Gabi turned to the door to avoid making any more promises.

She threw herself into the front seat of her car and slammed the door behind her. Macon Brent. Gabi fastened her seat belt, her mind making connections. Wasn't Macon a fae name? She'd known a Macon in school, and he'd been a pure, infuriating fae—despite the species segregation in the town proper, a lack of teachers meant even the fae deigned to share classrooms with witches and elves.

Maybe Skye was right about the boyfriend, or maybe someone didn't like a fae dating a witch. The town was still rife with prejudice and separation between species. At least this was a more solid motive than Gabi'd had before. And the cheating explained why the killer wanted to punish her. Gabi needed to Skype Rick Ali and update him—this changed things.

"Why are you always in my kitchen?" Joy complained as Gus ate the last of her cereal. She felt better, steadier, for having them here, and it seemed less likely that Paulina could get in and pry her wand from her fingers with her coven as a barrier between them. But still. Her cereal...

"Because you have a big table," Eilidh replied, chopping a sprig of sage. "My house is full of family right now, Salma's mum doesn't like us going round, Maisie and Gus don't have a real table—"

"A breakfast bar *is* a real table," Gus argued fiercely around a mouthful of dry cereal.

"And none of us are brave enough to go to Victoriya's house," Eilidh finished, her knife hitting the board with soothing thuds.

All valid points, Joy had to admit, her soul soothing to watch them do normal, familiar—albeit irritating—things. She jumped when the front door slammed open without so much as a courteous knock, but her heartbeat settled as logic set in.

Not Paulina, she told herself. *She wouldn't dare come here.*

"What's up, fuckers?" Victoriya asked in lieu of hello, dropping into a chair and kicking her boots up onto the table where Maisie laid curled up. The fix slitted yellow eyes in her friend's direction.

"Do we think this will work?" Joy asked, scuffing her feet on the tile floor and eyeing the copper pan on the stove beside her with more apprehension than she used to. She turned a bit of green sea stone over in her hand, worrying it smooth.

Victoriya snorted.

"Don't be pessimistic," Salma chided, breezing into the house like a goddess. She approached Joy, assessed the pot, and stirred the clear concoction. "We have to try. If we help Gabriella catch this killer, we don't have to jump at every shadow."

Maisie made a long, high sound from the nest she'd made of Joy's hat and scarf on the table.

"Oh yeah," Gus said, rumpling his brown hair and looking at Salma with a rueful wince. "I might have punched an old man in the supermarket. And before you all look at me like I'm a monster, I didn't *mean* to. It was right after we left the morgue; I was a little on edge."

"Morgue?" Joy asked, her mouth falling open and her heart clanging in her chest. "When did you—?"

"Long story," Victoriya cut in, trying to spare Joy the details. "How'd you hit him, Gus? Straight in the face, punch to the gut, or did you box his ears? Give me details."

"I'm surprised you weren't arrested, Augustus." Salma sighed, spinning a golden ring around her finger. "You're lucky Gabriella wouldn't detain you for long."

"Yeah, that's a thing," Victoriya said, stretching her pale

arms above her head for no apparent reason other than to show off the deep cut sides of her faded vest. "Since we're besties with the law now, *can* we be arrested? Or do we have a free pass for any crime?"

Salma gave her an unamused stare, pointing the stirring spoon in warning. She said nothing but her expression spoke volumes.

"Asking for a friend," Victoriya added with a grin.

"I don't think that's how it works," Joy told her, peering into the pot on the stove. It was just starting to bubble, all according to plan. It was a relief to see a potion brewing normally—a few months ago, there'd been a period when no spells had worked at all, thanks to a mischievous and stubborn naiad corrupting their water source. Salma had been hurt—badly—and for a tense, terrifying period, Joy was scared they'd never be able to heal her.

Now, Salma wisely ignored Victoriya, removing a leather-bound notebook from her pocket to check the potion's instructions. Salma's grimoire was full of so many things Joy couldn't keep track—spells and incantations, potion recipes, runes and their meanings, plus the properties of every herb and flower. And more.

"This spell should reveal the species of who we're looking for. We *all* need to be focussed on the same person —the killer—or it won't work. Eilidh, will you be okay to do this? You don't have to."

"I'm fine." Eilidh's voice was quiet but strong, and more than a little annoyed at Salma's fussing. Joy looked between them, sensing something unspoken, but Salma just nodded and turned off the hob, putting down the spoon.

When the water had cooled, perfuming the kitchen with herbs and fresh flowers, Salma set the copper pan on a wire rack in the middle of the kitchen table, sweeping aside a demolished Tupperware of calming shortbread biscuits, and nudging Maisie's nest aside.

On her friend's instructions, Joy grabbed several mason jars off the big cabinet against the wall—the shelves bowed with the weight of spell ingredients—and handed out St John's wort, fleabane, and ground ivy.

Chairs scraped as Gus and Victoriya stood—spells cast much stronger when a coven stood in a circle. Without instruction, the six of them took their places, and Maisie climbed to her feet, too, her eyes bright and fierce.

"Good," Salma praised. "Now add each element —slowly."

A steady calm washed over Joy as, in turn, each of them added a herb or stirred clockwise or crushed another ingredient into the concoction. This was familiar; this was home.

"Alright, *now!*" Salma ordered, her voice rich and compelling, and Joy crowded close to the table with the rest of her coven.

Five wands lifted—ash, birch, elm, hazel, and crystal— and they all peered into the perfectly transparent potion. It should have been murky with hers floating in it, but it was as clear and glimmering as opal. It worked.

Joy let out a rough breath. But just because it had worked didn't mean they'd find the killer.

Salma grabbed a ladle and with a look of unwavering confidence that inspired the same in Joy, she put a small amount of the potion into mugs for each of them.

Joy clutched her amethyst wand tight to remind herself it was still hers, still here. She could still feel the wrench, the emptying of her soul, when Paulina snatched it from her hand. But she had to put that out of her mind; only a clear mind would work for this.

Joy held the cup tight when Salma handed it to her and

waited for her cue with a mix of nerves and butterflies. If they found the killer, if Gabi could prove it was them, Joy would be safe.

"Drink on three. Maisie, can you reach?" Maisie gave a *yip* of confirmation. "One. Two." She made eye contact with them all, settling nerves with her unwavering strength. "Three"

Joy lifted the mug and threw the liquid down her throat like a shot. Warmth instantly sloshed in her belly, and a thrumming rush built, making her shudder. This wasn't exactly *usual*, but witchcraft was so changeable that a spell rarely worked the same way twice, even if it had the same outcome each time. There were too many changeable factors.

All at once, and without really meaning to, Joy's mouth opened and she intoned, "Witch."

Her coven spoke all at once, voices overlapping, creating an eerie harmony.

Joy shivered and shoved the cup aside to touch her mouth with shaky fingers. The witchcraft had given her an answer, but it felt like it had *used* her. She noticed the thrum had faded, and she exhaled all at once, stumbling back from the table until her back met the countertop. But her lips still didn't seem to belong to her.

"Let's *never* do that again," Gus rasped, visibly shaken as he lit the end of a smudge stick to dispel the power of the spell. His hand shook like Joy's, she noticed.

"I agree. That was foul." Salma drew a chair and dropped heavily into it. "Joy? Are you okay, honey?"

Joy swallowed, inhaling sage-scented air that didn't quite fill her lungs. *Was* she okay?

It was Victoriya who came around the table and touched her, fingers grabbing Joy's chin hard enough to bruise. Victoriya lifted Joy's head, scanning her eyes, and Joy stared back at her friend, gradually coming back to herself.

Victoriya's mouth pressed into a dangerously thin line when Joy gasped, "I'm alright."

Victoriya dropped her hand and stepped back, looking pissed off or worried or both. "You let the power take control."

"I didn't."

She hadn't. But what Joy had felt, the magic taking over her, using her as a mouthpiece ... that would haunt her for a very long time.

"You're weak because of all this shit," Victoriya growled, stalking around the kitchen, almost pacing. "Your ex showing up, and being dragged into this investigation, and being locked up and all the fucking rest. Sit out the next spell."

Joy's mouth fell open at the clear order, and she spun to entreat Salma, gripping her wand amethyst tight enough that her bones creaked.

"Do as Victoriya says," Salma said gently, looking surprised to hear the words coming from her own mouth. Her expression was cloyingly sympathetic when she added, "I won't risk you, Joy. We'll be fine with the five of us."

Joy hung her head, feeling small, feeling useless. If they didn't want her, that was fine. She'd find a way to prove her worth.

"Fine," she agreed, and went to stand by the window as far away from the table as possible, looking out into the garden as her chest caved in. She hadn't felt like this since she'd been freed from the cells, this sinking feeling that she'd be easily forgotten.

She gasped, jumping out of her skin when something bit her ankle.

Maisie. Bristling, the fur standing up on her back, and her eyes narrowed.

Joy glanced away after a moment's eye contact. Maisie had always been exceptional at picking up on other people's feelings, but since she'd been limited to a single form, it had become a real *sense*.

She knew exactly how Joy was feeling—ashamed and embarrassed and a bit like she wanted to cry.

"Sorry, Mais," she whispered.

Maisie only looked more put out. When she failed to communicate her thoughts, she spun in a whoosh of fur, her tail whipping across Joy's legs as she returned to the table where the rest of their coven was debating how to cast the next spell.

The spell to *see* the killer.

Victoriya had glimpsed painted fingernails, they explained, finally telling Joy what had happened while she'd been locked up. But painted nails weren't helpful when half the female population had them.

Gabi needed proof of the murder, and if this worked, the killer would be locked in the cells under town hall to await trial. Joy would be safe.

"Joy?"

She glanced up to find Salma's worried brown eyes on her. "Do you have a mirror? Big enough for us to all see."

"You're scrying?" Joy blinked.

Salma nodded. With the mirror, scrying was safe, at least. It would show them a scene in the past. If they used something like a locator spell or a sight charm to see the killer, there would be no defences between them. It would reveal the killer as they were at that very moment—and the killer would see them right back.

Not even as a last resort would they use it. The coven had all agreed, even before Joy had got out of the cells. If they used one of those spells, the killer could see Gus, see *Eilidh*, and come for all of them. It wasn't worth the risk.

Joy chewed her lip. "There's a mirror upstairs, in my mum's old room. It should be big enough. Do you want me to—"

"No. These two will stop nosing through my grimoire and get it."

Victoriya and Gus complained instantly, but ended up carrying the mirror down anyway when Salma levelled them with a stern look. Joy numbly watched them set the mirror face-up on the table, watched them link hands around it and focus intently on the silver glass. Joy herself saw nothing, since she wasn't part of the circle, but she knew when the mirror had revealed something. Victoriya stiffened. Eilidh gasped.

Eilidh's gasp turned into a cry, then tears, and to Joy's utter shock, her friend dissolved into broken, wrenching sobs.

Joy's hands fluttered uselessly as Eilidh wrenched away from the mirror, the table, and the others. Shuddering, her blonde hair stuck to her teary face, she fled down the hall.

Victoriya and Gus linked hands to close the gap; Joy knew the instinct—the witchcraft—that drove them as they kept staring, unfaltering, into the mirror. Usually, that power was her friend. But after the hold it had taken on her, she wasn't so sure tonight.

Joy felt worse the longer she looked at them, functioning fully without her, not even noticing she wasn't part of the circle. Her heart aching fiercely, she tore her stare away and went after Eilidh, frowning when she found the front door hanging open to let the crisp sea wind into the hallway.

Gripping her wand in a white fist, she went out after the younger witch. There was a killer free in the town; it wasn't safe for Eilidh's to be out alone.

TWENTY
JOY

Joy's stomach roiled at the thought of what her witch sister had seen in the mirror. She intently scanned the steep road, but when she saw it was empty, Joy frowned and circled her house to the back garden.

She found Eilidh on a wooden bench next to the big ash tree in Joy's back garden, her pink face and blonde-teal hair lit in shadows and amber light by the solar lantern by the back door. She had her knees pressed to her chest and looked utterly miserable. Comforting her friend, at least, was something Joy could do. She sank onto the bench beside Eilidh, the wood creaking as she put her arm around her friend's shaking shoulders.

"It's alright," Joy murmured, tucking Eilidh closer. "Cry as much as you need."

When Eilidh fell against her, Joy brushed damp strands of hair from Eilidh's cheeks, scanning the garden as she always scanned her surroundings now. No one but her and Eilidh cast shadows on the lawn and herbs. They were safe.

But that didn't mean they were *okay*.

Joy's heart clenched the longer Eilidh cried, and worry

pressed her to ask what was wrong. But she held back, nor wanting to upset her further.

For minutes she let Eilidh cry and cling to her, smoothing her hair back. Joy's whole body was cold, her hands going red and her nose numb, but she refused to leave until Eilidh was okay.

"That girl you found?" Eilidh murmured, her eyes fixed on the grass at their feet, her lip caught between her teeth. But there was a familiar hardness to her eyes that Joy had always admired, to be so strong at such a young age. "It was … it was Freya. My cousin."

"What?" Joy breathed.

Her stomach swooped, the body on the beach flashing behind her eyes, the images cruelly vivid.

That was Eilidh's cousin...

"Oh, Eils," Joy whispered and wrapped her arms around her friend tighter. The ache in her chest intensified as the realisation settled in. Eilidh had been through so much these past few days. And she'd just soldiered on as if nothing was wrong. "You should have told me."

She tried not to be hurt that she hadn't.

And poor Freya. Joy's chest hurt even more as she remembered the girl's body. The blood on the beach, the body splayed, face carved into, the wand snapped beside her. Joy fought to hide what it did to her, remembering too clearly how it felt being without her own wand. She clutched it in white knuckles now, the amethyst warm and reassuring.

Eilidh rested her head on Joy's shoulder. "I was worried if I told you, it might make everything so much worse."

"Worried about *me?*" Joy frowned.

She was used to being the friend worrying about

everyone else, not the one being worried about. It was a strange feeling, but she was more than a little touched.

"Why would you be worried about me?"

Eilidh lifted her messy head to give Joy a *look*. "You were accused of murder, Joy. That bitch locked you up— and Gabi was so angry—and I *knew* the conditions had to be bad, to make her that angry. Before, when she was showing us the ... showing us *Freya*, she seemed calm and serious."

"Uptight," Joy corrected with a faint laugh that eased up the panic's grip just slightly. "That's just her; she doesn't show her feelings." Joy smiled, then remembered what Eilidh had said, and her breath hitched. "*Gabi* was angry?"

Eilidh nodded, her hair brushing Joy's jaw. "I thought she was going to kill Paulina, to be honest. I'm glad it's her looking for the bastard who killed Freya. She doesn't seem like she'd let *anyone* go unpunished."

"No," Joy agreed, "she wouldn't."

Eilidh nodded, and they fell silent again, only the murmur of the nearby sea filling the quiet.

Joy squeezed Eilidh into another hug, so many emotions vying for control inside her, all of them building into an ache in her chest, lungs, and throat. It wasn't fair that Eilidh had to lose her cousin, but death was never fair. Joy had learned that cruelly quickly when her mum died. It still made her angry though.

Eilidh sniffled.

Joy almost asked if she was alright, but the answer was *obviously not*. When Joy lost her mum, she'd quickly got tired of that question. So, she waited for Eilidh to speak instead of pressing her.

"We saw—in the mirror—Freya drank this tonic and then—all of it. We saw *all of it*."

"Oh, gods. Eilidh..." Joy breathed.

She's watched her cousin's murder. Joy couldn't begin to imagine how furious and grief-stricken she was right now.

"It was a woman. Like we thought." Eilidh inhaled jaggedly, huffed in frustration at her own breathing, then stubbornly forced her breaths to steady. It was such an Eilidh thing to do that a bit of Joy's pain eased. Stubborn and brave and determined to crush any sign of weakness; that was Eilidh.

"Freya—she was still alive, just *barely*, when her—when that *bitch* cut her face."

"Shit." Joy was going to be sick, and that was just at the *thought* of it. What were the others feeling? They had *seen* it. Joy silently wiped away Eilidh's tears, her heart drumming in her rib cage.

Eilidh growled a sudden breath. "I don't get it. What the fuck is it meant to *mean*? Freya didn't do a single damn thing wrong. She was a normal fucking girl and I—" Eilidh's voice became too thick for words; she made an angry sound and flicked away her tears.

"She didn't do anything wrong," Joy murmured, stroking her friend's hair. "She didn't deserve that. And I promise you, we'll find her killer and make her pay."

Eilidh nodded but didn't say anything for a while. And then she took a ragged breath and asked, "Can I have some hot chocolate? With cream and marshmallows?"

"Of course." Joy rose, pausing when she realised Eilidh didn't plan to come inside with her. But maybe she needed a moment alone. The hot chocolate had been an excuse. "I'll be back in a minute. Do you have protection spells?"

Eilidh nodded, looking at the beds of herbs and medicinal flowers. She patted her pocket with a shaky hand.

"Three. And I can grab something from the garden if I run out."

Joy arranged her face into a sort-of smile. "I'll just be a minute. Don't leave the garden—promise?"

"I'm not going anywhere, don't worry."

When Joy didn't budge, Eilidh added, "I promise."

Joy nodded and crossed the lawn, a strange mix of numbness and riotous emotion making her stomach roil. As soon as she was out of sight, she crumpled.

She walked back to the front of the house if only so she could collapse out of sight of Eilidh. A pained sound rose, but Joy pushed her hand against her mouth and held it back.

TWENTY-ONE
JOY

It was all too much—finding the dead girl, being locked up, thinking she would be executed, Gabi coming home, and now this: the body belonging to Eilidh's cousin.

It took a long, long time for Joy to get herself under control, standing under the porch next to a tinkling wind chime of sea glass. Dragging a hand over her face a last time, Joy straightened and, as if she was walking into hell itself, opened her front door.

She braced for the night to get even worse as she made her way to the kitchen, every step tightening that pressure on her chest. Not even the woodsy scent of her new decorations took the darkness from her mood.

Joy found her coven waiting for her, worried and paler than usual. Not still in the spell, not reliving a murder. Not even discussing the brutal details of it. Just standing there, staring into space, silent. Even Salma looked sickened.

"How is she?" Gus asked, looking past the lacy curtain on the window to where Eilidh sat on the bench. His voice was a wretched thing, empty of any humour.

"Better than she should be," Joy answered quietly, robotically crossing the room and flicking on the kettle. The cold from outside had seeped into her bones and all she knew in that split second was a memory of her mum saying *there's no ache a cup of tea can't soothe.*

Maybe Eilidh had the right idea with hot chocolate, Joy thought as she reached for the tub of cocoa.

"Are you alright?" she asked, masking her emotions. "Eilidh told me what you saw."

Everyone had kept this from her—all of them. They hadn't thought Joy could cope with knowing the body was Eilidh's cousin. As if she was weak. As if she hadn't survived losing her dad, then her mum, and then Gabi.

"We're fine," Salma said, attempting to soothe her as she dropped into a seat at the table, her brown fingers knitted into a knot.

"I'm not fragile," Joy replied, harsher than she'd intended. "I won't break."

It felt good to say it out loud, even if she'd rather do anything else than fight with her coven.

"What?" Salma blurted in shock.

"Of course you won't break," Victoriya said, lacking her usual sharpness.

"You should have told me about Eilidh's cousin," Joy said firmly, and turned to look at Salma, at Gus and Victoriya and Maisie.

Gus dropped his gaze to the floor, but Victoriya heaved a rough breath and asked, "When? When you were locked up? Or after, when you'd just got out of a jail cell? When was the right time, Joy?"

Joy shook her head, trying to be angry so it would fill the widening hole inside her. She turned back to the hot chocolate, tipping sugar into a polka dot mug. "If you don't trust me—"

"Don't be a fucking *idiot*." Victoriya stormed across the kitchen, grabbed Joy's arm, and wrenched her around and into a hug that was more combative than comforting.

Still, all the tension and anger dropped out of Joy, and she hugged Victoriya back tightly. The hole in her chest filled just slightly.

"Sorry," Joy mumbled into Victoriya's warm leather jacket.

"Shut up," Victoriya sighed, releasing her. "We were protecting you, dumbass."

"Oh," Joy whispered, a lump swelling in her throat as she poured boiling water into Eilidh's cup, simply so she could avoid the looks of pity from her coven. She expressly did not want to cry again; she'd only just got her breathing back under control.

Joy cleared her throat and asked, "What did the mirror show you?"

"A lot," Gus said with a shudder.

Victoriya got the cream from the fridge before Joy could go for it and thrust it out like a cat gifting a dead mouse.

"The killer's a blonde with sharp nails," she said, red lips pressed into a thin line. "She's slim and pretty tall, but the angle we saw was behind her, looking down as she walked past the high street and towards the beach. So, that's all we got. That and a weird glimpse of shitty wooden houses and snowy mountains that I fully blame Augustus for."

"What did *I* do?" Gus protested, scowling.

"You weren't concentrating." Victoriya's eyebrows pressed into a frustrated V. "The image skipped."

Gus crossed his arms over his jumper, his glower intensifying. "Maybe *you* weren't concentrating."

"Alright," Joy cut in before they could start bickering. "So, it didn't show you her face?"

"Nope," Victoriya confirmed. "Total waste of time."

But if she was a slim blonde woman ... it wasn't Paulina. A tight knot of fear eased in Joy's chest. It wasn't the killer who'd locked her up, and who would do it again as soon as the chance was provided.

Joy looked between her friends, and realised none of them would meet her eyes. Even Maisie, usually so forthright with her eye contact, glanced away.

"What else is wrong?"

"The mirror broke," Salma breathed gently, her gaze apologetic and sad. "We needed a balancing presence. I didn't realise until the glass shattered when we ended the spell. All our witchcraft tried to get out at once, separately, instead of working together."

"Oh," Joy choked out, looking past them to the mirror laid on the table. Not only had it shattered but most of the glass was gone, swallowed by magic.

Her mother's mirror. Joy's throat closed up, her eyes burning.

"It disintegrated," Gus explained, wringing his hands. "We really suck at spells without you."

"Oh," Joy murmured in a different tone. So, they *did* need her...? "*Oh.*"

Maisie made an exasperated sound in her throat, and Joy finally grasped what she'd been trying to say earlier. She wasn't useless or unwanted. In Maisie's eyes, she was as important as Gus or Salma.

"It doesn't matter about the mirror," she said finally, pushing back her tears and checking Eilidh was still on the bench outside. "I don't use that one anyway."

And this house was *full* of her mother's trinkets and possessions. It was silly to feel so gutted over one thing.

She poured milk into the hot chocolate and slid it along the counter for Victoriya to pour a mountain of cream on top.

"I'll take it," Salma volunteered, removing the mug from Victoriya's hands before she could protest. Her chest a bit lighter, Joy watched through the window until Salma sat beside Eilidh, drawing her into a hug.

"Are we getting paid for this?" Victoriya asked, crossing her arms over her chest and leaning against the counter.

When everyone shot her the same look, she added, "Seriously. I think we should get paid for all the shit we're doing for Pride."

"Gabi doesn't get paid much," Joy told her. "Just enough for rent and food and stuff. I doubt she has any extra for herself let alone you, Victoriya."

Gus came to lean against the counter beside Joy, gazing out the window. "Do you reckon people'll start taking Pride casseroles and cakes like they used to with her dad?"

Joy smiled at the unexpected—and forgotten—memory. Back then, dishes and cookware had forever been piled on the table of the Law House, and even more were stacked in the fridge, as payment from thankful families and gifts from doting old ladies.

"Probably," she said, and hoped people appreciated Gabi as much as they did Bo.

"So, *no* pay," Victoriya grumbled and squirted cream directly into her mouth. "Which means *no* shiny new wand holster for me. Why are we doing this again?"

"Because we're good, charitable people," Gus offered, tapping her bottom lip in thought.

Victoriya snorted.

"For justice," Joy input, twisting her wand in her fingers. "And it means Paulina isn't going to lock me up again. And *anyway*," she added quickly to cover up that vulnerability, "do we *really* want to live in the same town as a murderer?"

Maisie made a throaty sound.

"Hell no," Gus translated.

"Are they even *in* Agedale anymore?" Victoriya asked around another mouthful of squirty cream. "How do we know they haven't run off? There's no way they're local with the power we sensed. No witch in Agedale feels that old. Not even elves or *fae* do. And I don't mean OAP old. I mean *ageless* old."

"Old as balls," Gus agreed sagely.

Joy frowned. Elves may live to a hundred and twenty, and fae might reach double that number, but the way her coven spoke about this witch, she was *much* older.

Older than two hundred and fifty years? Who the hell *was* this killer?

Gus rapidly tapped the speckled countertop, chewing his bottom lip. "Why did they come *here*? Why not one of the bigger towns? Not to be critical of a psycho, but wouldn't it make more sense to go for a big city like Manchester where ordinary cops wouldn't notice the witch-craft? I know there's a supernatural police department in every major city but, seriously, murders in small towns *never* go unnoticed. In bigger places? Happens way more often."

"Maybe they *wanted* to be noticed," Victoriya said, narrowing her eyes. "It could be a notoriety thing."

Joy didn't like this direction of conversation *at all*. She didn't want to think about a killer being so close to her home, leaving a girl on the beach that was essentially Joy's back garden. But she was part of Gabi's investigation, and she'd begged to help, so she couldn't get spooked now. She had to put her big girl pants on.

"Gus has a point," she said, gripping her wand in a white-knuckled hand. "It doesn't make sense that someone this old and powerful came here. Is there anything we can do to find out why?"

Victoriya let out an abrasive laugh, fear mingled with the sharpness. "You really wanna get inside the head of that bitch?"

"No, thank you," Joy replied quickly, her whole body flashing cold.

"Then no. There's no way we can find out why she came here *or* killed Freya. That's Pride's job."

"Which we're helping with," Gus pointed out.

Victoriya lifted a shoulder, conceding the point.

Joy looked at Victoriya from the corner of her eye. Tonight, despite everything, she'd been less ... snarly. "Did something happen?" she asked. "With your mysterious suitor?"

Victoriya made a sound in the back of her throat. For months now, she'd had a crush on an older man she saw around the community centre where she taught dance classes. She wouldn't tell the coven anything about him except he was too attractive for his own good—and for hers—and he was *completely* oblivious to her advances. Joy, Gus, and Eilidh had been desperate to find out who he was for *ages,* but they'd had no luck.

"Just kiss him, V," Gus suggested seriously. Victoriya swung towards him—it was a *very* touchy subject—but Joy caught her by the lapel of her leather jacket before she could smack Gus upside the head.

"*Please* don't trash my kitchen with your world-ending

anger," she begged.

Victoriya huffed, wrenched her jacket free, and said, "I'll consider sparing you."

Joy smiled, pleased.

Somehow being with her friends and teasing Victoriya had lessened her hurt. And when Victoriya crossed her arms over her chest, looking scowly but pleased, Joy found herself distracted as she asked, "So *did* anything happen?"

Victoriya glared, but she also blushed. "I might have given him my number after work yesterday. He *might* have texted me."

Joy grinned. She worked hard to suppress the urge to yank her friend into a celebratory hug.

Gus got there first; he pushed off the counter and slung his arm around Victoriya's neck. "Look at you, getting the D. I'm proud of you."

"I got his *number*," Victoriya hissed, ripping his arm from her shoulder, blushing fiercely now, all the way to her ears. "That's it. Just a number."

But Joy could tell she was delighted, no matter how surly she was. "I'm happy for you, Victoriya."

Victoriya scowled instead of glaring and throwing a harsh word, which was evidence enough of her good mood.

"*Oh joy*," she drawled, turning towards the hall, "your girlfriend's here." She paused, and added, "Pun intended."

And sure enough, there was a knock on the door. Gus made the sign of the cross, albeit with heavy mischief and sarcasm.

"How did you know?" Joy asked her friend. "You're not a seer."

"No, I'm a listener. You can hear that car a mile off."

Joy laughed at the unexpectedly normal reply and went to answer the door.

TWENTY-TWO

GABI

Gabi would have been at Joy's house an hour earlier if she hadn't driven past a couple violently arguing in the street. They both had to be pushing eighty, but they had some *serious* lungs on them —and tempers to match. The husband had been sneaking to the pub behind his wife, Helga's, back. Helga handled learning this fact badly; right as Gabi was driving past, Helga lifted the two-foot gnome from her shrubbery with a hovering spell and hurled it straight at her husband's head.

Now, the woman was cooling off in a town hall cell. Her husband was in A&E, still tipsy and ranting loudly.

Speaking of the town hall, Gabi needed to figure out how to tell Paulina the conditions of those cells needed improving *ASAP*. Somehow, she needed to phrase it, so it seemed like Paulina's own idea.

She'd ask her dad; he was better at cleverness and intrigue.

By the time Gabi had pulled up outside Joy's house, she'd lost all the mental energy she needed to deal with the coven. Not that Salma, Eilidh, or Joy were difficult. But Maisie ... she'd taken a liking to Gabi's perfume and insisted on claiming Gabi's coat for her bed. Every single time Gabi was near. And Victoriya and Gus could give her a headache in two seconds flat.

Somehow, she managed the night without snapping, only disappearing twice to the toilet for a moment's peace.

It had been hours now since the coven left, and Gabi had lost track of the time.

With the house empty, Gabi and Joy took a bottle of wine and a Tupperware box of ginger biscuits into the living room. Salma baked the biscuits, her speciality, and gave a warmth to both Gabi's tongue and her mood. She'd forgotten what it was like to be around witches, the special things she'd once taken for granted. Enchanted food, like Joy's mum used to make.

God, she'd missed this.

Again, there came that tug in her belly, urging her to stay in Agedale. Her plans for a city career seemed very far away right now.

"Poor thing," Joy sighed, swirling the rosé in her glass.

It was the first time Gabi had seen Joy put down her wand, though it remained in clear sight on the coffee table, Christmas lights catching in the facets of the amethyst.

"He was still crying when you left?" she asked, her eyes big with sympathy.

Gabi nodded, leaning back into the sofa and casting off the day's aches. Her face was warm from the alcohol, and red from the electric fire across the small room. She wondered if her eyes were glossy too; Joy's certainly were—they now sparkled rich chocolate brown.

"I don't think he could hurt an insect, let alone murder

his girlfriend," she sighed. Macon had been the deadest of dead ends. Hence her exhaustion.

"You were always a good judge of character," Joy murmured, staring into her wine. "Unlike me."

"Hey," Gabi said, loudly. Too loudly; she winced at her volume. "Don't be so hard on yourself. You're great. It's not your fault people are assholes."

Joy shrugged. She was a sad drunk. If they opened another bottle, she'd start weeping.

Gabi reached across the coffee table between them—for some reason they'd forsaken the furniture, alighting instead on the carpet—and patted Joy's hand.

"You give people a chance when they don't deserve it. That just makes you a good person." Gabi set her drink aside, not liking the impulse to kiss Joy that kept thumping through her blood. She took her hand back, and set it firmly on the floor, then switched the topic back to something safe.

"If anyone had a motive, it was his mother."

"Whose mother?"

"The boyfriend's."

"*Ohhhh.*"

Joy's sweet, guileless smile was doing unacceptable things to Gabi's stomach. Butterflies and somersaults, the whole damn circus. She shouldn't feel this way about her ex.

Their argument was a line in the sand, keeping Joy on one side and Gabi on the other. She couldn't cross it without dredging up all that bitterness and hurt and history.

Gabi had stolen Joy's last night with her mother and had caused her unspeakable hurt. She couldn't just walk back into her life and kiss her again, couldn't feel this way again.

But she *did* feel this, and she did want to kiss her.

The wine. It had to be the wine.

She said, "You know how well relationships between two species go down. The mother is ... traditional. Staunch. She hated Freya."

"Doesn't mean she did it," Joy said, munching a biscuit. "Maybe she just didn't want her son to get hurt by Freya."

See, this was why it was so difficult to stay professional around Joy. She saw the best in everyone, even people she didn't know. It was something Gabi both admired and couldn't fathom. She didn't give *anyone* the benefit of the doubt. In her experience, they didn't deserve it.

"Maybe," she replied, but didn't truly believe it. Her first task tomorrow was finding out as much about Mrs. Brent as possible.

Joy snorted and shuffled around the coffee table.

"*Maybe*," she parroted in Gabi's neutral tone. "You always agree with me, even when you don't."

"I don't know what that means," Gabi replied, aware of the closing distance.

Not good. *Not fucking good*.

Her heart pounded, a trill of nerves joining the circus in her belly.

Joy snorted again. It was fucking adorable. Gabi suppressed a groan.

"Means," Joy said, close enough to reach out and pat Gabi's face, "you're being too *nice*. I won't break if you tell me I'm wrong."

She placed her hands on either of Gabi's cheeks, giving her a searching stare, and Gabi almost groaned at the touch, heat pooling inside her.

"You look the same. Same face, same dark eyes, same straight hair. Same grumpy frown." Joy brushed her fingers over Gabi's aforementioned frown, and Gabi shuddered, every part of her aching for more. She held herself still, but it was a losing battle; sooner or later she'd fall. "Did we travel back in time? Are we back there?"

Gabi swallowed, her hands flexing, a fraught moment away from grabbing Joy, hauling her close, and kissing her breathless.

"No," Joy sighed, dropping her hands and inching away. "No, we're still here."

"Do you wish we were back there?" Gabi dared to whisper, surprised when her voice came out hoarse.

Joy nodded, a fall of pink hair hitting her face from her untidy ponytail. She looked so sad, and that threw ice water on Gabi's desire.

"So I could fix it," she murmured. "So I could say sorry. Not even ... not even so I could fix *us*, because I missed that up so badly. But I don't want you to think I hated you. I never did. Not *ever*."

Gabi blinked, dropping her gaze. Her face had warmed even more. She felt unreasonably like she was about to cry.

"I never hated you either," she said, voice still raspy and raw. Gabi wasn't a fan of how her emotions were on full display, ragged and fragile. "I just wanted to say sorry and to make it right. To take back that night on the beach, so you could be with your mum in those last hours."

"She'd have been furious with me, you know?" Joy said, a flicker of a smile on her mouth. "For shouting at you. And then for what I said... She'd have told me to stop being so mean and stupid and *blinded* by how much it hurt. She'd have told me to say sorry, and maybe I would have stopped being angry before you left. Maybe I'd have apologised and fixed it all."

"Maybe doesn't matter," Gabi said, lifting her eyes to

Joy's face; she was close to crying, her face blotchy and her mouth set. Gabi wanted to touch her, but couldn't find the bravery, too afraid of rejection. "We can fix it now. I'll go first." She sat straighter and kept eye contact. "I'm sorry."

Joy gave a tentative smile, her eyes as glassy as brown crystal. "I'm sorry, too. More than you'll ever know."

"There," Gabi said decisively. "All fixed."

Joy looked more relieved than Gabi had ever seen her. Then the look in her eye changed, something Gabi couldn't interpret, when she said, "You can't drive like this, you know?"

"I know."

She was a grade A idiot for drinking so much.

Joy patted the sofa. "I'll bring you a cushion and blanket."

Gabi caught Joy's hand as she rose, a selfish compulsion she couldn't fight.

"Thank you," she said, her ragged emotions betrayed when her thumb swept along the pulse point in Joy's wrist.

Joy nodded quickly. She looked flustered. Gabi should *definitely* not like that. Not at all. But she did. She didn't let go for a long moment.

She knew how this could play out—she'd tighten her grip, pull Joy back down so she tumbled into Gabi's lap, and she'd kiss her until they were both gasping for air.

But her eyes snagged on the messenger bag she'd dumped on the table; she remembered the case files within and released Joy's hand.

Professional. Friends. Crime-solving and nothing else.

Ugh, Gabi was so fucked.

"A cushion would be good. Thanks, Joy."

When Joy nodded and scurried out of the room, Gabi let her head fall back against the sofa, a groan in her throat.

The silver lining was she couldn't make this any more awkward while she slept.

The morning, however, would be a different matter.

TWENTY-THREE

JOY

Joy walked past the elegant peaks of the elven community, the mini-town of tents in all manner of shapes, sizes, materials, and colours. She was late to work, thanks to an emergency errand for Mor Margaret in the Apothecary. Joy listened for the rise and fall of elven songs. It was a haunting, high melody that loosened something in Joy's bones like a healer's touch. Beauty. She desperately needed it today.

The community was silent today, like the universe was trying to tell Joy something.

She still took the long way around the beach to the nature reserve. She might have been in a rush, but she couldn't walk past the spot where she'd found Freya.

Joy's mind kept lingering on Gabi and the way she'd looked last night, her eyes a little glazed from the witch biscuits and wine. The memory was just enough to help Joy convince herself the beach was safe.

How many years had she walked this same stretch of sand, and inhaled its brine and storm-air scent? How many of those days had been nightmarish? *One*, she told herself, *just one, just an aberrant thing*.

When she reached the reserve, she stomped her feet on the stone ramp to knock the sand off her boots, repeating her mantra. *Just one day, just one day*.

But she was graced for more tragedy and trauma, and she wasn't surprised when a strangled cry cut through the air. It sounded like an animal being killed—

A shadow shoved out of the reserve building and past Joy before she could run away. Bony elbows and angles slammed into Joy's front, knocking the air out of her lungs as she tumbled off the ramp and into the sand.

The person kept running. It wasn't the killer, just an exceptionally rude jogger.

"Don't apologise," Joy growled under her breath, outraged and offended, "it's *fine*."

She grunted as she pushed to her feet, sand now stuck to both clothes and skin. Awesome. This was *just* what she needed after being an hour late to work. She was supposed to start at twelve, but it had taken her half an hour to find her keys—snaffled in a bundled up cardigan she fully blamed Maisie for—and another half to help Mor Margaret. She didn't need some careless prick in a hoodie shoving her into the sand.

Or robbing the reserve.

Joy's breath quickened with dread, and her heart sank as she realised she could be sacked for this. She fumbled for her keys, set them to the lock, and realised the door was open. Of *course* it was—the prick had come from inside.

Something dripped onto Joy's boots and for a second, she just stared at that speck of red, and then gaped as another drop fell. Her eyebrows furrowed, Joy looked down at herself, her coat, her sleeves.

Oh, god.

Breath whooshed out of her when she saw blood on her sleeve. She was *bleeding*. Bright, crimson drops of confusion. She was bleeding?

When that asshole shoved past her, they must have nicked her. But this was too clean a cut to be done with fingernails. This was a knife's doing. Joy stared at the shallow cut on her forearm, about five centimetres long, and struggled to process it. She'd been *cut*.

Disinfectant, a calm voice advised. *And a bandage*. Both of which were kept in the first aid box under the little counter in the front room of the reserve—which had been converted into a little gift shop to generate money.

Biting back a groan, Joy pushed inside and—

Froze.

There was a *lot* of blood. So much that Joy's breathing quickened even more, her hands starting to shake.

Blood had splashed across the floor she'd polished clean yesterday, and splattered across the display of leaflets, and over the educational boards she'd been improving these past few months.

And over the figure slumped on the floor.

Oh God.

"Mr Ivers?" she gasped, rushing through the blood to kneel beside the bloody form of her neighbour—and her mum's best friend. She bit the inside of her cheek and ignored the pain flashing from her own arm. It was growing worse with every minute, burning fiercer.

Joy had almost always known Neil for his kind smiles and gentle personality. And somehow, he was here in the reserve, with dark liquid soaked into his checked shirt, his jeans, and his face—

Gods, there was a cut on his cheek, just like—

Joy shut that thought down. His chest was cut, and he was bleeding heavily; that was more pressing. Her hands shook harder.

What would Gabi do? *What would Gabi do?*

"Neil?"

Her neighbour, her friend, was bleeding on the floor, his shirt and coat ripped open, his skin cut apart. She reached out to touch him, her fingers searching for a pulse in his neck. Alive. He was *alive.*

It was only then that she realised his jumping chest meant he was breathing, too.

Get it together, Joy!

Gabi would phone the police. But Gabi *was* the police. Shit. *Shit.*

Joy let out a shuddering breath and stumbled over to the rack of nature-themed items available for purchase. She grabbed a tea-towel with rare birds on it, ripped off the tag, then pushed it hard against the bleeding wound on Mr. Ivers's chest. He didn't so much as grunt, even though it must have caused him excruciating pain.

Leaning all her weight on one hand, Joy fumbled for her phone with her other and scrolled through her contacts until she found Victoriya's number.

"What now, Mackenzie?" she barked, answering.

"I need your mum," Joy gasped, panicking as the towel soaked through too quickly. It was only a small wound, but it was bleeding fast. And if the cut on his face—just a line, not a word, *but still*—meant he'd been hurt by the same person who'd killed Freya, witchcraft could be involved. Blood thinners, anti-healing hexes, *curses.* Gods, *curses...*

"*Now,* Victoriya! Put her on the phone or give me her number and I'll call her myself." Joy sounded nothing like herself. It was an eerie, out of body experience to hear her own voice.

"What's happened?" Victoriya demanded. "Where are you? *Mum!*"

"I'm at work—the reserve. Someone must have broken-in. When I got here, they knocked me over and ran, but then I found my neighbour inside. He's bleeding and I—I don't know what to do."

"Which neighbour?" Something had changed in Victoriya's voice, but Joy didn't have the energy to place the tone.

"Mr. Ivers, the man in the green house beside me," Joy replied, struggling for air as panic raged. "Long dark hair, early forties. He's a professor." Joy gritted her teeth against a sudden throb of pain in her forearm but with her eyes on Neil, her own pain was nothing.

The phone clicked off.

Joy gasped, horrified and alone, as Neil bled out, another tea-towel soaking through.

She screamed, jumping hard when a loud sound startled her. It took a panicked second for Joy to realise it was her phone ringing.

Joy frantically swiped to accept, smearing blood across the screen.

Mrs. Stone's cool voice was a blessed relief. "Tell me exactly how he looks."

Joy described it all, the bleeding, the cuts. Her voice shook. In the background of the call she could hear traffic, a horn screaming, and Victoriya swearing.

"We're almost there, Joy," Mrs Stone said, her voice soothing. "You're doing a really good job. Keep pressing on the wound. Just another minute."

Joy gasped out a pathetic reply, crying too hard now to

see. She was so beyond relieved that someone was coming who could properly help Neil. Mrs. Stone was a professional. Everything would be okay.

Joy was a damned idiot for not carrying healing spell ingredients. A basic one wouldn't save him, but it might help increase his chances. Or at least she should carry healing crystals—those would heal a papercut. Anything was better than the nothing she had now. The only crystals Joy had with her were for calming, and they'd thoroughly failed her.

Joy pressed the towel to Neil's chest for two agonising minutes, and she started to suspect help would never arrive. The ticking of the clock on the wall seemed endless, each tick driving her mad. With every second, he lost more blood.

But footsteps rushed up the ramp outside, and then Mrs. Stone burst through the door, looking capable and assured. The sleeves of her grey shirt were already rolled up and her black hair was swept into a bun. She was calm in the face of the blood and injuries, a contrast to Joy's pure panic.

Joy stumbled to her feet and moved out of the way as Mrs. Stone took over, saying her colleagues from the clinic were on their way. A long ebony wand was in her hand, and the other busily lined up bottles of green and pink and clear tonics.

Victoriya stood in the reserve doorway, gripping the frame with white knuckles, her face slack as she stared at the bleeding man. She came closer on unsteady legs, looking so unlike herself that Joy could only gape as Victoriya dropped to her knees beside Mr. Ivers and swore softly in Spanish.

Everything was a blur after that; the gift shop was

suddenly full of people, Joy was ushered out onto the beach, and she ended up hugging Victoriya as her friend silently sobbed, shaking hard.

Joy sensed when Victoriya's shock turned to fury, her whole body stiffening like iron.

"The *bitch* did that," she snarled, her voice raspy and hoarse and somehow more dangerous than normal. "Did you see? His cheek? If you hadn't come when you did, she'd have killed him."

Victoriya grabbed Joy's hand and squeezed hard enough to realign her finger bones, her eyes bright and wild. "You saved his life."

Joy opened her mouth to argue but quickly shut it, realising Victoriya was right. She'd interrupted the killer. They'd slit Neil's stomach, had begun marking his face, but whatever witchcraft had poisoned the beach around Freya, that her coven had sensed on the girl's body ... Joy had stopped *that* happening to Neil.

The person who'd run out of the reserve, who'd shoved Joy into the sand, and fled. That had been *the killer*.

Oh, god. Joy had been so close.

She shuddered, gripping Victoriya's hand just as tightly even as burning pain throbbed through her forearm. She used her blood-smeared phone to call Gabi.

TWENTY-FOUR
GABI

Gabi resisted the urge to bang her head against the frosted window. This morning with Joy had been awkward; Gabi left after breakfast, claiming she had to get to work. Which wasn't a lie. A full morning later, Gabi was hungry and frustrated and inadequacy was starting to set in. Every time she didn't accomplish something fast enough or good enough, she felt like she just *wasn't* enough.

Freya's sweet boyfriend was not only innocent but had been revising with his geeky friends the evening Freya was killed and had stayed at the friend's house until the following morning. No chance for him to sneak out, either—suspicious parents had locked and alarmed all the doors, thinking the lads would rifle the booze cabinet and sneak off to the beach.

His mother, however much she hated Freya, was with her toy boy all night and the following morning, while her husband was away at a 'golf retreat' with *his* bit on the side.

Gabi had finally got home from questioning them, with

a headache the size of China for her trouble, and a failure complex even bigger.

She should have known she couldn't do this, couldn't solve a murder.

Plus, the worst part of all this: her theory of Paulina being the killer had gone out of the window when the coven glimpsed the killer in their mirror. Blonde hair could be easily faked with a wig, but to go from Paulina's size to rail thin ... it wasn't possible. Which meant Gabi had no clue *whatsoever* who had killed Freya.

Why now? This time she did bang her head against the window, knocking a fine dusting of snow onto the path below. Why had Freya been killed *now*? What had changed? What had triggered the murder? Freya had been the same as ever, according to more than ten people, and she'd got back together with Macon Brent. Which meant the catalyst had been in the *killer's* life. Not the victim's.

Gabi gnashed her teeth. She'd never figure this out. A killer would go uncaptured, free to hurt someone else, and it'd be all her fault. She'd fail herself, her mum's memory, *and* Paulina's trial week, all at the same time.

Gabi's mobile buzzed.

She peeled her head off the cold glass to retrieve it.

"Pride," she answered in a flat voice.

But as she listened to Gus speak, a renewed enthusiasm and determination filled her.

"That *does* sound suspicious," Gabi agreed, grabbing her bag off the back of the chair. "I'll be there in five."

GUS'S HOUSE turned out to be a terrace like Gabi's, only his was at the fringe of Agedale. Furthest from the beach, where the houses were less pristine and split into two flats. Gabi trekked up a bare wooden staircase that looked like it had been cleaned last decade, heading for the top floor. The whole place smelled like mildew.

At least the beige wallpaper wasn't peeling. And it was quiet, which was more than she could say for her own neighbours sometimes.

"I know," Gus muttered when he met her at the landing, his shoulders tense beneath a faded band shirt. His brown hair was shoved back from his forehead in an artful quiff today, his self-deprecating smile not lighting bleak eyes. "It's a shit hole. But it's cheaper than anywhere else."

"I didn't mean to judge," Gabi rushed out, a twinge of guilt in her stomach. She'd never had to worry about money, thanks to the town's mutual adoration of her dad. "It takes me a while to turn off my perception when I'm ... in detective mode."

God, she hated struggling for words. She avoided Gus's eyes when she reached the top, a single wooden door ahead.

"I get it," Gus replied easily, warmly.

A weight lifted off Gabi's chest at his easy forgiveness.

With a gesture of his sharp chin, Gus led her into a modest flat that was much cleaner and tidier than she'd expected from a guy in his twenties living with a fox. Then again, he was always dressed in clean, lavender-smelling shirts and dark jeans—not a rip in sight—and he clearly made an effort with his appearance, so she ought to have expected this. He closed the door behind her, and she spotted the fox bundled into a nest by a large window that looked onto a fire escape.

"Hello," she said to the witch, pleased when she made a responding noise.

"Huh," Gus murmured, blinking at Gabi as he headed into the kitchenette and began gathering things.

At her questioning glance, he explained, "People don't say hi to her like that. They say it sneering or with a laugh or something. Cause she's a fox, y'know?"

Gabi frowned, judging those people hard. "She's also a person."

"I like you, Pride." Gus grinned, a smile that lit his entire tanned face. "And Maisie *loves* you. Sit down. I don't have tea, but I've got cola. Will that do?"

"Thank you," Gabi said politely and took a seat at the breakfast bar that separated his small kitchen from the living room—a carpeted square with a beaten up sofa, a TV, and a portable radiator. On top of the TV was a cheerful snowman teddy bear with blushing cheeks and a stuffed carrot nose. The whole place smelled of toast and lavender and some other sweet smell. A witch tonic, maybe.

There were certainly hallmarks of witchery in the flat. Gabi peered at an army of plastic cereal containers filled with herbs, fifteen of them lined along the kitchen counter with their contents scrawled in Sharpie. Their living, greener siblings filled the empty spaces of the apartment, plants dangling from airers and door hooks and draped around the cupboards. Despite her first impressions, Gabi found herself warming to the place.

Maisie made a sound in her throat, startling Gabi, but Gus only screwed the cap back on the coke bottle and laughed.

"There," he said, crossing the room to shove the window open so Maisie could jump out onto the fire escape. "The joys of outside."

He grabbed two glasses of coke from the kitchen worktop and said, without preamble, "I saw a woman run up the road, shifty-looking. With everything that's happened, I paid attention. Our flat looks onto the main road through Agedale. That's why I asked you to come here instead of going to yours, so you could see for yourself."

Gabi was stunned for a second before she recovered and got out her notebook to write every detail down.

"I was sitting there, dicking about with job applications —contemplating how best to word my *many* talents—when a shadow caught my eye. Do you know how many people around here would be skulking around in a black hoodie? One. Me. Anyway, this hoodie-wearing person comes sprinting down the main road and disappears into the back streets behind the bakery. I can show you the direction she came from and where she went."

Gabi got legit butterflies.

"How could you tell it was a woman?" she asked. "Or are you just saying that because you sensed the power on Freya's body was from a woman?"

"No." Gus shook his brown head and took a gulp of coke. "Tight hoodie. Boobs, bum, thighs. I'd say it *could* be a trans guy, but since I'm the only pariah around here for being a different gender than I was born ... definitely a woman."

Gabi made no comment but felt a twist of anger inside. This backwards town and its bullshit discrimination.

"Does that make you uncomfortable?" Gus asked, fiddling with the glass in his hand. "Me talking about being trans?"

"No," Gabi responded evenly, giving him a serious, open look. "It makes me angry at every bigot in this town. Makes me almost miss Liverpool."

"But Liverpool has no cute pink-haired witch, right?" he teased, waggling his eyebrows.

Gabi shot him a look, then flicked her eyes back to the window. "Show me where this hooded person came from."

"Don't try to change the sub—"

But Gabi's phone's shrill call interrupted her. Joy's name flashed on the screen. Delight rippled through her, but on its heels came panic.

Why was Joy calling? What had happened?

"Joy?" she demanded. She couldn't remember the last time she'd seen that name on her phone.

All she heard were sobs and gasped words in reply, and Gabi shuddered as icy fear spread through her.

Gus came closer, his brow knitted in concern. Maisie climbed back through the window, eyes on Gabi.

"Joy? Sweetheart?"

There was a crack of silence, and then *Victoriya* hissed, "Get your arse to the clinic. If you don't find this bastard, I'm going to fucking *kill* you, Pride."

Horror swirled in Gabi's stomach. For a second, she just reeled, nausea rising.

Why was Joy sobbing? What had *happened* to her?

Gabi grabbed her car keys in a shaky hand and bolted out the door.

OF COURSE PAULINA and her pretty shadow took this moment to corner and interrogate Gabi as she raced down the high street. Of course they fucking did.

"I don't know anything yet," Gabi replied, as polite as she could make her voice, which wasn't very. "If you let me do my job, I will tell you when I have something concrete. I don't want to waste your time, Paulina," she added to soothe over her irritated tone. "Telling you theories instead of facts won't help anyone."

Paulina pursed her lips, her eyes flicking to the golden sun badge on Gabi's collar. "Act *faster*. Are you so incompetent that you can't do your job, Gabriella? I thought you had a knack for this sort of work."

Gabi wasn't a violent person, but she desperately wanted to knock that mocking smile off Paulina Montgomery's face.

"I'm competent," she said slowly, as if explaining to a child, "but I'm not *omnipotent*. I am one person doing the work of a whole team, and right now I need to be at the clinic"

She wanted to yell that she was doing everything she could, short of never sleeping and wasting time on silly things like bathing and eating.

Paulina's expression narrowed further. "I expect you to do *better*. I want this killer caught yesterday. Do I make myself clear?"

Maybe if Paulina hadn't wasted Gabi's time by arresting Joy, she might be fucking closer.

Trying not to grind her teeth, Gabi replied, "Yes, ma'am."

Paulina nodded and, finally satisfied, stalked off, leaving Gabi behind with her blonde assistant.

"Don't mind her," Katrina said in a sweet voice. "She's just under a lot of pressure right now." She laid her hand on Gabi's arm without permission.

Gabi pried the woman's chipped fingernails from her jacket and said, "She isn't the only one."

It may have been rude to just walk off, but she didn't have time to waste chatting.

Two victims, one alive from what she'd been able to

piece together. One who might have seen his attacker. And Joy caught up in the middle of it.

Gabi fought to settle her nerves as she stalked up to the butter-yellow clinic. She could do this. She could make Agedale safe again. Make Joy safe again.

She didn't want to think about the alternative.

TWENTY-FIVE

JOY

Joy had barely processed her relief at seeing Gabi, storming through the cold, yellow corridor, her long black hair flying behind her and her coat flapping open—she was like an angel burning with glorious fury—before Joy's face was against Gabi's shoulder and Gabi's arms were crushing her close.

"I thought you'd been hurt," Gabi cried, drawing back to touch Joy's face.

Joy could do nothing but look at her, caught off guard, stunned by Gabi's hands as they moved to Joy's elbows, as if unwilling to let her go. Her eyes roved over Joy's body, as if unable to believe she was okay.

Joy's face burned hot, the end of her nose tingling, warning tears were close.

"I'm alright," she rasped after a too-long moment of silence. "I'm not hurt."

A nurse had patched up her arm in what felt like seconds while Joy stared at the healers working on Neil, and it had stopped throbbing ages ago.

"But Neil, my neighbour, is really hurt. I found him

bleeding, and there was so much blood, Gabi, it was everywhere."

"Shh," Gabi soothed, stroking her back. "You're okay."

"I think—I think the killer shoved me. No, I know *someone* shoved me and I think it was the killer. It's too big a coincidence for it be anyone else and—"

"Joy," Gabi said calmly, ducking her head to trap Joy's stare. "It's alright. Take a deep breath."

Joy struggled at first, but after the fourth attempt, she filled her lungs with a trickle of oxygen.

"There was so much blood," she breathed again, stuck on that fact, unable to move past it. She shook, a primal shudder. "It's all over me," she hissed. "It's all—it's everywhere. I—I tried to clean it but—"

Her words, her panic, her disgust ... all of it paused when Gabi left a kiss on Joy's temple.

To someone else, Gabi said, "I'll be with you in two minutes."

To Joy she murmured, "Come on, sweetheart," and guided her down the hallway to the ladies' toilet.

Joy didn't understand why until Gabi started removing her clothes. She checked to make sure no scandalised women were going to come out of the stalls, relieved when they were all empty.

"None of your clothes will fit me," Joy rasped, still feeling the blood on her hands even if her fingers themselves were numb.

She knew, on any other day, the sight of Gabriella Pride stripping would make her face blush and her body pulse with heat, but now she only watched, feeling ... emptied.

"*This* will," Gabi said, removing the black vest she wore under her smart shirt and coat. "It has some stretch. Take your top off."

Joy didn't argue, and found Gabi was right—her vest was stretchy enough to fit Joy's curves. She swallowed, gratitude and confusion and shaky fear rattling around inside her body.

Gabi put her white shirt back on, but she buttoned her heavy wool coat around *Joy* instead. It came halfway down Joy's calves and was long in the sleeves, but she instantly felt better to be out of her bloody shirt. She'd worn black trousers today—her single attempt to look professional, not that her boss cared—so if any blood had spilled onto them, it wasn't visible. And she couldn't feel any wetness in the fabric.

Relief slowly loosened the fist gripping her lungs. She lifted her head when the comforting weight of Gabi's hands settled on her shoulders, before sliding up her neck to frame her face.

"Coffee, tea, or soup?" Gabi asked, her steady brown eyes trying to convince Joy everything would be okay.

"I don't need anything," Joy replied in a scratchy voice. She'd already been given clothes and more physical contact than she'd dreamed of in a year.

Gabi tucked a messy lock of pink hair behind Joy's ear. "Coffee, tea, or soup?"

Joy surrendered. "Tea."

With protectiveness blazing across her face, Gabi put her arm around Joy and led her back to the hallway. She kept that arm around Joy as she got tea from a vending machine, and then settled Joy in a padded green-and-wood seat.

She was treating Joy like a spooked animal or a scared child, but Gabi's care made Joy feel a little bit better, so she didn't complain as Gabi led her to a seat and left to talk to the healers and nurses.

Joy sipped the hot, insipid tea and stared at the door across the hall, where Victoriya's mum and her colleagues were treating Neil. Joy's throat closed up and tears threatened when she thought of what could happen, that the healers might not be able to save him.

He'd always been a friendly face, helping her carry heavy bags, chatting about the weather, inviting her to Christmas parties when his wife used to throw them. He'd made sure her coven knew that Joy had been locked up when he saw Paulina drag her into the town hall. He didn't *deserve* this. There'd been so much blood on him. Joy's hands shook around the paper cup, spilling a drop to the linoleum floor.

Who would *do* this to him?

Joy spent a long time thinking about him, replaying her memories, and realisation struck slowly.

His wife.

Was she the wife who'd sent Victoriya on her way, mistaking her for one of Neil's students?

Joy peered up and down the hallway but didn't see the woman. She'd always seemed distant to Joy, a self-made distance that spoke of everyone else not measuring up to her standards. If that was the kind of woman Mr. Ivers liked, well ... he should *love* Victoriya's sharpness.

If he didn't die from blood loss or infection or a number of other threats Joy's mind sped through. Her eyes filled with tears again. If she'd gone straight to work, if she hadn't lingered helping Mor Margaret...

Joy jumped when a body threw itself into the chair beside her, and pale fingers snatched the tea out of her hands. Victoriya looked *young*. Her hair was tied back in a hasty ponytail, her face clear of its usual war paint, and her lips were so strange when Joy was used to seeing them a dark red. The only red on her today was her bloodshot eyes, and the blood stains on her jeans and T-shirt. No make-up, no malice. Joy had never seen this side of Victoriya. She *hated* seeing it now.

"What the hell *happened?*"

Joy tore her eyes from Victoriya and saw Gus striding towards them. For a second, she only frowned at the empty space behind his feet, and then she realised animals weren't allowed in the clinic. The nurses wouldn't make allowances even for witches trapped in fox form.

Joy stumbled through an explanation, and then they sat for three hours while the nurses and healers—most of them fae who'd deigned to help all species thanks to the high pay Paulina offered—worked their magic on Neil.

When Salma finished her shift, she joined them, and Eilidh came sprinting through the doors a few minutes before school was supposed to let out, her eyes puffy and red from crying—from worrying that someone else would be taken, like her cousin had. Joy tucked her friend under her arm, and they sat like that for a long time, in utter, fearful silence.

Gabi paced. Once she'd taken Joy's and Victoriya's statements and spent an hour tapping at her tablet, she was left with nothing to do but wait for an update on Neil, or for Victoriya's mum to make her own statement. But Mrs. Stone was busy trying to save Neil's life.

Gabi paced, and paced some more until Victoriya snarled for her to sit the hell *down*. She finally did, taking a seat next to Joy, but her leg bounced, and her fingers tapped, and she was no less restless.

"Maybe you should go home," Joy suggested, her shock long worn off. Other emotions had flooded back in—fear, hatred, disbelief, and now, for Gabi, worry. "I'll call you when we're allowed to see him."

Gabi started to speak, but the door across the corridor swung open and Gabi sat up straight, her attention fixed on the nurses who exited.

This was it. The moment when they'd find out if Neil would live or die.

TWENTY-SIX
GABI

Gabi was used to being level headed and unflappable, but for the past three hours a jittery, impatient beast had taken possession of her body. She'd found out everything she could about Neil Ivers in the first thirty minutes of waiting, and now she was antsy. Neil was a good man, it seemed, though his moral standing had been thrown into shade by Victoriya's reaction to his attack. If someone as dangerous as Victoriya was fond of him, he couldn't be completely innocent. Unless that was the allure. Gabi couldn't say; not only was the man injured and locked in a hospital room, but men weren't of any interest to her.

Her thoughts were disconnected, blasting from one subject to another like a tornado. She returned, as always, to the attack. It wasn't safe to assume Neil Ivers had been hurt by the same woman who'd killed Freya, but Gabi worked on that assumption for now. Joy had interrupted the killer and forced them to abandon the murder. But why not kill Joy? Why only injure her, shove her into the sand, and run? Shock, panic, or some other reason?

Joy had interrupted the killer and saved Neil Ivers. Would the killer find a second victim to fix that? Gabi needed to speak to her professor immediately, needed to go home and look through everything she'd collected so far. Joy must have been thinking along the same lines because she suggested Gabi go back to the Law House and promised to tell her if something happened with Neil.

But then the door opened.

Gabi shot to her feet, hopeful and nervous, her stomach fluttering. *Please let him be alive. Please let him be conscious.*

"Are you all for Mr. Ivers?" a middle-aged male nurse asked, his glasses slightly askew on his red nose—the only bit of colour in his pale face.

"We are," Salma confirmed with a polite smile, putting her hand over Victoriya's and squeezing to keep her still.

"I shouldn't really tell you anything unless you're family." His sympathetic green eyes said he was about to break the rules. "But since you've been waiting here for hours, I'll tell you he's stable."

"He's going to be alright?" Joy breathed. The wand in her hand was shaking badly, throwing specks of purple-tinged light all over the floor.

The nurse nodded, a worn smile on his face.

"Can I see him?" Victoriya asked in a voice unlike any Gabi had heard from her. Faint, exhausted—desperate. Eilidh reached out and caught her arm, squeezing tight enough to dent the sleeve of her jacket, but Victoriya didn't attempt to shake her off. And for her, that was akin to clinging to her friend and sobbing into her shoulder.

"Sorry. No visitors for the time being."

Victoriya snarled, but it was half hearted at best.

Gabi tugged down her vest and approached the nurse, straight-backed and calm-faced despite the torrent inside her.

"Do you know when I'll be able to speak to him? I'm Gabriella Pride." The name, as it had done before, spoke for itself. The nurse became more guarded.

"Not until tomorrow at the earliest."

Gabi nodded, suppressing a growl of frustration. But she'd suspected as much. "Thank you," she said, and made herself sit back down. A killer was out there, potentially hunting another victim; sitting and waiting was fucking useless. But she still parked her backside in a seat.

She wanted to pace, to *demand* to see Neil, to examine and photograph his injuries, but that was impolite and, more importantly, it would get her nowhere. The nurse at least looked less wary of her now she was sitting. Gabi saw the moment he realised Gabi was part of the group, waiting not by coincidence but by friendships. Well. Friend*ship*, but the nurse didn't need to know that.

"Where is he?" a strident voice rang through the corridors.

Gabi raised her eyes to the ceiling with a sigh, recognising that voice a mile off. This damn woman. A cloud of real fur with diamond earrings pushed through the double doors into their corridor, the thin woman almost swallowed by her giant white coat. Her long legs were like twigs above skyscraper heels. She really thought she was something.

Gabi gnashed her teeth when the woman's eyes swung to their little group. Judging, and finding them lacking.

"Who are you?" she demanded, her red upper lip curled back from her teeth and her coil of blonde hair wobbling on her head.

Gabi could easily punch her, right here and now, but she flattened her hands on her knees. *Professional. You are a Pride.*

"Gabrielle," Lana Ivers said when she spotted her, a laugh in her voice. She intentionally got Gabi's name wrong. Every damn time. "I heard you'd followed in your daddy's footsteps. How nice for us."

Gabi pressed her palms harder to her legs. *Calm. Cool. Unmovable as a mountain.* Never mind that this bitch had insulted Gabi's mother so badly she'd cried when Gabi was five years old. Never mind that Lana had sued Gabi's aunt's pub for some asinine reason, dragging her through court, putting her through *hell*, and leaving the Tipsy Witch with half its regulars at the end of the court case.

Cool. Calm. Unmovable as a mountain. It became a little easier when Joy's hand covered Gabi's.

"Mrs. Ivers," the male nurse said, his face too serene. *Everyone* had an opinion on Lana Ivers—saint or bitch, depending on what she'd done for or *to* you. "Your husband's in this room—you can't see him—no visitors—*please*, madam."

Lana did not give a single shit about respecting rules. She swung the door open, and a laugh burst out of her, tinkling and high. "Neil, you miserable, pathetic fool."

Victoriya was on her feet in a blink, and then across the corridor, baring her teeth at Lana with a snarl.

It happened so fast that Gabi couldn't get to her feet before Victoriya had the woman pinned to the doorframe by her throat. Not that she'd have stopped Victoriya.

Salma took a few steps to attempt to, trailing ivy and a comforting earthy scent, but she reconsidered. Maybe she was remembering Lana's laugh, or her snide words. Her husband had been attacked and was in Gods knew what state, and she'd *laughed*. No one stepped in to stop Victoriya. Not even the nurse.

"*Victoriya Regina*," a horrified voice cut through the tension, followed by a rush of footsteps. "Let that woman go *right now*."

Lana laughed—and choked when Victoriya's grip tightened. Even with her face red, hair coming undone, and coat askew, she somehow croaked, "Do as mummy says, *Victoriya Regina*."

Victoriya Regina did not.

"Either you both stop this, or you *both* leave." Despite Mrs. Stone's worn, frazzled appearance, she somehow gave the impression of a woman not to be tested. Gabi had a feeling she'd throw them both out with her bare hands.

Victoriya dug her nails into Lana's red neck, one final warning before she let go, and then hauled herself back with visible effort. Her hands shook, her body quivering with barely-leashed rage. The death threats didn't leave her eyes, though.

Lana simply straightened her expensive fur coat and smiled lazily. "Nice to meet you, sweetie. Whoever you are. Let's do this again some time."

And without even a glance into her husband's hospital room, she sauntered off.

Gabi did not like to think of the Ivers' divorce proceedings. The poor man wouldn't be left with a single penny. But it was worth it, to be rid of that bitch.

With the atmosphere in the hallway shifting away from violence, Salma closed the distance between her and Victoriya and bundled the girl into a hug. Gus, too, got up and joined them, and Eilidh pressed close, her tear-worn face now lined with sympathy and anger. Joy rushed to her feet to crush Victoriya in her own worry and love.

Gabi felt in the way; she moved aside and sat back down, her pointed ears burning. Her feet wanted to take her far from here, but she wouldn't walk away from Joy when she was still shaky.

Gabi was a little surprised when Victoriya's mum—the renowned healer and psychometric Regina Stone—sank into the seat beside her.

"You as honourable as your dad?" she asked without preamble. Wisps of dark hair had come loose from the knot on the back of her head. Gabi tried not to stare at them as she puzzled the woman's question.

But she'd heard so many stories about Regin—the people she'd saved, the cases she'd helped her dad with over the years—that she didn't hesitate to answer.

"Yes," she replied, meeting Regina's green eyes.

"Good. You keep an eye on my daughter while she's caught up in this case of yours."

"I will," Gabi said seriously.

Regina patted Gabi's arm, reminding her of the absence of her coat—her armour. "Anytime you need my help, you can ask. And there's a hot meal for you at my house any time you want to join us for dinner. Your dad, too."

"Thank you," Gabi breathed, her professional mask slipping in the face of this unexpected kindness. She knew Regina and her dad had been friends for years, but she'd never expected that to extend to *her*.

Regina patted Gabi's arm again and stood, disappearing into the room across the shiny corridor. Gabi had meant to thank her for keeping Joy as calm as was possible before the medics got to Neil, guiding her through the phone and in person. It was too late now.

"Victoriya," Regina hissed a moment later, popping her head out of the door and gesturing with her chin at the room. "Quickly."

Victoriya didn't hesitate; she shot for the open door on wobbly legs. When she stepped over the threshold, all her fury evaporated. She slumped, pressing a hand over her mouth—but when she dropped it, she was smiling, just slightly.

"I thought you were dead," she said in a hard voice.

"Not just yet," Neil croaked from within the room.

"Good," was all Victoriya said before she spun on her heel, looking more like herself than she had all day as she blew through the hallway to the exit and out into Agedale.

"Gus," Salma said, lifting an elegant hand to stop him as he started following his friend. "Let her be."

Gus stopped in the middle of the hall, looking awkward. He scratched the back of his neck, rumpling his hair. "Then what are we doing? Are we staying?"

Eilidh shrugged, folding her arms around herself. Looking as if the day had hit her all at once. Gabi didn't know how she would have felt, to be Eilidh, to have her own cousin—

No.

She swallowed hard at the image, those memories, that *hurt*. She shied away but forced herself to finish the thought. She didn't know how she'd feel to have her cousin be killed, ripped from the world, and for that killer to hurt someone else.

Hurt? Furious?

Lost, she decided. Gabi would feel empty and afraid and lost.

Pretty much what she'd been feeling this whole time they hadn't spoken.

She felt keenly the slice of grief Joy must have felt in the days after her mum's death, and she knew exactly what had made her lash out, and push Gabi away.

"We should go home," Salma murmured, looking at the exhaustion on her coven's faces. "Mrs. Stone will tell Victoriya if there's any news, and Victoriya will tell us."

Regina's nod confirmed it before she shut the door to Neil's room again, taking care of whatever mysteries healers needed to take care of inside.

"I'm leaving too," Gabi input, standing. "You can keep my coat for now, Joy. I don't need it."

She did need it. More than anything. She felt exposed and vulnerable, her skin prickly and tight, but she knew Joy felt worse. So she just unclipped her badge from the wool lapel, pinned it to her shirt, and let Joy keep her coat—her armour.

"Thank you for staying," Salma murmured, coming over to press Gabi's hand between both of her own. In a quiet voice, she added, "I'll make sure Joy gets home safe."

"Thank you," Gabi replied earnestly. A little bit of her worry eased. Not much compared to the giant pile of things she had to worry about, but some.

She felt like she was running out of time. When would the killer try again? Tonight? Tomorrow?

Joy's arms eased around Gabi when Salma stepped back, and Gabi tugged her closer on instinct, dragging her scent into her lungs.

"Thank you for looking after me," Joy said, her voice muffled.

The words fanned across Gabi's open collar, raising goose bumps on her skin.

"Always," she replied, running a hand down Joy's back, over her wind-knotted snarl of hair. "Be careful," she added.

"Don't go back to the sanctuary. I need to collect evidence from it."

That was the first thing on her list of endless to-dos.

"I've already told your boss to leave it alone. Also, he doesn't expect you in work until Monday. He said something about recovery and needing time and sending you well wishes."

Joy laughed softly. "He's nice. Kind of over the top, but nice."

Gabi smiled wearily. She noticed Joy was not letting go. Neither was she. "Are you alright?"

Joy nodded, her head bumping Gabi's chin. "Are you?"

"Me? I'm fine," Gabi replied, her brow knitting.

"So, you're *not* worrying enough for ten people? Your mind's *not* doing that thing where it thinks everything at once, and you forget to breathe, and your heart gets palpitations?"

Gabi had no reply. To be known so well... She tightened her grip on Joy.

"I'll be fine," she promised. Her lips brushed the top of Joy's head before she could remind them that Joy was her *ex*. She stepped back with effort and found Salma and Gus doing their utmost best to look elsewhere. Eilidh was just watching them with very soft eyes.

"I'll call you later," she told Joy. "You can give me your statement over the phone. I'll record it."

"And print out a transcript to memorise and annotate?" Joy teased.

Gabi already missed the warmth of Joy's body. "I'm nothing if not thorough," she played along.

She went to shove her hands in her pockets, but realised she wasn't wearing her coat, and felt awkward.

It should not have been as difficult as it was to walk to her car.

TWENTY-SEVEN

JOY

Gabi looked so tired when Joy called her that night, her sore, red eyes obvious even over Face-Time. Joy bet she hadn't stopped working since the moment she left the clinic. She was tempted to put off making this statement now just to give Gabi a break, but it might be important. If she left it much longer, she'd start to forget. Not that she knew much—she'd seen only an indistinct shape in a hoodie, but that matched what Gus had seen, too.

Joy and Gabi spoke for hours, smoothing out the snags in Joy's memory, going over the details of the case. *Nothing* connected Freya and Neil Ivers. There was nothing in common in the days before they were attacked—Freya had spent all her time at the food drive and Neil had been teaching, both at the school and at the community centre's night classes.

They'd come to a standstill and Joy could tell Gabi was sinking into despair.

"Salma had an idea," Joy said hesitantly. "It might not

work, and it'll probably be ... difficult. But her mum's a seer. If she's having a good day, she can focus on truths and lies, and tell you anything about *anyone*."

"And on a bad day?"

"She has hallucinations. Hears voices." Joy bit her lip. "She believes they're part of her visions."

"They aren't?" Gabi didn't look as hopeful as Joy had hoped she would.

"She has an illness that makes her see them. We don't usually bother her because we could make a good day into a bad one, but ... with everything, and Mr. Ivers being hurt and ... Salma said we should. Mrs. Nazari might be able to help."

Gabi looked thoughtful. Still tired, but contemplative at least. "We've got nothing to lose."

"Great!" Joy gave Gabi her brightest smile and watched Gabi's frayed edges knit back together. "I'll tell Salma. We can go tomorrow afternoon. Oh—can you bring some of your dad's cinnamon shortbread? Mrs. Nazari would love it; Salma says baked goods make her happy."

"I'll bring some," Gabi promised, giving Joy that soft look that turned her insides to mush.

"Thank you." Joy wanted to keep talking but couldn't think of a good excuse. "I should go. I need to feed Jilly—that's Neil's dog. Unless you need to talk some more...?"

"Go, Joy," Gabi said with a smile creasing her golden face. "Text me where and when to meet you tomorrow. I'll see you then."

"Yeah." Joy was aware her smile became too soft, too loving. "Bye, then!"

She ended the call before her face could betray her anymore, flushing red hot. She'd already blurted that she still loved Gabi. She didn't need to do any more damage.

Despite Gabi admitting she had feelings for Joy too, they were managing a friendship, and working together well. She didn't want to mess that up, especially when people were at risk.

Joy flashed back to finding Neil with a vivid jolt, blood everywhere she looked, but she fought her way out of those memories.

Jilly needed her; she'd be hungry.

Joy grabbed her keys off the sideboard and tucked a sachet of a protective spell into her pocket. Jilly would make her smile again. Dogs had their own brand of magic, special and more powerful than witchcraft.

———

IT TOOK a whole hour of sitting in Salma's box bedroom in the eaves of her sage-scented home for Salma's mother to feel ready to talk to them. But just Salma and Gabi. Even though the rest of the coven had come, a whole coven of unfamiliar faces would overwhelm Mrs. Nazari. So most of them had squashed into Salma's miniscule room, ducking their heads to avoid hitting the sloped ceilings.

Joy perched on the sliver of windowsill beside a trio of potted plants and a singular cactus, overlooking a patch of sad grass and the rows of matching houses behind Salma's. The rest of her coven occupied the single bed under draping boughs of ivy and honeysuckle and plants even Joy didn't know. Maisie had burrowed under the pillows, but her eyes were wide open, grave.

Joy knitted her fingers together around her wand—she still couldn't let it go—and watched Gabi with Salma. It was strange to see Gabi in a colour other than black or grey, but black clothes made Salma's mum unsettled. She'd startle and panic, and whatever clarity and calm she'd had would spiral into fear and absence. So Gabi was wearing a very pale green vest, the taut muscles of her arms exposed, and white trousers that Salma had dug out of a cramped drawer in her older brother's bedroom.

Only Salma still lived at home, but she had four siblings, scattered across the world in various supernatural and non-supernatural cities and towns. Joy struggled to picture so many personalities clamouring in this house and understood a little of why Salma often watched Victoriya and Gus bicker with a fond smile.

Gus's phone blared a morose metal song—Gabi calling —and then they could hear the conversation as Salma and Gabi joined her mother in the sitting room. They didn't tell Mrs. Nazari many details—Salma expertly left out anything that could trigger her but told her mum enough about the murders for Mrs. Nazari to be able to help. Even though she suffered hallucinations, she was still a fearsome seer.

"Mama," Salma said warmly, her voice crackly over the phone.

Joy pressed her knees to her chest on the windowsill, watching the phone for no real reason—it wasn't *showing* them anything. But Gus, Maisie, and Eilidh were doing the same.

Victoriya had never turned up. She'd texted Salma, *I'm busy*, and hadn't offered any other explanation. They all knew she was still upset because of Neil Ivers's attack. Joy and the others weren't dumb. It was common knowledge that Victoriya liked an older man. Were they supposed to think it was coincidence that Mr. Ivers was hurt and she'd gone ballistic? They hadn't spoken about it, despite Gus's pointed attempts, but now they knew the identity of

Victoriya's mystery man. And they all knew she was shaken and scared, so they left her alone.

"Give me that," Salma's mum said, her voice a thicker version of Salma's Moroccan accent.

Joy wondered if she'd snatched the item they'd brought with them to help her tap into her sight—a scrap of Neil's shirt where the killer had torn it open.

"Is she a mirror? A reflection? A trick?"

"I don't know, mama," Salma replied in her calm voice.

"A trick," Mrs Nazari repeated, sounding surer. "You think she's one person, but she's two. A witch, and a dealer of justice. Old. Older than the witches here. As old as ours, Salma."

"She's from another country?" Salma asked, surprise clear in her voice.

"Yes. The mountains. Snow. Europe?"

"Can you be any more specific?"

"Mountains," Mrs. Nazari repeated firmly. "That's what I see. Not a sign or landmark, no word or name. But I see land, I see Europe. Are those biscuits?"

"Yes, Ma'am," came Gabi's respectful voice. Joy heard the lid crack off the Tupperware.

"Thank you, mama," Salma murmured. "That's more than we could see."

"Do you know her name?"

"No." Salma paused. "Do you?"

"It's hard to see. She's twisted it, hidden it."

Joy met Gus's eyes, then Eilidh's. Her frown matched theirs. Hidden her name? She wanted to voice her confusion, but Salma had given strict instructions not to speak— they'd be able to hear it on the other end and Salma's mum was freaked out by any voices she didn't know the origin of.

Which, Joy thought, was reasonable. If a voice came out of nowhere and spoke to Joy, she'd be pretty freaked out, too.

"Hidden it where? Where's she hidden her name, mama?"

"That mountainy place. They know it and fear it, but we haven't learned to. Yet. That's why she's come here. No. She was ... brought."

"Is she alone?" This was one of the most important questions. They'd all felt a female presence and Gus had seen a woman from his window, but what if there was more than one person?

"Alone," Salma's mum confirmed. "But someone knows she's here. She's not listening to him anymore, though. She's found too many naughty people."

Salma was quiet. Joy wondered if Gabi was scratching all this down in her new notebook—Joy had noticed she only had a few pages left yesterday and had plenty of blank notebooks stashed away. It was a casual gesture, but it was clear it had meant something to Gabi by the way she tucked her hair behind her pink ears.

The book was the brand Gabi liked, which Joy was sure had not escaped her attention.

Gus nudged her, and she frowned, realising she'd zoned out.

She tuned back in just as Salma's mum said, "Lying. Lusting. In that order."

There was a moment and then Salma said, "Are there any details? Can you tell me what lies, mama?"

"The girl lied to her boyfriend about her fidelity. The man lusted over a girl who wasn't his wife."

"Lust," Salma breathed, her tone sending a shiver down Joy's spine. "Does this have anything to do with the seven sins?"

"No."

"You're sure?"

"Yes. They were bad. Naughty, not nice. That's why they're dead."

A shuffle of bodies and then Salma said, "Thank you, mama. That's all really helpful. Do you want a cup of tea before I go?"

"You're a good girl," Mrs. Nazari said, a smile in her voice. "I'll have a cup of the good tea. From the tin."

"Alright, mama. Gabriella?"

Half a minute later, the door to Salma's room opened and Gabi and Salma edged their way around the bed and drawers that took up most of the floorspace. Gabi was barely looking where she stepped, her pen moving feverishly across the paper, phone balanced dangerously. Salma took it from Gabi's hand and ended the call.

"So," Gus sighed, looking fed up. "That was helpful."

Maisie made a low noise of agreement.

Salma gave them a sharp look but didn't comment. "Gabriella. Did you hear anything to help you?"

"Maybe," Gabi replied, finally glancing up, a lock of short dark hair falling into her face.

"I'll go find Victoriya," Gus offered, sliding off the bed to his feet. "Tell her what's going on."

Check if she's alright, he meant.

Joy gave him a smile, thankful. All *her* calls and texts had been unanswered.

"We should leave; I don't want to upset Mrs. Nazari. Salma, are you coming?" Joy asked.

Salma shook her head. "I have a second interview for that job."

Joy tried to smile, but too much weight pressed on her. If they failed to find the identity of the witch, someone else could be hurt. Killed. "They called you back?"

Salma nodded. There was something unsure about her smile. Joy's heart gave a sympathetic flop—when she'd interviewed for her job at the nature sanctuary, she hadn't slept at all the night before, and she'd fluffed all the prepared speeches she'd written. Not that her boss cared. He was so laidback he hadn't noticed when she'd accidentally said orgasm instead of organism.

"You'll be fine, Salma. You're perfect for the job," Eilidh said, squeezing Salma's arm.

Their unofficial leader gave them a weak smile and went to make her mum a cup of tea, while the rest of them crept down the stairs and out the back door.

Eilidh left to reassure her dad she was safe—he'd left her ten texts and three missed calls in the last twenty minutes alone—and Maisie skulked after her to make sure she got home safe, leaving Gabi, Gus, and Joy to walk towards the high street in silence.

"At least we know *some* things," Joy said, attempting to break the heavy quiet.

Gabi smiled, a little forced, and—

They all jumped a mile when Gabi's phone trilled, Gus hissing a vulgar word.

"Pride," Gabi answered.

Joy focused on getting her heart rate to a more reasonable level, allowing herself a quick scan of the road as if she was bored and waiting for Gabi's call to be done, not looking for evil witches who punished people when they lied.

"Alright," Gabi said into the phone. "I'll be there in ten minutes. Thank you."

Joy looked expectant when Gabi put the phone away. Gus just scuffed his Converse on the pavement.

"Neil Ivers wants to talk to me. He saw who attacked him."

Joy's stomach swooped. She and Gus shared a glance. They were getting closer. But did they really *want* to be closer to a witch cruel enough to try to kill someone just for liking a girl who wasn't their estranged wife?

J oy's hand folded very securely around Gabi's elbow as they marched down the clinic corridor, Gus close beside them. They were really ought to have for Eilidh and Victoriya—Maisie was still banned from the clinic—but Gabi pushed the door to Neil's room open and walked briskly inside.

Her blood pumped fast with excitement, dread, and a knot of other emotions. She was done waiting; she wanted her suspicions confirmed.

"Tell me," she demanded without preamble, shutting the door behind her—and Joy and Gus who apparently wouldn't be left out.

Neil was propped up in the hospital bed, a flock of flowers on either side of him adding riotous colour to the butter-yellow room. His brown hair was plastered to his face with sweat from whatever healing tonics were flooding his system, and his eyes were glazed, but they pinned on Gabi when she entered, and his jaw clenched.

There was nothing weak or uncertain about his voice when he matched Gabi's briskness.

"Paulina's assistant. Girlfriend. I'm not sure which she is."

While Gabi reeled, he pushed himself higher on the pillows. She suspected it was only sheer determination that kept him conscious, let alone upright.

Her stomach flipped. Her mind instantly began making connections, working through the shock that threatened to ground her to a halt.

"I'd been at work all morning—" Neil began angrily.

"At the school?" Gabi clarified. He worked two jobs as far as she was aware—the school and community classes.

Neil nodded. A wave of dizziness clearly washed over him; he hissed and gripped the bed tightly. "I was on my lunch, having my sandwich on the beach for a bit of fresh air."

The beach beside town hall, Gabi noted to herself.

Gods—*Katrina* was the killer. Gabi struggled to process it, but the coven had seen manicured fingernails and a blonde, slim woman. That fit. Plus, the faked witness statement. Katrina could have easily warned them to change his statement once she'd seen Joy in the cells.

And the witchcraft Gabi had sensed, which the coven had confirmed was odd and unusual... Katrina was new to town. She could have any sort of witchcraft.

Fuck, she'd been so close to Joy... Gabi's blood boiled, but she ground her teeth and made herself pay attention to Neil.

"She grabbed me. She made it look natural, friendly, but the grip she had on my arm ... I couldn't shake her off. She said if I drew attention to us, she'd kill everyone I loved."

"You went with her?" Joy gasped, her hand pressed to her chest. In the doorway, Gus was pale with horror.

"I tried to run," Neil said, his voice turning weary when

he looked at Joy. "I wanted to get to the phone in the nature reserve, but I should have kept running. I only boxed myself in. She caught me easily, as strong as she is."

Neil shook his head, hands shaking above the pale sheets—anger, Gabi thought, not fright. "I should have known something was wrong when she first spoke to me. I'd seen her around the community centre—that's how she knew me, because she took an exercise class there and I taught on the same evenings—"

"Neil," Gabi interrupted. Her heart beat as fast as hummingbird wings. "Paulina's assistant, Katrina, is the woman who attacked you?"

A witch from Europe, that's what Mrs. Nazari had said. Katrina was German. Gabi was already whipping her phone from her pocket and navigating to Google to type in 'German witches', which brought up a hundred pages about ancient witch trials.

"Yes," Neil answered confidently, swearing when he swayed without warning. Joy rushed over to support him and helped prop him back against the pillows.

"Be careful," she murmured to him. Gabi didn't understand how she could be caring and fussing this way, when all Gabi wanted to do was run out the door and arrest Katrina.

She narrowed the web search by adding 'kills the naughty' and after scrolling through the top five hits, she paused.

Stilled.

ONCE THOUGHT OF AS A GODDESS, *Perchta lives in the snowy mountains and cold valleys ... watches over the good children and punishes the bad ... can appear beautiful, white as ice, or old, haggard, and monstrous ... sometimes the leader of the Wild Hunt ... she knew who had behaved and left them a silver coin, but if anyone misbehaved, she would slit their bellies open and stuff them with straw and rubbish and vile things ... marking them as bad, naughty...*

GABI SPEED-READ the stories of Frau Perchta, also known as Berchta, Perahta, Frau Faste, and Kvaternica. That last one ... it was so damn similar to *Katrina*. Mrs. Nazari said she'd twisted her name.

It all fit.

Gabi took a pen and legal pad from her satchel and thrust them at Neil. "Write down *exactly* what happened to you. I'll be back later to collect your statement."

She paused, near the door, her body like a coiled spring. "Normally, I'd ask a witch to stand at your door in case you're in danger, but since Paulina is a suspect in this too, I'd rather not trust anyone in her coven."

"Don't worry about me. I'm sure I'll be fine," he said with an ill-advised shrug. "Who's going to hurt me in a hospital?"

Gabi frowned, contemplating. She couldn't leave him vulnerable. It didn't sit right.

"My aunt has a gun and strong elven magic. I'll ask her to guard you." She was already pulling out her phone. "You'll be safe."

She left the room before he could delay her any longer.

"You're not serious," Gus said, catching up to her, Joy on his heels. "The waif-y blonde woman from the front desk? *She's* the killer?"

"It all fits. It's her." Gabi didn't hear his reply, already phoning her aunt. When she readily agreed to guard Neil,

Gabi rushed out her thanks and slid the phone back into her pocket, feeling steady, feeling scared.

She knew who the killer was. She could catch her and stop her hurting anyone else. But she had to confront this cruel witch herself.

With temperamental elven magic that was nothing to write home about—and a baton. Why hadn't she applied for a taser?

Because she'd naively thought she wouldn't be walking into a life-or-death situation in her first week.

"Gabi." Joy's hand slid into her palm, squeezing. "Are you okay?"

"Of course," she lied, fooling nobody. "Just thinking."

She quickly explained everything she'd found to Joy and Gus and watched them turn pale.

The things Frau Perchta did ... slitting people open, stuffing them with rubbish, punishing the naughty, there was no denying *that* was the killer they had here in Agedale. A Christmas spirit, a wicked woman comparable to Krampus. Old and ancient and deadly.

Gus's phone buzzed, interrupting whatever Joy was going to say.

"Huh?" he said, holding it to his ear. "No. Why? Her mum said she'd locked herself in her room and didn't want to be bothered."

Gabi and Joy both stared at Gus with panic when his voice changed, suddenly breathy. "Say that again."

"Gus?" Joy demanded, her knuckles white around her wand.

"Our flat's the closest. I can be there in ten minutes. Alright." Gus was wan when he lowered the phone, his breathing jagged.

He said, "Victoriya's gone missing. So have the ingredients for a connection spell from the apothecary."

Joy's swore. "She wouldn't do something that stupid."

"She *would*."

"*What?*" Gabi asked urgently, cursing her lack of witchcraft knowledge. "What has she done?"

Gus's tight eyes darted around the clinic hallway. "She's gone after the witch. You know, the psycho murderer."

"We couldn't do a connection spell because it's too dangerous," Joy said quietly.

"She'd *see* the killer," Gus explained, practically vibrating with nerves, "but the killer would see her too. She'd know Victoriya was coming."

"*What?*"

They all jumped, stunned to find a very pale Neil gripping the doorframe to his room, slumped against the wood. "Victoriya's done a connection spell?"

Joy nodded weakly.

"*Go get her.*"

Gabi swallowed. This was far beyond the realm of dangerous, into suicidal.

"Why are you all just *standing here?*" Neil roared. His raised voice drew the attention of the male nurse, who looked momentarily stunned to see him out of bed, and then outraged. "*Pride,*" Neil pleaded.

"I'm *thinking*," Gabi ground out. "If we go charging in there without a plan, we could get her killed."

"She could already be killed," he argued, furious. Gabi couldn't *think* with him shouting at her.

She walked off without another word, her head pounding She couldn't do this. She wasn't *enough*. It wasn't doubt telling her that—it was the hard truth. Confronting a witch to arrest her might have been doable, but she couldn't confront a witch to save someone's life. She wasn't a hero or a fighter. She just couldn't *do* it. She'd fuck it all up. Victoriya's blood would be on her own hands.

"We have to go," Gus breathed, catching up to her. Joy was at Gabi's side then, gripping her hand again, her eyes wide and face pale. "I said we'd meet Salma and Eilidh at my flat."

"Right," Gabi murmured. It was the only word she had.

"We'll do a spell to find Victoriya, and then make protection and offensive spells. Then we'll go in there and get our girl back. It'll be fine."

Gus was convincing himself more than Gabi and Joy. But Gabi appreciated the snippet of a plan. She had direction, and a purpose.

"Tell me what you need for the spells." She drew herself upright, turning to meet Neil's hard gaze. Telling him without words that she'd get Victoriya back. "I'll go to the apothecary in town and make sure you have enough."

BETWEEN THEM, Joy and Gus scrawled a list for Gabi, and while they ran to Gus and Maisie's flat to prepare the location spell, Gabi rushed down the road to the stuffy apothecary. It was a serious battle to keep herself together as she marched across the road and into the dim, narrow shop. Even the rich, herbal scent couldn't calm her.

The shopkeeper gave Gabi a funny look—an elf walking into a witch shop sounded like the start of a joke—but when she slammed the list on the counter and said it was for Joy Mackenzie, the crone wasted no time in helping Gabi round up everything she needed.

When Gabi pulled out her purse, the ancient witch

waved her hand and wished her good luck. Whatever it was about Gabi's expression, the woman knew something was wrong.

"Thank you," Gabi forced out, the bag of herbs and vials cradled in her arms. She fled the shop and ran flat out down the high street to Gus's flat, praying she remembered how to get to it.

Her breathing remained steady but her heart beat so fast, her mind running even faster. This was how her fear manifested: she couldn't slow her thoughts. *Failure*, those thoughts called her, *inadequate*. And if she failed Victoriya, failed Joy, failed her mum and her dad and their legacy, they called her *killer*, too.

Gabi's heart found a way to beat faster.

She craned her head, scanning the terrace houses that'd been split into flats, and was relieved to see Joy standing on Gus's fire escape, waving to get her attention.

Gabi ran faster, sped up the stairs, and arrived at Gus's open door, breathless. Scared in a way she'd never been before. If she failed, Victoriya would be *killed*. This wasn't a nameless suggestion of a victim—it was Victoriya, Joy's friend, Gabi's own acquaintance.

Gabi's throat closed up, but she tried to conceal her fear as she helped the coven finish the location spell.

"This is taking too long," Eilidh snapped, sitting cross legged on the bare floorboards, tending a pot of clear water, her seagull familiar circling high above and her hand clenching a feather necklace. Beside her, Maisie was bolt upright in her fox form, her eyes darting from witch to witch at every tiny movement.

No one argued. Gus merely kept mashing a paste with a pestle and mortar, sage smouldering in a bronze dish between them. Salma had abandoned her interview and was brewing a tea that, when thrown at an opponent, would smother them in smoke. Joy sat in a circle of delicate pink and purple crystals, breathing hard as she used her witch-craft to cast a defensive spell, readying her gems for when they'd need them most.

Gabi watched from the wall she leant against, feeling even more like an intruder than ever, at least until they finished, one by one, their individual protection and defence spells, and came to the spell that mattered most: the location spell to find Victoriya.

The five of them gathered on the rug spread over the floorboards, sitting in a circle, hands linked.

Gabi's breath caught at the oppressive air that strangled the room with little warning. If this didn't work... She wished she understood *what* they were casting, just this once.

But then Salma said, "Gabriella, put your hand on Joy's shoulder. Make sure you're not touching her skin, just clothes."

Gabi's heart quickened. She was in danger of throwing up.

"Oh," Joy said as Gabi did as instructed despite her fear. Joy craned her head back to look up at Gabi. "Now you'll be able to see what we see."

Gabi's tongue stuck to the roof of her mouth. She couldn't tell them that she wasn't sure she *wanted* to see it, that the hairs on her arms stood on end at the thought. Yet she held onto Joy, and only braced herself for the images that would flood her.

A shudder wracked her; she swore a soft wind of warning blew through the living room.

Salma nodded a signal to the rest of her coven.

Gabi's stomach twisted.

And then they were all leaning to look into a bowl of clear liquid, the coven adding ingredients with little prompting, and Salma cracked open a well-used book and began to speak.

Gabi had never heard someone speak an incantation before, the cadence of Salma's deep voice was startling, the rich, almost musical tone of her words magnetic. Gabi was already off balance, out of her depth and afraid, and *then* she felt as if she'd been plunged into an icy pool of water.

Cold but into her everywhere—the tips of her fingers, the back of her neck, all the way from her toes to her scalp.

The room blacked out, and only the comforting solidness of Joy's shoulder under her hand kept Gabi from yelping and darting away. She held on tight, fingers curled into the wool of Joy's jumper as the world spun.

A moment later, the space around her lit in stages but it wasn't Gus's living room. They were in a room lit in warm shades of gold and orange, with rows of filing cabinets and bookshelves around them, most untidy and unorganised.

Gabi found herself on the floor, too-pale hands bound in front of her grimy shirt. A deafening, drowning pain pulsed from her back as if she had been kicked or stabbed.

It took a moment for her to realise she wasn't alone; Katrina leant over her, her hair as icy as Gabi felt inside, her lips plump and coated in a pretty peach lipstick. She looked exactly like she had when Gabi first saw her: friendly and warm and beautiful in a ghostly way.

Gabi laughed, but it was someone else's laugh that came out of her. Sharp—confrontational. "Nice. But I think your other face is prettier."

Katrina said nothing, only tightened the rope around Gabi's hands until it dug in painfully. The witch took a clear vial from her pocket and unstoppered it, holding it to Gabi's mouth.

Gabi gritted her teeth in refusal, but it was like someone else pulled the strings of her body. She had the sense of another body somewhere else, but this one hurt, the pain louder than anything.

"You were naughty," Katrina said slowly, as if explaining to a child. "So you'll drink this and be punished."

Gabi snorted but did not open her mouth.

"You lust after a married man," Katrina said. "It's my job to punish you."

Gabi mashed her lips tighter together. Her hands were sore, her leg muscles straining.

A slick kind of power pressed against her throat, and then her lungs were burning. Her mouth gaped open without her permission, and she choked on the liquid that was shoved down her throat—

Gabi stumbled back, crashing into Gus's front room, into her own body again, her breathing a torn mess and her eyes watering.

She could still feel her wrists, the chafe of rope around them, and she shuddered even as she tried to lock her body.

Joy shook badly enough that her want shot prisms of light across the floor; Gabi reached for her again and rubbed comforting circles into her back. The touch calmed Gabi too, allowed her to shake off the phantom sense of being Victoriya.

Eilidh and Gus looked equally rattled.

Only Salma seemed calm, though Gabi knew a forced calm when she saw it.

"Where *was* that? Does anyone recognise it?" Her dark eyes pinned every one of them, searching.

"I do," Gabi rasped, feeling hollowed out. Raw. "It's the records room at town hall."

Salma inhaled sharply, digesting the info.

"Take a moment, and then we'll make the worst offensive spells we know."

They wouldn't just be armed with defence spells but ones to hurt, too?

Gabi needed a whole day to recover, but when Joy turned and pushed to her feet, Gabi realised tears carved shiny paths down her cheeks. A protective rush woke Gabi up and shoved off whatever weakness had gripped her.

She opened her arms and Joy tipped forward into them; within seconds they were hugging tight, Joy's chest shuddering as she cried.

When Joy finally stilled, Gabi ran a hand down her hair and said, "I need to call someone. I'll be a minute. Will you be okay?"

She'd been slowly resolving herself to make the call since this morning. She hadn't spoken to him in years, but for this, for Victoriya, she would.

Assuming his number hadn't changed.

Joy nodded and wiped her eyes with her sleeve. "Go, I'll be fine."

That was an overstatement, but Gabi took the out she offered and headed for the door, digging her phone from her pocket. Her chest pulled tighter, but her voice was steady when she said, "It's Gabriella. I need your help."

"Give me a time and place," Peregrine Morris replied, not even hesitating.

Gabi crushed down spiky emotions and told him, "One hour. Town Hall."

She put the phone down before he could say anything else and squeezed her eyes tight against the tears stabbing them. He sounded different, so much older and deeper, but it was still *his* voice, the voice she had grown up hearing.

Peregrine, who she'd thought was her cousin for so long, her older, serious, grumpy—but *always* reliable—cousin.

Peregrine, who had kept the secret of being her brother, and broken her heart with the deception.

All too soon Joy's pockets were filled with sachets and crystals, and her coven was moving as one down the stairs of Gus's apartment building into the cold, pale afternoon outside. The sea hissed over the sounds of traffic on the main road, and a few houses back, kids were running wild, laughing and shouting.

Normal—it was all too normal. Victoriya had been taken. Or worse, had given herself over like a sacrifice, so she could get revenge. In between bouts of fear that had sweat sliding down her spine, Joy was struck with disbelief and anger at Victoriya's naivety. To think she could take on a witch like the killer by herself...

"I should warn you," Gabi said in a tight voice as she unlocked her car and the others climbed in.

Joy hovered, her eyes on the straight line of Gabi's shoulders, the shadows in her eyes.

"I called for backup. He's meeting us at Town Hall in twenty minutes, along with my dad."

"Oh," Joy said, relief unwinding a tiny knot in her chest. "Good. Thank you."

She didn't know what to make of Gabi dancing around talking about them, but she had to admit the most severe of her panic lessened at the idea of having Bo with them.

Gabi nodded and opened the driver's side door, but Joy stopped her with a hand on her wrist. It was too easy to touch her, even now with the world going to hell around them, with one of Joy's best friends in mortal danger.

"Are you alright?" she asked, quietly enough that her coven wouldn't overhear.

"Ask me when Victoriya is safe," she replied, ducking into the front seat.

She knew the urgency in Gabi, the anxiety twitching her fingers, clenching her jaw. It was quickening Joy's own heartbeat, telling her that even wasting these precious seconds asking if Gabi was okay was endangering her best friend.

Joy froze while Gabi tore away from Gus's flat, pain arrowing through her heart. She'd never thought of Victoriya that way before. Her best friend...

Joy swallowed, straightened her spine, and marched around to the passenger side, slamming the door behind her.

There was no time to think about Gabi's backup, no time to think of all the terrible things that could be happening to Victoriya. The car thundered to life, and before Joy could go over the plan one final time, they were racing down the high street towards the beach.

Before she'd fully prepared herself, they were there.

Town hall loomed beside them, elegant and square, the columns out front shining in the pale light. People milled from one end of the high street to the other, shopping or socialising, and a woman darted out of the town hall's glossy golden doors, a briefcase in her hand and a harried look on her face. There was no sign that a woman was being held hostage inside.

Joy didn't feel ready. Even with her pockets full of spells, they'd soon run out, and then what would she have to save her friend? Raw power and her wand?

It suddenly became clear that Joy might not make it back out of the town hall. Against a witch who had killed Freya, who'd tried to kill Neil, and who carved judgement into people's faces and sliced open their bodies, filling them with trash... yes, there was a chance this was the last time Joy would see daylight.

So, when she climbed out of the car, her bones already shivering with fear, she made sure to fill her lungs with the salt and citrus air in case she never tasted that familiar brine again.

Eilidh alighted on the pavement beside her, clutching her talisman, and the others seemed to pause and follow Joy's example. She made sure to wipe everything but her conviction from her face.

"We're going to get her back," she said to Eilidh, to Gus, and Maisie, and Salma.

Victoriya was *theirs*—theirs to love, theirs to protect. Joy had already lost her mum; she would *not* lose anyone else she loved.

Eilidh straightened at the look on Joy's face, pushing back her nerves and meeting Joy's determination with something steely and hard on her tear-reddened face. Gus didn't raise himself from his slouch, didn't take his hand from inside his jacket where it was clenched around his thick ash wand, but he did nod. Maisie brushed against his ankle, but even she looked afraid, her belly closer to the ground, her eyes in constant shifty movement. Only Salma stood tall and calm, though she had to be fighting to keep that mask up because Joy knew she was as afraid for Victoriya as the rest of them.

"Let me take the lead," Salma said, letting her eyes linger on each of them. They all knew this could be the last time they stood together like this "Stay behind me. I have training for these situations, I know what to do."

Only Salma had been trained in combat—by her brother, who was part of a secret witch corps in the army.

They started up the wide stone steps towards the columns where Gabi waited for them, stiff backed in her coat, her baton at full length in her hand. Joy expected her fear to relax at the sight of Gabi but this close to Victoriya, tied up and hurt—and to Katrina, violent and gloating in the vision—Gabi's steady glance didn't begin to touch the knot in her chest, the twisting of her gut.

But Joy held her head stubbornly high. Sunlight caught on the facets of her wand, the jagged amethyst tip. It didn't matter if Joy was ready or far from it. Victoriya *needed* her, so she would be brave, and she would enter that Town Hall and get her friend, no matter who she had to fight, no matter how many offensive spells she needed to use.

Joy's eyes slid to two figures lurking in the town hall's old stone doorway. One was Bo, leaning on a honey wood walking stick, his dark hair whipped around his chin by the wind and his eyes as hard as Joy had ever seen them.

The other was younger. Tall, dark-haired, and strikingly beautiful. But that beauty was marred by the grim expression on his face, the slash of black eyebrows, and by lips pressed into a thin line. His eyes though ... warm amber brown shone with emotion. It wasn't fear, Joy realised with confusion, but something sad. Hurt.

Joy tracked his attention to Gabi and felt a swell of protectiveness rise, but she quickly shoved it away. This was the backup Gabi had called for, the elf that had made her look so haunted.

Eilidh touched Joy's elbow to get her attention, a question in her vivid eyes and Theodore—her seagull familiar—echoing her confusion with a cry from where he perched on a nearby lamppost.

Joy had no answer for her. She didn't know who he was, other than an elf, but that was obvious from his olive green and black leathers, his chiselled features, and the gently pointed ears just peeking out from his long, dark ponytail.

Gabi glanced at the man, who stared solidly back at her, but there was something so empty and lacking about Gabi's face. Even as something inside Joy thrashed against standing here while Victoriya suffered inside, she stepped beside Gabi, close enough to touch, wanting to erase that blankness.

It was such a practised emptiness that she had to be feeling something intense beneath the calm mask. Whatever was between Gabi and this man, it was big and prickly with pain.

The elf's green eyes flicked away first, and Bo came striding forward, his hand white on his cane.

"You've heard about the witch murder," Gabi said in a tight voice. Her eyes went to her dad and stayed there. The elf nodded; Bo's expression did not change. "The killer is inside, in the records room, and she has a girl with her—one of my friends. We're going in to get her to safety, and to arrest the killer. She's blonde, young, slim and well put together. It's Paulina's assistant Katrina if you've ever met her."

The elf made a sound in the back of his throat. "The simpering one."

His voice was deep—deeper than even Bo's—but the

emotion that writhed in his eyes was there in his voice, too. Instead of the velvet it might have been, it was raw and gravelly. His eyes jumped past Gabi, to Joy and her coven, and something in his bearing reminded her of a soldier. "We'll go in first and subdue the killer to give you time to get your friend out."

Gabi nodded, her eyes lingering on Joy. "Stay behind me. Watch your back—and above you."

She looked over Joy's shoulder, to where Gus, Eilidh, Maisie and Salma were listening too. "If you get the chance, take Victoriya and *get out*. Go to the clinic—it's the nearest guarded place. Agreed?"

"But—" Joy began.

"Joy." Gabi's voice was soft, somehow more powerful than a shout. "I'll be okay. I have Peregrine and my dad if something happens."

Joy opened her mouth to say something dumb. *I don't want to lose you again. I want to stay with you. I'm scared, I'm so scared.*

"Be careful," she said after a moment.

Gabi squeezed Joy's hand and then let go.

Joy's heart rushed fast, her back prickling with sweat, but her steps didn't falter when she followed the elven warrior and the two Prides up the stairs and into the town hall that hid a murderer.

G abi's heart pounded as she ran through everything in her head one final time. She should be calm, her emotions kept far down to allow her to do her job, but with Joy here and in danger, that calm was impossible to hold onto. This was the last thing she wanted—Joy and the others walking into a situation with so many variables and a killer who targeted witches— but there was no keeping the coven away from when Victoriya was in danger. Besides, Gabi needed their help facing the witch killer, as bad as that sounded. She was one woman, and very aware of her limitations when it came to power.

Peregrine stormed into the town hall in front of her, dark haired and as immovable as the statues of Agedale's founders in the lobby. With him here, there was no way in hell Gabi was going to find calm.

Her best friend, her cousin—*liar, betrayer, brother.*

Hurt speared behind Gabi's rib cage but she wrenched her stare away from him. She thought of Victoriya, snarling and threatening the first time Gabi had met her, seething with fear for Joy. Gabi pictured her fierceness stripped from her after Neil had been attacked, and imagined she looked a lot like that scared girl right now, with her hands bound and Katrina—*Perchta*—taunting her. Likely hovering over her with the same knife that had carved Freya's cheek.

Focus came quickly at that image, and Gabi held it in an unrelenting fist. Her back straightened; her lungs filled with a clearing breath.

The reception desk was empty. The quiet of the lobby was notable as their steps echoed; usually people scurried from hallway to hallway, conversations making a dull hum. A scant few people moved through the building but quickly, silently, with their heads ducked and shoulders hunched.

Unease grew inside Gabi despite the lock on her emotions. She allowed herself a single assessing glance behind her to make sure the coven—to make sure *Joy*—was close and prepared, wands in hand, protective spells at the ready.

Griswald, the guard from the day Gabi met Victoriya, stood by the lifts, barely a head shorter than them and nearly as wide. Peregrine's shoulders tensed perceptively, his hand twitching, but Griswald made no move to stop them; he didn't call out to ask them what they were doing. He simply stood by the lift doors, staring into space.

"Griswald," Gabi said in as pleasant a voice as she could muster. "I'm looking for Katrina, have you seen her?"

The mountain of a man only blinked. Peregrine looked over his shoulder to share a look with Gabi, and it was easy —too easy—to communicate her thoughts to him even after so many years apart. It was a talent that came with growing up together.

"I have a warrant to search this property," Gabi went on, producing the paper from her pocket. It was forged but he didn't need to know that. Griswald gave no response, but Gabi had a sinking feeling he wouldn't let them into the lift.

"This is not going to be easy," Gabi heard Peregrine murmur.

Her dad nodded his agreement, his dark eyes flitting around the room, searching for nooks that could hide a witch, for CCTV, for exits and doors to other rooms. Gabi knew because she was doing the same thing. There were three doors on this level—one to the slope that led to the cells, one to Paulina's office, and one to a lushly appointed meeting room. Her dad broke off from the group to search all of them, his left hand curled at his side, elven magic within reach.

"Empty," he declared, re-joining them, the sound of his walking stick slapping the tiled floor like a war drum. "All of them."

"I had a feeling," Gabi replied, her heart speeding.

They'd seen the records room through the spell, but it felt like a trap, as if Katrina had *wanted* them to come. The practically empty lobby, the guard by the lifts, the sense of something being *wrong*...

Again, the image of Victoriya, scared and bound and bloody, spun through Gabi's mind. She had to act quick, even if it meant throwing procedure out of the window.

"What are the chances Griswald has been hexed?" Gabi asked in a low voice.

"High," Salma answered from behind her. "See his eyes?"

Gabi looked into the guard's face ... the change was difficult to describe, like ice forming over his eyeball and melting, then icing over again, repeating the process. A spell, then.

"Peregrine?" Gabi asked blandly.

With a long look at her—he was nowhere near in control of his emotions and every bit of hurt and hope and fear shone through his hazel-brown eyes—Peregrine rolled his shoulders and exhaled a long breath.

Gabi's arms prickled, hairs standing on end as his magic worked. Griswald inhaled sharply and began to sway. The thud of him hitting the ground made Gabi flinch. She didn't let herself dwell on any of it—the innocent man they had used offensive magic on, the longing in her brother's eyes for her to hear him out, the startled cries of the witches, or the shivering that wanted to move though Gabi at the sight of Peregrine affecting the air, making it a strange sort of anaesthetic on the guard.

The things he could do ... Gabi could not begin to imagine them.

"Second floor," Gabi said, punching the call button on the lift. It opened with a too-pleasant ding and breathless, quiet, they crowded in.

A trap, her subconscious warned. But what option did they have? Forsake Victoriya to the witch killer? Let a murderer go unpunished, free to kill again?

Gabi found herself pressed between Eilidh and Bo. She wanted to relax when her dad's hand brushed her shoulder, wanted to let that comfort find its mark, but she needed to stay vigilant. The moment that lift door opened, they were in danger. And even if her dad was here, everyone was *Gabi's* responsibility as the current Pride.

Peregrine whispered a direction in Elteri, coordinating their exit, and it squeezed something fragile in Gabi to hear it spoken after so long.

She and her dad used English or the little Mandarin she knew, and all her fellow students at uni had been witches or humans. That didn't stop the elven language being second nature; when Peregrine slanted a look at Gabi, she nodded.

Bo would take the left, Peregrine the right, and Gabi would be a step behind them, in the centre. Covering the witches.

She held a hand behind her, signalling the coven to hold back, as her dad and Peregrine exited slowly, hands twitching at their sides as they magically communicated with their surroundings, connecting to the wood panelled walls, the concrete floor,]the canvas paintings lined along the corridor beneath swinging white lights.

Gabi didn't bother calling on her own magic—despite being a child of two talented parents, her magic had always been sporadic. It could as easily deny her request as react to it, and it was safer to rely on consistent weapons. She held the telescopic baton at her side, already snapped to full length, and swept the corridor with her eyes as she stepped out of the lift.

Eight doors, four on either side of the hall—bright white monoliths in the dark wood corridor. All of them were shut.

At the far end, two glass doors led to a staircase. Gabi had no idea where it would bring them out. She hadn't seen a staircase connect to the ground floor. The roof maybe, or the next corridor up? At least it was a second exit; she made a mental note of it.

"Stay behind us," Gabi murmured to the witches. Not because they were harmless and needed protecting, but because a spell from Katrina could easily take all of them out at once. If Gabi, her dad, and Peregrine went down, they needed the witches to be okay so they could get Victoriya out.

That was what they had all agreed on—the three elves would distract Katrina while the coven rescued Victoriya.

Gabi couldn't remember exactly which door led to the record room, so she looked to her dad. Bo was laser-focused on the second door on the left, his hand trembling on his stick, brow creased with the effort of calling elven magic.

Gabi's breath caught when the door collapsed, solid wood turning to liquid that splashed around their feet. It rushed like a stream down the corridor before rushing back together and solidifying into a wooden door on the tiled floor.

At the open doorway, Gabi tensed and raised her baton as she fixed her attention through the door. No sign of movement so far, but that didn't mean it was clear.

With a nod, Gabi sent her dad and Peregrine through first. It was the most logical course of action—with their magic, they could better defend themselves—but it still sent a sharp pain through Gabi, to send them into the unknown in her place.

From the doorway of the well-lit room, Gabi watched her dad and Peregrine search the room with both eyes and magic. It didn't take long for Bo to wave her inside.

Gabi's heart pounded as she stepped over the threshold and into the old-paper-scented room, adrenaline pumping through her system even as she tried to master her emotions.

It looked exactly as it had when Gabi had last been here —rich wooden planks hugged the bottom half of the walls, cream paint above it, and waxed floorboards reflected the lamplight, filling the space with greenish light. Around them, rows upon rows of chrome filing cabinets stretched from end to end of the room, utterly normal, not a file out of place. But when Gabi inched further into the room, a heavy copper smell joined the scent of old books, and Gabi's stomach turned.

What if they were too late? What if Victoriya was already dead?

Gabi tightened her grip on the baton, clenching her jaw. Her eyes jumped from one silver filing monolith to the next, to the open door at the back of the room that led to a small, empty office, to the shadows lurking deep in the aisles.

Peregrine and her dad stormed down the aisles formed by cabinets, their hair and skin lit an emerald hue by the office lamps perched on top of each row.

Gabi's eyes kept returning to the door to the back room; she dragged a deep breath of air into her lungs and followed the tinge of blood, unsurprised to find it led to the door.

She made a gesture to *hold back* for the witches who'd begun to creep into the room despite orders to do otherwise. But Joy let out a cry and rushed past Gabi, a blur of pink.

Gabi swore, her stomach cramping tight as she raced after Joy. Her heart pounded uncontrollably fast, sweat rolling down her spine, down her chest.

She swung her head from side to side, waiting for Katrina to charge at them from a swath of darkness. But the only people in the room were Joy's coven, rushing after Joy with Gabi, and her dad and Peregrine, who had taken up positions by the door in case the killer came back. Because with the heavy miasma of blood in the air ... it was clear Katrina had been here, that the spell had shown them the truth.

Where was she now?

Gabi flinched at the sound of flesh hitting the floor; Joy fell to her knees near the far corner of the back room, in between two rows of tall cabinets. With her heart in her throat, Gabi hurried over to her, dreading what she would find. It was like walking through thick mud, everything inside her begging her not to look. But she had to.

Victoriya was slumped sideways on the floor, hands and ankles bound. Gabi desperately scanned her for signs of life, and with relief so severe she had to tighten her posture so as not to sag, she saw Victoriya's chest rise and fall.

She was breathing—unconscious but alive. *Alive.*

Gabi swore softly, staggering at the last second, scanning the unconscious witch with what remained of her analytical mind.

There was a cut on Victoriya's cheek—from being hit with a fist, not cut with a knife the way Freya and Neil had been—and a slash on her arm, but neither were deep enough to account for the heavy, metallic smell in the air, the iron coating Gabi's taste buds every time she inhaled. Gabi had a feeling they had interrupted Katrina before she could really begin. She'd clearly given Victoriya the tonic to knock her out, but she hadn't had the chance to kill her. Good for Victoriya, but dangerous for someone else.

Whoever's blood scented this room, it wasn't Joy's friend's. That was a small relief, but it didn't last long. Someone had been badly injured, possibly killed.

When the coven reached their side, Gabi tried to block them from the sight of their friend, unconscious and pale, looking so much like a discarded doll. But they muscled past her, and Gabi didn't fight them; she'd have wanted to see her, too.

Maisie made a soft, questioning sound, like Victoriya would open her eyes, smirk, and respond. Gabi hated to see the hope in Maisie's eyes go dull.

Eilidh grabbed Gus's hand when he staggered forward with a rough curse, and Salma's face went slack with fear.

It hurt her to see the witches' pain. Even if Victoriya was alive, they were still hurting, and Gabi felt an echo of it behind her ribs.

She flattened the emotion out of her voice, drew herself up straight, and said, "Take Victoriya and go. If Katrina is still here, Dad, Peregrine, and I will subdue her."

She met their eyes and softly added, "We'll get his bitch in handcuffs so she can never hurt anyone again. I promise you. But getting Victoriya to the clinic has to be your priority."

Joy opened her mouth to argue but one look at Victoriya, pale and bruised and bloody, and she set her mouth in a thin line and nodded, her eyes misty with tears.

"Quickly," Gabi urged, helping Joy stand.

Touching her was a mistake. Gabi wanted to scoop her up and get her out of here, to drop everything else until Joy was safe. She knew emotion was clouding her judgement, but it didn't help the instinct being so strong that Gabi could barely release Joy's hand.

Joy had the rest of her coven with her; she would be safe. Gabi's hand flexed when she returned it to her side, *barely* managing not to reach for Joy again.

In a rough voice she said, "Run and don't stop running until you're at the clinic."

Between them they got Victoriya up, supported her between them, and headed out of the back room.

"I don't want to leave you." Joy's brown eyes were glassy with fear. She flicked away a tear that escaped.

"I'll be fine. I can handle myself; this is my job."

Gabi couldn't look at her a moment longer. She swung her gaze to Salma, but it was *Eilidh* whose eyes were clear and alert, her stance defensive. Salma was staring at Victoriya, her hand pressed to her throat as she breathed wildly. Gabi met Eilidh's eyes, putting the responsibility of the whole coven on a sixteen year old girl and feeling like shit for it. "*Go.*"

"Naughty," a smoky, lilting voice drifted into the room.

Gabi froze as the word snaked through the high ceilings, sending chills down her sound.

"Stay back," her dad barked—either at Frau Perchta or the witches, Gabi couldn't tell.

"Nice."

Gabi spun, wishing she had a long-distance weapon, wishing her environmental magic was reliable. She was suddenly *very* aware of the coven beside her, and their immediate danger.

Maisie let out a threatening sound at Gabi's feet, but what could she do? What could *any* of them do, against a witch as old and psychotic as Frau Perchta?

"Nice. Nice. Nice. Nice."

In the doorway, like a pale spectre, Katrina appeared, her eyes bright as she looked at each of them, her tan suit incongruous with the insanity in her voice. Her eyes slid to Bo, to Peregrine, and both of them went ramrod straight in response to her perusal. Her judgement.

"Nice. Naughty."

"Back off," Bo ordered again, gravel in his voice.

"Two," Perchta breathed. "Two of you have been bad. But don't worry. I can absolve you."

THIRTY-ONE

JOY

"Oh god," Joy breathed.

Her heart leapt into her throat when Gabi shielded her with her body. Joy wanted to step around her, to shield *Gabi*, but she was frozen in place.

Her heart raced so hard she could feel it against her ribs. Perchta was the most beautiful woman Joy had ever seen, with straight icy hair, soft features, a warm smile, and a statuesque body. Her voice was delicate but the words themselves chilled Joy until she trembled. This was who had killed Freya, who attacked Neil Ivers and hurt Victoriya.

Katrina.

She'd visited Joy in her cell, even brought her a bottle of water; she'd been *kind*. What a lie. When she'd recoiled from the water on Joy's hand, had she been trying to *hurt* Joy Esther than heal her?

Looking at Perchta now, it was hard to reconcile her image of the killer—wizened and twisted, with cruelty in every inch of her sneering face—with this pretty woman.

Katrina took a step and Joy flinched. Everyone did. She was still staring, trying to catch up to the danger of the situation, waiting for the pounding of her heart to convert into the screaming urge to *run,* to *flee.* But she could only stare, breathing so fast, at the woman who had hurt her friend and her witch sister.

But behind them, Victoriya moaned, and Joy slammed back to reality with a start. Anger, clearing and pure, burned out the fear. This monster had hurt Victoriya.

Joy snatched a sachet from her pocket and ripped it open so she was ready. She couldn't let Katrina get to Victoriya again. She wouldn't. It was the only thing she was sure of. It was like Gabi had said—Victoriya was their first priority.

Around her, Gus and Eilidh reached for their own spells, wands gripped in fists. Joy had been so focused on getting to Victoriya, on not thinking about what might have happened to her, that she hadn't contemplated the idea of *fighting.* Making offensive sachets was one thing but ... *this?*

Joy flinched back a step when Salma yelled a short incantation in her native Arabic, the words like a call to arms. She drew her arm back and hurled a bottle of potion, the crash of glass shattering over the filing cabinets making Joy's breath short.

She didn't know how to fight. She didn't know what to do, and horror filled her with ice when Katrina lunged across the threshold.

Move! Joy screamed at herself. *Do something! Don't just stand here waiting to be killed!*

Peregrine was inching steadily closer, no doubt calling up elven magic, but Katrina shot forward and grabbed him. Joy stumbled closer in instinctive panic, her wand snapping up as Katrina pulled him close and whispered a word.

From across the room, it sounded like *whiskers,* but Joy sensed it was witchcraft, black and cruel and controlling. It must have been part of an incantation because as Joy lurched forward to help, to do *something*, Katrina opened her mouth again—

Peregrine yelled in pain, Katrina grinning—until Salma's shattered potion finally took effect.

Thick, silver smoke bubbled up and filled the room, and Joy froze between one step and the next, unable to see in front of her. A grunt came from across the room, followed by a feminine growl of frustration.

"*Peregrine?*" Gabi demanded, shrill with panic.

"Fine," he rasped, though he sounded anything but.

What were they supposed to *do?* Joy cast a frantic look through the smoke for her coven, for Gabi and the others. But the billowing silver magic obscured everything, even Victoriya, and Joy's chest tightened, rationing every breath.

Katrina was moving through the smoke; Joy knew it. She could be inches from Joy, could be right behind her, poised to kill Victoriya.

Joy spun with a ragged gasp, her wand trembling in front of her and every breath loud in her ears. A heavy silence had filled the room; it settled around Joy like a noose.

Across the room, someone spat a foreign word—an elven word—and Joy grabbed onto the deep, bass sound of Peregrine's voice with relief. Whether he was a stranger or not, he was on their side—someone Gabi trusted.

Joy's eyes roamed the room that had become shapeless and infinite thanks to the smoke, panic making her restless and itchy.

She jumped so hard she spilled some of the sachet; a groaning, metallic sound cut across the room, louder than a scream. It sounded like the whole world was pulling itself apart around her, and Joy didn't even hear her squeaking shoes when she stumbled back.

A firm arm caught her around her waist, and Joy flinched away with a bright cry, jamming the end of her wand into the unwanted arm.

"It's me," Gabi rushed out, her arm tightening.

Joy gasped, the sound halfway to a sob. She knocked her wand from Gabis arm and slumped back against her. Fear had hollowed her out, made her a shell of panicked breaths and shivering.

She flinched as the metallic shriek rent the air again, but Gabi was calm, the weight of her arm reassuring.

"That's Peregrine. You need to get out of here, Joy." Joy could've sworn Gabi placed a kiss on her head. "Can you, Gus, and Eilidh get Victoriya out?"

No. No, she couldn't. She couldn't breathe, couldn't stop the tears now rolling down her cheeks, couldn't tear her eyes from the mask of smoke around her.

But a memory grabbed hold, of hands being bound, a brow creasing with pain as a scream tent the air— Victoriya's scream, Victoriya's hands, heard and seen through the spell. Joy wouldn't let her friend down. She made herself nod. For Victoriya, for her coven, she could try.

"I'll—I'll get her out," she whispered, finding her throat sore.

Her knees tried to weaken again when Gabi pressed a kiss to the side of her head, but she locked them.

"I know you will." Gabi squeezed Joy tight, so close that Joy could feel the hard bones of Gabi's hips against her. Warm tears dripped down Joy's cheeks, but she wiped them away, holding onto that sense of fear she'd felt from Victoriya.

Gabi kissed her forehead, and then her arm was gone from around Joy's waist.

Joy grasped with frantic hands, trying to pull her back, suddenly full of the burning hot fear that she'd never see Gabi again.

That wasn't the last time I'll hear her voice. It wasn't.

She swallowed her dread and dried her face. "Salma? Bo?"

Squinting into the smog thick around them, she tried to make out the beige and white blur of Katrina's clothes, the shapes of Bo and Peregrine, or the familiar figures of her coven, but Joy saw nothing but fog.

"We're here," Gus replied, closer than Joy expected, and a yelp escaped her lips.

She reached out until her wand brushed his stomach, and a new sort of strength filled her. Gus was alright — he was here, tangible.

"Eilidh's here too, and Maisie. We've got this." His voice shook but the fact that he was attempting a pep talk in the middle of this ... Joy squeezed her crystal wand until her hand stopped shaking.

If Gus could be brave enough, so could she.

"We need to get Victoriya out of here," she breathed.

But she hadn't taken one step before a shout cut the room, and her heart crashed to the floor.

"Katrina!" Gabi yelled, already too far away from Joy. "You are under arrest for the murder of—"

Gabi's voice cut off with a grunt and Joy stumbled in the direction of her voice, fury clenching her jaw. She had the wild idea to march across the room and fight Katrina herself if she had to.

"Freya Faulkner," Gabi finished in a strained voice.

Gus grabbed Joy's arm in a tight grip. She threw a

panicked look in his direction. The smoke was clearing enough for her to make out his wand, raised and steady. His eyes, bleak.

"Victoriya," he reminded her in a raw whisper, and Joy's heart thudded in her chest. He was right. Victoriya was unconscious and vulnerable. And Gabi had given them an order.

"I'll find us a path out," she murmured, throwing a glance around the room. The shadows of the filing cabinets were visible now, the smoke thinning above them, but Joy could only make out the vague forms of people many feet away. One tall and broad, the other thin—the elves if she had to guess, but the latter could have been Salma.

It was difficult to tear her gaze away from them, but Joy made herself follow Eilidh around a row of cabinets to where Victoriya was slumped, her hands bound, pale.

She didn't respond to any attempts to wake her, so the three of them lifted her between them. Joy grunted at Victoriya's weight, but at least her hands had stopped shaking.

"This way," Joy whispered.

They managed to get her a few steps before Gus lost his grip with a hissed curse and Victoriya almost slipped from their grasp. If only they'd thought to prepare a spell for this —they could have supported her with a cushion of air. But without a potion, incantation, or tool to guide the witchcraft … raw witchcraft was *not* an option.

Raw magic was seductive; it corrupted and corroded. Anyone who used it ended up manipulated by the power instead of the other way around. Witches had been eaten from the inside out, others melted or turned to stone. Unchecked, the power ran wild and cruel.

Joy took a steadying breath and scraped a plan from the depths of her terrified mind.

"We need to stay low," she whispered, meeting her friends' panicked gazes. "Hide behind the cabinets."

Gus nodded, his shoulders heaving with every breath. "We should stay close to the walls."

"Guys?" Eilidh whispered. Her eyes were hard as she scanned the rows of filing cabinets around them and then assessed Victoriya's prone form. Joy had never seen this side of her friend before. "We can't cast anything when we're carrying Victoriya. What if..."

What if Katrina found them?

Gus shook his head, looking around for answers.

There was no easy way out, no answers, so Joy said, "We just run. If she finds us, you two take Victoriya and I'll ... I'll cast something."

She'd lost the spell sachet, and she wasn't sure what she had left, but she tried to match the determination in Eilidh's eyes, tried to feel deserving of the trust in Gus's.

Beyond them, it was silent. The lack of sound was almost worse than hearing vials smash and Katrina passing judgement. The creaking, rending noise of Peregrine's magic had gone quiet too. Katrina could be *anywhere*, but Joy could either allow that to paralyse her or she could get her friend to the clinic.

She had to trust Bo and Peregrine to have Gabi's back, and had to trust Gabi to protect herself, too.

"Mais?" she whispered.

Maisie made a low sound, her bright eyes fixed on the end of the aisle—empty for now—and her ears swivelling to follow whatever tiny sounds were beyond Joy's own hearing. "Keep watch."

Maisie made a sound of agreement, tucking close beside them.

"We run on three," Gus breathed and counted them down.

One.

Joy was glad he was taking the lead, that he was fighting his fear even though his face paled with every ascending number.

Two.

It was too quiet, her breaths loud in her ears. Where was Katrina? Was she hiding in the shadows, waiting for them to walk into her claws?

Three.

Joy erupted into action, her thighs and arms burning as they bore Victoriya's weight. She followed the tilt of Victoriya's body forward and turned it into a run, relieved when Eilidh and Gus caught Victoriya's falling chest and matched Joy's speed.

Their footsteps were too loud. Katrina would hear them, find them.

Her lungs ached for breath, less from the exertion than from panic. She swivelled her head to scan the smoke, her ears alert for the tiniest sound; even Maisie's claws on the floor made her jump with a gasping breath.

At the far end of the row, Eilidh's grip faltered, and they were forced to stop. Setting Victoriya down, her head lolling to the side, Joy peered around the furthest cabinet, at the door—hanging invitingly open but far away.

"Okay, we—" she began.

The world filled with sudden sound, like trees crashing to the ground, wood torn apart.

Joy's eyes shot to Eilidh's, to Gus's, to Maisie's, and with a silent agreement, they grabbed Victoriya and flung themselves around the cabinet's corner.

Joy panted for breath, her lungs straining as they ran at full speed across the room. Even sandwiched between the aisles and the wall, it was too open. She could see Bo, his hands lifted towards the ceiling. That cracking, tearing sound got louder.

Bo was all she could see. No Gabi, no Katrina, no Salma. Joy didn't have time to panic; they reached the doorway, and somehow spilled out into the hall without the killer jumping into their path.

"Get to the lift," Gus rasped as they struggled to manoeuvre their friend.

Joy's arms were badly aching from holding up Victoriya's legs, and her hand was cramping from holding so tightly to her wand, at such an awkward angle, but she gritted her teeth and endured it.

She threw a look behind them, but no psychotic witch had pursued them.

Eilidh ducked out from supporting Victoriya to jam the call button on the lift. When it didn't light up, a heavy feeling dropped over Joy, acceptance absent of surprise. Eilidh hit the button over and over, growling through gritted teeth, but it remained dark, and the doors remained shut. The exit was barred.

Joy matched her friends' horrified expressions. "She locked us in."

THIRTY-TWO
GABI

Whose blood can I smell? It was the only thought circling Gabi's head. She kept low to the ground so the filing cabinets would hide her from Perchta, trying in vain to get her emotions to calm. With her baton extended in front of her and fine hairs standing on end, she took small steps towards the end of the row, where her dad and Peregrine crouched, their hands flat on the ground. They had to be planning something big to be coordinating their magic like that, pooling it into one powerful source.

Gabi needed to be with them when they unleashed it. Not because she could help, but because being outside the epicentre could be fatal.

She took another few steps, trying to make as little sound as possible. She couldn't afford to worry about Joy, about the coven, but the fear was persistent, pressing into her in careless waves.

She hadn't seen Perchta since Salma filled the room with smoke. The fog had cleared now, but it had left a metallic tang that, added to the cloying scent of blood and iron, turned Gabi's stomach.

Where *was* Salma? Gabi craned her head as she finally reached her dad.

"You okay?" he mouthed. His eyes were pinched with concern as he scanned her, but at her nod, he turned his attention back to the magic pouring into the floorboards. Peregrine bowed over his hands, his face creased with the strain and sweat beading on his forehead. Gabi felt a pang of worry but shoved it off. He knew what he was doing with magic. Unlike her.

She scanned what little she could see between the cabinets and caught her breath. Was that Perchta's tan suit moving through the faint mist clinging to the ground, or just a shadow? Was it the witch killer coming to finish what she'd started with Peregrine—a line of blood trickling from his neck—or was it Salma fleeing the records room? As much as Perchta's lilting judgement had chilled Gabi's blood earlier, she wished the killer would taunt them now, so she at least knew where the ancient witch was.

"Gabi?" came a low whisper in Peregrine's velvet voice. Her eyes snapped to his, and she pretended not to feel the hurt and recognition that hit her. Had it been a mistake all these years to push him away?

No. She'd heard him out before, right after she found out he'd been sitting on the secret ever since her mum died. She hadn't forgiven him then; she wouldn't now. But she couldn't let that get in the way of their survival. For the sake of survival, she would trust him.

"Get ready to run." He jerked his head in the direction of the corridor, the door still hanging open.

Gabi dared to look over the top of the cabinets to plan her route to the door. It wasn't massively far but it would be *open* and provide plenty of opportunity for Perchta to spot her.

Gabi ducked back down, crowding closer to Peregrine and her dad, and fought to keep her emotions off her face. Perchta was nowhere to be seen but neither had Salma. Had Perchta gone after Victoriya? After *Joy?*

The air rippled, her only warning.

Gabi bit down on a shriek when the world rocked and creaked and tore apart. Her heart beat faster, adrenaline dumping into her blood like electricity. She threw an assessing glance around the aisle, but what she saw made no sense.

What the hell? In all her life, Gabi had known nothing like this.

The boards on the floor peeled back like leaves shrivelling, the wainscoting on the walls tearing itself free with a visceral groan, panel by panel, and at the far end of the room all that wood came together, *coalesced.*

Amber floorboards and dark, stained strips, and random lighter shards from wherever her dad and Peregrine could pull them from. Groaning and cracking, the wood twisted and twined together like a woven ball and then formed a shape. A *man.*

A wooden man, seven feet tall, stood in the heart of the room, groaning like a creaking ship as he took a step.

Gabi's breath went jagged, and even as she recognised the magic as elven, fear beat through her, sweat dripping into her eyes as she crawled backwards, away from that thing. His face was smooth wood, only hollows where eyes should be and a black, gaping hole for a mouth. It hung open in a silent scream.

Only the floorboards under her and her family had been

left; everything else had been consumed by the magical being.

Crawling backwards, Gabi slammed into something solid, and a hand caught her arm and squeezed. Flesh and blood, not wooden. She snapped around, prepared for a fight, but her eyes landed on Peregrine's, hazel brown—twin to her own. All the breath flooded out of her.

His teeth were gritted, his jaw locked with the effort of controlling the wooden man, but he still spared a second to reassure her.

"That's ours," he grated out.

"Walk," Bo yelled, his arms lifted high to command the wooden man.

Gabi glanced between them, her fingers clenched around her baton, waiting for a cue to jump in and help. Or bolt to the door.

She flinched hard when the wooden man creaked and moaned, picking up his giant leg to take another step.

The coven are relying on you, she reminded herself, and locked her body, forcing back her jumpiness. She hastily focused herself the way she was trained. She couldn't afford to flinch again.

"What are *you?*" a silken voice purred.

Gabi snapped to attention, turning towards the source of that voice. A few rows away.

She ducked and crept towards the central aisle, leaving her dad and Peregrine to control the wooden man. With her free hand, she unhooked the handcuffs from her belt, her pulse tapping rapidly in her throat. Screw running for safety. If the wooden creature could distract Perchta, Gabi could get cuffs on her.

She glanced over her shoulder, locked eyes with her

dad, and gestured with her finger to draw Perchta away, keep her occupied so Gabi could creep up from behind.

More low wooden groans filled the air as the huge man manoeuvred himself; Gabi peered around the steel cabinet to see him lead Perchta away. The witch was prowling, long white hair trailing her every step, her heels clicking when moments ago they were silent. No wand in her hand, just manicured red nails. Were they somehow longer than before?

Gabi gripped the baton and cuffs hard, sterling herself. *No doubts, Gabi, no doubts.* And while Perchta was focused on the puzzle of the magical creature, Gabi launched at her.

Her wrist snapped out, locking one cuff around Perchta, and Gabi exhaled a single shaky breath. Scratches ran up the witch's forearms, mostly healed but still visible—Freya's final attempts at survival. Gabi reached to bind the other wrist, but Perchta turned eerily quickly.

There was nothing human left about her, no humanity in her eyes. This was pure hunter, pure evil. Gabi's body went cold at the sight of her grin, and she knew it was a lost battle. Too slow. She should have grabbed both wrists at once.

All Gabi could do as Perchta used the handcuff to wrench Gabi closer was raise her baton and bring it swinging into Perchta's side. The witch howled, but the sound tapered into a laugh, and she inhaled a long drag of air, millimetres from Gabi's face.

Gabi shuddered hard. A predator—Perchta was like no killer, no criminal, Gabi had ever faced. And Perchta was *scenting* her.

Gabi reared back to bring the baton down again, but Perchta spun quicker than Gabi could stop her, and the handcuff was ripped from her grasp. She sailed through the air, slamming into a solid filing cabinet on its lethally sharp corner, and grunted as the breath was knocked out of her. Her ears rattled at the loud noise of impact, a headache flaring.

The pain hit a moment later, her ribs screaming, instantly bruised, and Gabi hissed at the pain. She blinked fast, urging her blurry vision to clear.

When it did, Gabi used the cabinet to pull herself back to her feet—and swore viciously.

The wooden man was turning in circles, whorls of the floorboards visible in the bulging muscles of his arms. He looked ready for a fight, as was Gabi, but Perchta was gone.

THIRTY-THREE
JOY

The lift wouldn't open. The doors to the upper level were sealed shut and no breaking spell would open them.

Joy and her coven abandoned magic and switched to manual force. Gus dragged a metal chair from a disused office; Joy held her breath as he threw it at the glass portion of the exit door and ... nothing.

No splinter, not even a tiny crack. They were thoroughly, helplessly locked in.

An ear-splitting groan ripped the silence and Joy flinched into the nearest wall. Her heart threw itself against her rib cage. She locked eyes with Gus, Maisie, and Eilidh, dread pooling between all four of them, but the sound was coming from inside the records room.

Joy clenched her right hand around her wand, slipping her left into her pocket to touch a kambaba jasper for reassurance and calm. But she was so scared, the stone didn't even touch her dread.

"That sounds like the elves again," Eilidh murmured, her eyes on the open records room door as she edged closer to Joy and Victoriya, the latter splayed on the floor, showing no sign of consciousness.

Joy held her wand in front of her, readying herself to grab a potion, but the corridor remained empty of everyone but them. And Eilidh was right; it sounded similar to what Peregrine had done before.

"Shit," Gus said in a tight voice. "Look at Mais."

Joy swallowed, wishing it was as easy to swallow her fear as it was to push down the acid in her throat. Bracing herself, she turned in Gus's direction.

Maisie was single-mindedly scratching at a white door down the hallway.

Joy shared a look with her friends, and without a word spoken they lifted Victoriya off the floor, refusing to leave her behind as they followed Maisie's obvious hint.

Unlike the exit, this door opened easily when Gus leaned on the handle with his elbow, swearing at Victoriya's unconscious, heavy body. Joy wished Victoriya's eyes would fly open, wished they would bicker for some sense of normality. But Victoriya's eyes remained bruised and shut, her body remained limp.

Shuffling inside, Joy kicked the door behind them, shutting it all but a crack for them to watch the corridor. Joy released Victoriya to point her wand in a defensive position, surveying the empty office. Three desks were each pushed against a wall, with desk lamps, piles of paperwork, and glossy Macs organised on their surfaces. The contents had a rich, expensive feel. One desk even held a plum Givenchy bag left carelessly behind, with a folder and a hat sticking out of it.

Wait, that hat ... Joy's stomach flipped. The narrow brim was embroidered with silver whorls and slashes—the rank of a head witch.

"That's Paulina's," she breathed.

As if her words triggered it, a muffled groan rose from the back of the room, coming from behind one of the heavy wooden desks.

A little numb with shock, Joy took a step towards the muffled voice, her stomach one big, sick knot and her breathing so shallow her chest barely moved.

"Wait." Gus caught her arm, abandoning all Victoriya's weight on Eilidh, who tumbled into the nearest desk with a string of filthy words. "Are you crazy? That could be Perchta."

Joy shook her head, glancing from his pale, freckled face to the elaborate desk. Gabi used to talk about gut feelings religiously, like they were a djinn's wishes, something to be coveted and *never* ignored or misused. Joy hadn't understood then, but she was having one now: a gut feeling told her the office on the ground floor was Paulina's public office, but *this* room was where she got her work done in private.

Joy shouldn't have cared, not after everything the witch had done to her, but ... if she pretended not to hear, if she left the head witch behind, that would make her as bad as Paulina.

And she wouldn't give the vile woman that kind of satisfaction.

She shook off Gus's bone white grip, and rounded the desk with sure, certain steps.

Folded up on the floor, hands and ankles bound, was the head witch of Agedale. Her frazzled orange hair looked extra bright against the bleached white of her face, and fear widened her eyes, whether she'd admit it or not. Her cloak was ripped right over the embroidery on the hem, some of it missing, as if she'd discovered Perchta and put up a good fight.

But *fuck*, the head witch, the most powerful witch for miles, had fought Perchta *and lost*. Joy was gripped by a sudden pressing need to go back into the records room, find Gabi, and drag her to safety.

Instead, she pulled the embroidered gag from Paulina's mouth and asked, "Are you alright? What happened?"

"What the *hell* are you doing here, Mackenzie?"

Well.

Joy sat back on her heels, anger bubbling in her chest. She hadn't expected kindness and gratitude, but cordiality wouldn't have gone amiss.

"Your assistant *kidnapped* Victoriya. My witch sister. We came to get her back."

Paulina's bushy eyebrows rose. "You came to stop a murderer?" Wry amusement curled her thin mouth as she looked past Joy to Eilidh and Gus. "And failed, I presume?"

"No," Joy snapped, anger as hot as coals in her chest.

Not yet. She shook her head, remembering the faith and belief in Gabi's voice just before she vanished.

Not ever, Joy snarled at herself.

She glanced over her shoulder at Gus, looking as if he'd swallowed something noxious.

"Did you bring your athame?" If anyone would've, it'd be him or Victoriya. Victoriya because the metal channelled her fire, and Gus because he could use the narrow blade to etch sigils in the air.

With an even darker expression, he handed over the thin dagger.

"I'm not sure about this, Joy," Eilidh said tightly. "What if she's working with Katrina?"

"Working with that madwoman?" Paulina demanded. "Are you insane, girl?"

No one wasted breath answering that question.

Joy sawed the ropes, cutting Paulina free. Not because she was feeling merciful but because Paulina was head witch, and if anyone could break the spells on the exits, it would be her.

Paulina said nothing as she flexed her bruising wrists and stood, towering over Joy. But the head witch wasn't looking at her; she was scowling at the ripped strip of her own cloak, rubbing it between her fingers. Blood leaked from a gash on her leg and stained the dress beneath her cloak, which explained the scent of blood in the records room. Paulina must have caught Katrina before she could cut Victoriya.

"I suppose," she said sourly in Joy's direction, "you were not the killer after all."

Joy waited for an apology. After a moment, it appeared that *was* the apology. She just shrugged. She wouldn't forgive Paulina, even though the head witch had truly believed she was protecting her town and coven. Joy could understand the motivation, but her methods had left a scar deep in Joy's psyche. So, she merely nodded and waited for Paulina to start bossing them around. *Someone* needed to take charge of the situation and provide a safe exit.

But the witch's head whipped to the door when that ripping, creaking groan split the air, coming from the records room. Joy watched the blood drain from Paulina's face.

This time the ground beneath them rocked. Eilidh and Joy grabbed each other for stability. Gus flopped into a desk with a dark curse. Joy frantically searched for Victoriya, but she was safely propped in a desk chair.

Her coven was okay, they were safe. But what about Salma?

"Paulina," Joy began. "Could you—"

Paulina didn't look at them; she snatched her wand out of the Givenchy handbag on her desk, flicked on the desk fan beside her, and she was gone.

"No!" Joy jerked forward but she already knew what she'd find. Sand on the floor where Paulina had stood. Sand she must have kept in the bottom of the fan for escapes just like this one.

"Godsdammit," Gus spat. "Fucking coward."

Joy's heart crashed. She realised much too late that she'd given herself false hope, believing Paulina would save them.

But they weren't part of the main coven, they weren't Paulina's *chosen* witches. They were castoffs, unwanted.

Joy's eyes burned as she looked at her friends, all of them jumping when that wooden groaning drowned out the fan's whirring. Whatever was happening out there, it was too strong for comfort now.

"Gus," Joy said slowly. "Is there a sigil that can—"

"Get us out of here?" he preempted. "Probably, but I don't know it. I have about fifty memorised, but most are for doing the washing up and taking the bins out."

"Eilidh?" Joy breathed, trying to be positive despite her heavy heart.

"If there was a window, we could get to..." Eilidh shook her head. "But I don't know where Theo is." Joy glanced automatically above for the seagull usually perched high, but he was absent. "Do you think... Victoriya's pack has to know something is wrong, right?"

Joy shrugged, hopeless and heavy.

With Victoriya unconscious, she couldn't call her canine familiars. And with Theodore missing too, they really were alone down here. Alone except for Salma, Gabi, Bo, and Peregrine. Who they'd *left behind*.

Joy took a tight breath and met the eyes of her best friends in all the world.

"Stay with Victoriya. I'm going back out there."

It wasn't bravery or heroics; it was Gabi and Salma trapped in a room with a murderer, and Joy not being able to stand it. It was selfishness.

She shoved her hand into the army of pockets sewn into her coat lining, ripping open sachet after sachet and stacking them upright, within easy reach. She checked the two potions she'd been given—a freezing spell and a flash charm—and gripped the bulbous base of her wand. Gus immediately objected, and Eilidh reached for Joy's arm, but before she could chicken out, Joy raced out of the door, across the hall and into the records room again.

Inside it was too still, too quiet. A trail of blood began a few steps away and curved around the row of metal cabinets. Joy's pulse beat like a panicked thing in her throat as she followed it, her wand raised and surprisingly steady. She'd moved past shaking, moved past fear into a constant state of numb terror.

Gus and Eilidh followed her without a word, disobeying her only order, though Maisie must have stayed to watch over Victoriya. "Oh shit," Gus breathed, pointing to the end of the row as they passed the metal monoliths. The floorboards had been torn up, revealing the dull black floor underneath, and at the end of the row, like a ship wrecked on a rocky bluff, were splinters and boards and limbs made of wood. Separated, ripped apart as if by a giant's hand or by ... by a severing spell. Joy's eyes fell on a head, the wood smooth over its eye hollows and the cavern of its mouth. Her stomach turned over and she moved quickly on, searching the rows for a black ponytail, a wool coat, a baton in a pale fist.

No Gabi. But three rows of filing cabinets later, Joy sucked in air and ground to a halt. The male elf was collapsed against a half-open cabinet at the end of the bloody trail, his leg cut and a slash on his chest. Not deep enough to cut *into* him, to hollow him and stuff him with rubbish, but enough to show Perchta's intentions. Was he one of the people she'd called naughty, or was she attacking anyone at this point? And what *was* this—some twisted version of the Christmas list? Naughty, nice... Joy burned with anger even as her blood chilled.

Eilidh knelt at Peregrine's side, brushing long dark hair from his neck so she could place a dot of green paste there, healing or reviving or some other combination of herbs that must have been Salma's doing. She was the one who made tonics and poultices. Joy's heart twisted at the thought of Salma hurt like Peregrine.

Joy moved on. She felt bad for leaving Peregrine behind, but she kept moving anyway. Her friend and her ... Gabi were in here somewhere, possibly as hurt.

She heard the elf inhale a sharp breath, heard Eilidh whisper to him and Gus shush her, but then Joy was too far away. The numbness had spread within her. Now fear didn't touch her, not even as she neared the end of the room, where they'd first found Victoriya.

Gus cursed and jogged after her. When he touched her elbow, Joy had to fight to stop the scream in her lungs from erupting. She swung a glare on him, but he just lifted his wand to point at the back wall where a door stood half open, a slice of silver light falling onto the bare floor. That door had been shut earlier, Joy was sure of it.

She broke into a run, not caring that her footfalls were loud, that Perchta would know she was coming. She took a sachet in one hand, wand in the other, and shoved the door the rest of the way open with her hip. One glance around the room—a second, smaller records room full of cardboard boxes and ancient desktop computers, this one smelling of ink and toner instead of blood—and she saw Salma, tied to a chair and unconscious, and Gabi, fighting Katrina with a small, ineffectual knife.

Joy took a breath ragged with both relief—she was *alive* —and white fear—Salma was slumped and unconscious. Without waiting for Katrina—Perchta—to notice her, Joy reared her arm back and hurled the contents of the sachet into the air, diving into her armoury of crystals for a shard of nuummite, for fighting negative witchcraft and strengthening positive. The wand in Joy's hand warmed in response to the spell, the purple ashes of the sachet now at Katrina's feet, staining the bottom of her tan trousers, her shiny court shoes.

The fight froze, Perchta falling still.

Joy's shoulders sagged. She had a single minute before that spell wore off, and even though she had a potion that would achieve the same effect when this one wore off, she couldn't waste any time. Urgency pounded at her, telling her to run to Gabi, to untie Salma, but the anger hammering her heart led her to Perchta instead. Wand held at the ready, Joy ignored Gus behind her, catching Gabi around the shoulders, letting furious steps carry her to the witch who had killed a teenage girl. Who would have killed Neil and Victoriya.

Aware of the clock counting down, Joy grabbed Perchta's hands—too soft for hands that had taken lives—and wrestled them behind her back. She had to holster her wand while she fumbled for a sachet and a crystal, tipping the ashes burned in a fire so hot it would melt skin from bones onto the witch's hands. As soon as the ash made contact, the flakes turned to liquid metal, glossy and silver-white. She held the crystal securely over Perchta's hands, one hand touching her holstered wand, guiding the witch-craft with smoky quartz, Stone of Power, to wrap around those pale hands like shackles. But she'd barely made one knot of the liquid metal when someone knocked into the doorframe—Eilidh—and Perchta came alive, wrestling and angry.

"No," Joy breathed, urging the metal to move quicker, but Perchta wrenched and thrashed, and the smoky quartz slipped from her grasp, the sachet knocked to the floor where the rest of the spell pooled and hardened into a puddle of harmless white gold.

Joy fumbled to keep Perchta trapped by sheer willpower and physical strength but in one capable move-ment, she demolished the meagre bindings Joy had made and whipped around. Joy made to unholster her wand, but before she could close her hand around it Perchta's pale hand struck Joy's nose. A horrific crunching filled Joy's ears. Pain hit her belatedly and with enough force to blur her vision. Perchta knocked her wand to the floor and Joy's stomach dropped as it rolled out of reach. Perchta's eyes widened as they fell on Joy, her mouth popping open as she registered her attacker. "But you're a good one," she said, and released Joy. Her pretty face was filled with shock and alarm. She looked at her hands, where flecks of metal still lingered.

Joy had forgotten about the rest of the room, the rest of the world, but she jolted back to reality with a faint sob as Gabi crept up behind the witch. She was steady, upright, and Joy couldn't see any injuries. Somehow, Gabi slid her small knife around Perchta's neck and pressed it against the witch's throat. Perchta went perfectly still but she grinned

... as if the knife wasn't restraining her at all but she'd allow them to think so.

Joy swallowed, not daring to move even to get her wand.

"Joy," Gabi barked. "There are handcuffs over there by the desk. Quickly."

Joy tripped over her feet in her rush. The numbness had solidly worn off, leaving a shaking, terrified Joy in place of the version of her that marched determinedly into a room to save her ex-girlfriend and her witch sister.

Losing balance, she slammed into the desk, saw the glint of metal on the floor, and snatched them up. Her breath was tight, scraping up her throat now, but Joy stumbled back to Gabi. Perchta was clawing at Gabi despite the knife at her throat, though half-heartedly, like she wanted her situation to seem convincing. Joy didn't allow her eyes to stray to Salma, a coward for not wanting to see, to know if she was alive and breathing or not. Gus had vanished between the freezing spell and Perchta resuming her motion, and Eilidh too, but Joy had no doubt they were nearby. Helping Peregrine, maybe. Or Bo. Gods, Bo. Where was he?

A lump formed in Joy's throat as she made to hand the handcuffs to Gabi but realised, with a flood of cool fear, she'd have to do it herself. This was no different than binding Perchta's hands with witchcraft, Joy told herself. Except she was awake now, not frozen. And she was still going along with this when she clearly had enough witchcraft to disarm Gabi. Joy looked into the witch's eyes and faltered. Fear took her in its careless hold.

The witch changed. A blink, and the willowy blonde woman was gone. A grey skinned, colourless nightmare smiled at Joy with teeth too long and thin to be of any witch she'd seen before. Her eyes were cloudy yellow, and her hands were skeletal and made entirely of bone. The pant suit had gone, the glossy white hair replaced by a fall of white wisps, any humanity she might have had or pretended to have wiped away to reveal amused cruelty.

Joy stumbled back, a cry in her throat, and her instincts begged her to run, run as far and fast as she could. The cuffs slid from her grasp as she backed away and she shrieked as her legs slammed into a computer desk, knocking over a mug of coffee. The sound of the computer monitor rocking, liquid dripping to the floor, were as loud as gunshots and Joy shook, every breath rasping as she looked at the nightmare before her, and Gabi, still struggling to hold Perchta with that tiny knife.

Gabi. Joy met her eyes and wished the fear had magically melted. It remained, brutal as ever, but Joy straightened her spine, bent to retrieve the cuffs and her wand, and shoved herself back towards the hellish witch before fear could snare her again. Joy snapped one of the handcuffs rattling in her hands around the wrist of the witch. She didn't take her eyes off Gabi.

She lifted the second cuff, but Perchta opened her mouth and screeched, something inherently pleased about the sound, like a hellhound's laugh. The sound filled Joy's head, screamed through her until warmth trickled from her ears. Blood. She lifted her hands instinctively to cover her ears, pressing her palms hard to push out the screaming echoing inside her skull. She realised her mistake a second too late and cried out.

One hand cuffed but the other free, Perchta lashed forward. Her hands were outstretched, those fingers of shining bone narrowed to claw like points on the ends, and all Joy could think was they were poised to sink into Gabi. Her Gabi. And she would never let Gabi be hurt, *ever*.

Joy just *acted*. She slammed into Gabi, knocking her out

of the way as Perchta moved—so fast she blurred into a bone white smear on Joy's retinas. Joy's cry choked off as the claws of both Perchta's hands sunk through her coat, her flamingo-patterned top, and into the soft flesh of her stomach. Joy felt the discomfort first, the spears in her stomach ripping free, and as if watching it happen to someone else, she saw the blood well from her belly, flooding her clothes. Saw the blood too dripping from the tapered ends of Perchta's fingers, saw the witch raise them to her lips, her tongue darting out—and then the pain hit in full force and Joy slid to the floor, gasping, a howl building until she was screaming, on fire, her face wet with tears. The impact of hitting the floor erased everything else and blackness rose up to claim her.

G abi felt those vicious claws as if they'd gone into her own stomach. Even as Perchta moved, even as she grinned to find Gabi paralysed, staring at Joy bleeding and fainting, Gabi couldn't move. Couldn't breathe. Joy—

She was going to be sick. She stumbled a step towards Joy but swayed at the sight of the blood gushing from her stomach, pooling on the floor. Perchta took advantage of Gabi's horror to slam her against the closest wall, a bookshelf digging into Gabi's back. She barely felt any of it, not the discomfort, not the pain flaring in her shoulder. Her eyes were glued to Joy, gasping for every breath, unconscious as Gus and Gabi's dad swarmed her, magic singing through the room as Bo called power to defend her. Gabi just stared. Useless. Her chest heaving with every breath, eyes burning.

"Gabriella." Her dad—a whip strike of a word.

She shook her head. She couldn't. Couldn't go on knowing Joy had been hurt when Gabi should have protected her. Couldn't live when those wounds, that bleeding, were stealing Joy's life. Gabi staggered away from the witch grinning at her, sliding along the wall, not caring as she bumped into a computer desk, a stack of Xerox boxes.

The knife had gone, fallen from her hand when the claws pierced Joy's skin. Her baton was lost somewhere during the struggle. Useless. If she couldn't protect the woman she loved most... Utterly useless.

"Gabi," her dad warned again, and as claws snagged her wrist, the tips biting into her palm, Gabi realised it was a command not to pull herself together but to beware the witch killer calculating her next move. Gabi didn't care. She didn't have the energy.

"She'll be fine, Gabi." Closer now, but as Gabi focussed her eyes, she realised she couldn't see him. He'd used his magic to make their environment camouflage them. Gabi's head hurt.

"Get her out of here." Her voice came out harsh.

"I'm not leaving you, Gabriella."

Gabi's throat ached. "Get her *out of here.*"

She could feel him nearby, hesitating. The last thing she wanted was for him to leave but she kept seeing those claws slide into Joy. "*Go.*"

"I'll come back." And then the air swept by her, and she knew he was gone, him and Gus getting Joy to the closest thing to a healer among them. That should have brought some relief but this cold, aching nothing that had swallowed her had been building for a while, since she'd seen Perchta throw her brother over the top of a filing cabinet, then pursue him with a grin and a spell.

A wound had opened on his stomach as if by an invisible knife, and Peregrine... There was a lot of blood. Too much to come back from without the care of the clinic's nurses or some sort of battle healing. Why hadn't Gabi told the witches to prepare a battle healing spell? She went to drag her fingers through her hair, but the hand snarled around her wrist bit in deeper, drawing more blood. Pain, clearing and cleansing, trickled up Gabi's arm to her brain. A bad move on Perchta's part.

The witch was fumbling for something at her waist, but her transformation hadn't brought her clothes and whatever was in her pockets with her. Gabi had no knife, no baton, no taser because she'd been naïve and assumed she wouldn't need one. Weapon less, she reared her head back and recalled one of the most important lessons her dad had taught her: never forget the disorienting power of a head-butt. It was both a warning for her to avoid one and encouragement for her to give one.

Pain slammed into her skull as she connected with Perchta and she almost bit right through her tongue but managed not to as the witch screeched and reared back. Gabi brought the side of her hand down hard on Perchta's wrist, disconnecting her grip. Falling back on training and self-defence classes, Gabi wasted no time bringing her knee up to slam into the witch's crotch even as her vision blurred thanks to the headbutt. If she had her baton, she would bring it crashing into Perchta's ribs but absent of it, she used her fists to rain precise, damaging blows to the witch's stomach, chest, and throat, and swept her foot out to knock Perchta, while she was still fumbling for a response, onto her backside.

Panting, blood trickling from her wrist to the polished floor under her feet, Gabi reached deep into the begrudging power that lazed deep inside her. She felt for it, as Perchta got her hands under her and leveraged herself into a sitting position—physical blows would never keep this witch down, Gabi knew; it would take power to get her unconscious long enough to cuff her and lock her up.

Gabi's breath came tight, her stomach cramping, and abdominal muscles pulling tight as she tugged and tugged on her elven magic. Perchta balanced on her feet, crouching, and Gabi slid a step away, eyes roaming the room for her baton, for the knife. There, a metre or so away, laid her baton. Could she dive for it quicker than Perchta could get to her unsteady feet? Gabi couldn't trick herself that Perchta would stay unbalanced for more than a few seconds longer. She braced to leap the distance but a thin whisper of power wound through her stomach, up her chest, and down her arms. Gabi had never been happier to feel the uncomfortable tingle sweeping down her shoulders. She poured every ounce of her will and control into guiding that tingle.

Gritting her teeth as the itching turned to a thousand needles stabbing her arms, Gabi pushed her magic out, forced it to obey her, and exhaled all at once in both relief and inner pain as the boards and stone under Perchta turned from solid to liquid. The witch's feet sank into the puddle and Gabi let the straining tether to her magic snap back to her core. The floor, the boards, the ground beneath turned solid again and while Perchta's feet were trapped, moulded into the very floor, Gabi threw her aching body towards the baton, crashing to her knees hard enough that she had to fix her jaw to not cry out.

Perchta laughed as Gabi struggled back to her feet, her knees, thighs, and stomach all jabbing pain into her. Gabi gave the witch a wide berth even as she saw the knife was a few steps behind Perchta. She wasn't getting anywhere near that ashen grey *thing*—long, thin teeth were bared, Perchta's true face a stretched, angular thing with more bone than skin and more malice than humanity. Gabi shuddered as the witch—was she still a witch in this skeletal, naked form, mere cobwebs of a dress covering the fact that the mottled grey skin was shrivelling?—lashed her arms at her.

Gabi's need to know everything about this new creature pressed into her—did Perchta look like she was decaying because she'd failed to kill Neil, because she was starving, or did she always look this way? Did she need to kill for sustenance?

A drowsy groan had Gabi jumping and turning. She'd completely forgotten about Salma, her spacial awareness gone to shit. Gabi pinched her face as she stepped towards Joy's friend, trying to make herself more alert, more *awake*. Before, the fear had always given her an intense clarity. Now it had dulled her. Or seeing Joy that way... She couldn't think of it. Wouldn't let herself until everyone was out of this building and safe.

As Gabi searched a nearby drawer for a penknife, scissors, anything to cut Salma's bindings, she read Perchta her rights, officially arresting her this time around. Perchta only laughed a low, sensuous laugh that made Gabi shudder again. Getting cuffs on her ... that would be difficult. Impossible. Getting everyone else out while Perchta was trapped was the priority. Not for the first time, Gabi cursed this tiny town, its useless head witch, and wished Paulina would allow her a partner. But that would cost Town Hall too much extra money. Never mind that it could save lives tonight. Her dad was decent backup, but she needed a *partner*. Right now, she'd have settled for a gun.

"Hey," Gabi said to Salma, finally finding a letter opener. It would do. She peered at Salma's dark face—was she more ashen than normal, had Perchta done more than just knock her out with a bump to the head?—as she sawed at the ropes holding her in the chair.

"Mama?" Salma slurred, her eyes blinking open but clearly unfocussed.

"It's Pride. Gabriella. We're in Town Hall. I'm going to get you to the clinic, Salma." She got through the last rope and put her arms under Salma, helping the witch stand. Salma leaned heavily on Gabi, groaning low in her throat, but she was becoming more lucid, blinking at her surroundings. She recoiled at the sight of Perchta, but Gabi held her steady. "Do you think you can walk?"

Salma swallowed a tight breath, but she nodded and took a step. Gabi took a moment to scan her for injuries, but it must have been just bruising and dizziness. And for her to be awake, Perchta must have used a less powerful strain of sleeping witchcraft.

"Why are you leaving?" Perchta asked in a whisper-soft rasp as Gabi and Salma crossed the threshold into the main records room. "Weren't we having fun, Pride?"

Gabi ground her teeth but kept walking, one arm around Salma's waist. The thought of finding everyone, getting them off this floor, out of this building and to the clinic, felt monumental. Salma swayed but stayed upright, leaning on Gabi.

"Where is my coven?" she asked.

Gabi shook her head, a knot in her throat. She didn't know. And Joy... Her breath hitched, sobs poised to shudder her chest and shatter her completely. She couldn't answer Salma, could only focus on putting one foot in front of the other as they passed filing cabinets and blood trails. She had to get out of this room. She could do that. Everything else... *One thing at a time*, she told herself.

Every step was like the world pressing down on her but finally they reached the corridor. Salma had said nothing else, asked no further questions, but Gabi knew she'd seen the blood. She leant against the wall, staring up and down the hallway as Gabi slammed the records room door shut. She wished she could call her magic to seal it firmly, but it ignored her, impetuous. At least she could tell, through her elven senses, that Perchta was still held by the ground in the office. She doubted it would last but if it gave them seconds, she'd take it.

Adrenaline was starting to wear off and reveal a dozen pains across her body. It was a battle to keep her mind on the here and now, to not think about those claws piercing Joy's stomach, the blood spreading across her coat, the floor. Gabi must have made a noise because Salma reached across them and squeezed her hand. Gabi was supposed to be capable and distant and calm, her emotions locked in a vault. Instead, this touch unleashed every one of her fears. Tears slid down her face. Was Joy dead? Gods, why hadn't Gabi told her she still loved her, that she'd fallen in love with her all over again, with the person she was now as well as the person she'd always been?

Gabi came so close to collapsing to her knees, to giving up and just staying there until Perchta broke free and came for her, but footsteps pounded at the end of the hallway and Gabi lifted her heavy head to see the glass doors at the end of the corridor stood open and a blur of black clothes and blue-blonde hair come flying out of them. Eilidh, her face red and eyes blown so wide Gabi knew adrenaline had to be the only thing fueling her.

"They got the doors open," she huffed, breathing hard, her shoulders sagging at the sight of them. "Your brother managed to open it." Oh good. Peregrine had made introductions. "Salma?" Eilidh asked.

"I'm fine," Salma said in a rough voice. She was still

dizzy, Gabi knew, but would never tell one of her witches that.

Gabi opened her mouth—to ask, to demand to know about Joy—but she snapped it shut. A coward, she didn't *want* to know. Couldn't face it. Not yet. "Where's my dad? Peregrine?"

"Upstairs." Eilidh's eyes lingered on Gabi. "Peregrine's ... he got hurt. I managed to heal his skin with a paste but the inside..."

Gabi shut off her hearing. Just blocked out the words. She reached for Salma's waist to support the woman and began what felt like a vast trek to the open doors at the end of the corridor. She didn't even ask why Eilidh had said they got the doors open, as if they'd been locked, or why they weren't using the lift.

She tightened her grip on Salma reflexively as they neared the doors, aware enough to scan the shadows and corners for anyone lurking, not that they'd had any indication Perchta had an accomplice. Gabi's heart was in her throat. First Joy and now... What if the last way she saw Peregrine was hurt by the way she was treating him? What if he thought she hated him? She wanted to punch him in the gut most days for what he'd done, but she didn't want him dead. She just couldn't deal with the betrayal. That he'd known they were siblings for so long and never told her. That he'd let her find out from a letter her mum gave her on her deathbed.

The door to the stairwell had been melted to the floor by elven magic, reforming in a messy puddle Gabi had to step carefully around. Did Eilidh say Peregrine had done this? He couldn't be dead if he'd done this. Could he?

"Almost there," Eilidh gasped, ducking under Salma's

other arm as the older witch swayed. "They already took Victoriya up and—"

And the horrifying sound of a door slamming open behind them killed all other words, any other reassurances she might have given.

Eilidh and Salma scrambled up the staircase but when Gabi lowered her arm from Salma, Eilidh turned wide eyes on her. Gabi just shook her head. She'd brought them into this building, risked their lives, hurt them all. Maybe worse.

"Go," she said, something inside her collapsing. She'd never see Joy again even if she survived the stab wounds to her stomach. But to make up for this mess, for endangering everyone ... that was okay. To get Eilidh and Salma to safety that was definitely okay. It was her job. "Up the stairs. Don't stop until you're out."

"We can't leave you here." Eilidh's face was tight, silver lining her eyes. "Peregrine's up there healing Joy. She's going to be fine, and she'll expect you to be around when she wakes up." That last part was a lie, but Gabi appreciated it, along with the other bit of information she'd given her. Peregrine was alright.

Without making excuses or goodbyes, Gabi turned, straightened her shoulders as if she could strengthen her bravery by a simple movement, and descended the few stairs to face the open door to the records room. And the sharp, grey figure framed inside it. Perchta ignored Eilidh and Salma, her beady yellow eyes fixed solely on Gabi. She'd been naughty now, she assumed. Good. Let Perchta allow the witches to leave. Let her fixate on Gabi. It was the least she deserved after letting the coven come into a situation like this.

Gabi sucked in a shallow breath, even that small movement straining the wrecked muscles of her stomach—her magic's price: physical weakness, physical pain. At least for her. For other elves, mere tiredness.

Her mouth went dry, her hands twitching towards the baton she'd once again strapped to her waist, as Perchta lunged out of the room, bits of the floorboards and concrete stuck to her feet, a trail of blood behind her. Gabi raised her weapon and struck hard and precisely at Perchta's throat. Pain had not kept her down before as much as surprise. "You," she snarled, her voice a pained wisp. Her grey face contorted with fury, the skin pulling tight to show sharp bones beneath. Her breath smelled of rot and iron. "You need to be punished."

Every bit of bravery had left Gabi. It was recklessness, it was Joy bleeding and Peregrine hurt and her dad in Gods knew what state, which raised her eyebrow and laughed. "Kinky, but no thanks."

Gabi's muscles stretched, screamed, as she dove out of the way, ready for the fury that propelled Perchta through the air towards her, claws pointed outward. On the stairs, far above, Gabi could hear shoes squeaking and she hoped it meant Eilidh and Salma were running as fast as their legs could carry them. Good. At least one thing had gone right.

"*He* wouldn't approve—he doesn't care about who's naughty or nice—but it's important. This is for your own good, Gabriella." Perchta lashed forward again but she was ready when Gabi dove, one clawed hand snapping out to curl around Gabi's arm, nails leaving even more shallow cuts on her skin. Somehow, they stung worse than her muscles, her rapidly-forming bruises. Gabi tried to lift the baton, but Perchta's hand squeezed her wrist so hard that her hand flexed involuntarily, and she gritted her teeth to not cry out. She couldn't spare a thought to wonder who Perchta was talking about and didn't care. The clatter of the baton hitting the floor, rolling away, was so loud Gabi flinched. Weak—she should have felt so weak, but to be here so the coven could get to safety ... there was strength in that.

"You've been a bad girl." Gabi's eyes watered as Perchta leaned close, her lungs filling with the witch's noxious breath. She was glad for the film over her eyes, so she didn't have to see the triumph on the witch's face, the satisfaction at having finally got her hands on someone deserving of her violent brand of judgement. "Lying to so many people."

Gabi thrashed in vain, trying to get her fists in Perchta's face in the absence of her baton but there was power moving around them now, Gabi could sense it, as it converged on her arms, pinning them to her sides. Panting for breath, while the rest of her body was unrestrained, Gabi shot her knee up and into the witch's gut. But Perchta's grip, both witchcraft and physical—claws and inhuman strength—did not waver. Gabi tried stepping down hard on her instep, did everything she'd been taught and learned herself over the years, but she was pinned, well and truly. But witchcraft was moving around Gabi, not restraining this time but something else. Her head swam and Gabi felt the sudden, delirious urge to laugh.

Even as a rasp of a laugh slipped out of her, as her eyes cleared of tears but glazed over with something else, she called on her elven magic. Dragged it from the depths like she was dredging an ocean. Laughed and urged that magic deep inside her to wake up, to cooperate. But concentration abandoned her as Perchta murmured a sinuous word and slashed a deep line down Gabi's forearm. The magic spun away from her if it had never begun responding, pain flaring, *scalding*, in her arm. Different to the other cuts. Cold, then burning. Gabi peeled her eyes apart—when had they shut? When had her sharp words dissolved to scratchy laughter?—and glimpsed silver. A knife.

A thought should have come then, some conclusion to draw from that knife, some connection, but Gabi just sighed and smiled and laughed. Wrong—she felt wrong—but also right, deep in her bones. She sighed again, letting her eyes fall shut.

"Lying to your father," Perchta went on, "about your work. You don't want his job. He thinks it's passion that keeps you in your job but it's duty—to him, to your mother."

Gabi shook her head. Through the haze of feeling right, something stirred. Unease.

"Lying to your brother," Perchta whispered. "You want a relationship with him but you're a coward."

Pain, pure and screaming and emotional, arrowed through Gabi, clearing the fog around her long enough for her to remember Peregrine's hopeful, hurt face as he stood waiting outside Town Hall. He'd come because she'd asked, at a minute's notice, and she'd treated him like she couldn't stand him, like she could barely look at him. She loved him —he was her cousin, her best friend.

"Lying," Perchta whispered, fanning rotting breath over Gabi. She gagged, bile rising, and that too pushed back the delirious fog. A spell? Or something Perchta naturally produced to disarm prey? "Lying still, to yourself."

Gabi's head slammed into the wall behind her as she recoiled at a cutting touch sliding down her cheek, a twisted caress. Not deep enough to bite into the flesh beneath, to carve her judgement but enough to remind Gabi of what was to come. And to pry Gabi's mouth open. Panic drummed into her, a thrashing wave, but Gabi didn't have the strength to stop Perchta's narrow fingers prying apart her lips. She tried to bite down, to cause any tiny amount of damage, and it was not logic and training controlling her now but pure survival instinct, yet nothing worked.

A glass bottle met Gabi's teeth and she choked as a sapphire blue liquid was forced down her throat. She gagged, coughing most of it back up, but Perchta ran the backs of her fingers over Gabi's throat and forced her to swallow a mouthful. Gabi clenched her stomach muscles, urging her gut to roil, to revolt, to purge whatever was working through her system, but she slumped before she could get her stomach to cooperate and Perchta's grip loosened. A hazy curtain fell over her surroundings, and then unconsciousness took her, leaving her to the witch killer's mercy.

THIRTY-FIVE

JOY

A gasp tore from Joy's throat. She hurt everywhere but especially her stomach, five points of stabbing pain jolting her awake. Her head throbbed as she groaned, the end tapering into a whimper, and she tried sitting up, but hands pushed her back down. Something solid and hard was under her, a table or the ground. The scent of fir trees and dust surrounded her, but Joy couldn't tell where she was, couldn't convince her eyes to open. The only sound she could pick out, other than her own strained whimpers, was someone's steady breathing very close by.

She shivered. Her coat. Where was her coat? Her crystals, her wand, the last potion bottle! She shuddered, cold skimming her arms, and tried to get up again, begging her eyes to pry open.

"Not yet," a male voice said, gentle and smooth. Deep, like secrets and shadows. The hands on her shoulders pushed her back down. "You're not fully healed yet."

"What?" Her tongue felt swollen, clumsy. Her nose pulsed, and she distantly remembered the crunch of bones breaking.

"It's Peregrine," he said, and Joy finally unglued her eyes, waiting for them to focus on his face. Long chin, good looking with his concerned chocolate eyes, crooked nose, and messy black hair hanging into his face. The elf who'd come with them, she remembered, piecing together events leading up to Perchta's claws stabbing into her soft belly. But then he added, "Gabriella's brother," and confusion fuzzed her mind.

"Gabi doesn't have a brother," she said, her tongue still feeling like a beached whale in her mouth. Too late, she realised that could have been rude, hurtful.

He glanced away but his hand didn't leave her shoulders, pressing down, keeping her from undoing the healing he must have worked on her. Pain wove through her, but it was nowhere near as painful as when Perchta had stabbed her. Gratitude instead unwound in her chest but more pressing was the lack of her coven, and Gabi and Bo's absence. "Where are we?" Joy asked, eyes rolling to take in the empty office around them. Dust covered most of the furniture, some of the pieces covered with sheets, and the back wall was stacked with unused chairs and tables. A storage room, then. That explained the dust she kept inhaling. And the forest scent was Peregrine himself. "Where's Perchta?"

"Downstairs still. We're on the third floor." His worried eyes met hers, hesitation in them. "The whole place cleared out when they heard me rip into those cabinets."

Joy didn't have a reply to that. She supposed it explained the wrenching metal sound that had drowned out everything else in the smoky room. That seemed like a long, long time ago. Joy gritted her teeth at a spike of pain that came from nowhere. She needed to go to the clinic, to get full healing and treatment, but she couldn't. Not yet. "Where's Gabi?"

Peregrine looked away. Joy understood the hesitation, the way he was handling her—as if she'd break. She stared at his sharp profile and felt her heart crumple, her face heat with oncoming tears. Downstairs? Gabi was still with that witch, that killer—

Joy scrambled into a sitting position, ignoring the flares of hurt along her legs, her wrist, her belly. None of that mattered. She was alive—she could get up, she could move, she could find Gabi. She paid little attention to the table beneath her, sheet-covered furniture around her, the gauzy light filtering through the windows. None of that mattered either. Nothing did except Gabi.

"I'm not done!" Peregrine tried to settle her down again, alarmed eyes on her, but Joy wrestled his grip off her. "I'm not the best healer on a good day. You shouldn't be straining yourself, Joy."

Joy looked him in the eye with her hardest glare and said, "The woman I love more than anyone else in the world is downstairs with a witch who's already killed one person and tried to kill three others." Herself included. Joy couldn't think of that, of the danger she'd be walking back into. She could only think of Gabi, her warm brown eyes, her slow-unfurling smile. "Let me up."

Peregrine let her up.

Her whole body screamed as she swung off the table she'd been laid out on, but she was steady enough. The adrenaline that had fled her earlier filled her veins again and gave her the strength to stumble out of the room. She reached for a crystal from her pocket and came up empty, remembering with a pang the absence of her coat. She spun, as if she could find it in this lonely corridor. For a too-long moment she stood there, a witch useless without her spells.

Peregrine touched her arm, tall and stone-faced at her side.

"Where's my coat?"

He shook his head. "I don't know. It was covered in blood the last time I saw it." He dug into a slim pocket cut into the chest piece of his elven leathers and Joy's heart leapt in her chest as he produced a long, tapering piece of amethyst with a rounded end and a jagged tip. A sob rushed out of her mouth, and she snatched her wand from him, holding it close to her chest.

"Thank you," she forced through her thick throat. "Thank you."

He nodded, watching her. Joy couldn't read his expression, but she was sure there was pity there, and the same worry from earlier. Gods—Gabi's *brother*? Joy shook her head, gripping her wand as her tears cleared. She didn't have time to think about it. "A witch should never be separated from their wand." Peregrine replied, a smile twitching his mouth. "My mum told me that once. My—my adoptive mum, I guess. Her best friend was a witch."

Well, Joy appreciated the woman—without her words she'd be wandless right now. And with it... Gabi's face flashed behind her eyelids as Joy blinked, looking the way she had when they'd stepped out of the lift. Determined to do the right thing, hellbent on protecting the town and Joy's coven, and scared deep down but not letting that stop her. Noble to the end.

Gabi had told Joy to run while she dove into the smoke to fight Perchta. *Not this time.* Joy wasn't running away and leaving Gabi to fight alone. Once was enough.

She locked eyes with Peregrine and said, "I can't leave her alone down there."

"I know." Peregrine smiled and Joy blinked, surprised. He began moving towards what Joy assumed was the staircase they'd ascended while she'd been unconscious. Her healed-over wounds pulled, and she winced but after she made the first step, the next steps came without much effort. "I was waiting for you to wake up and finish healing." He speared her with a look that reminded her she'd failed to do so. "And then I was going back down there to get my sister."

Joy nodded. His voice had changed into something determined and rough, and Joy could identify with it. They reached a door set in the wall that led to a staircase, a narrow window above letting a shaft of grey light into the area. Joy took a breath, leaning on the elbow Peregrine offered when she wobbled, and began to descend. They took each step in silence, the light fading until they were enclosed in flickering fluorescent light, until that heavy iron tang grew stronger, until it was all Joy could smell.

Because the silence and the fear were killing her, and because she couldn't get the imagined scene out of her head —Gabi torn apart, her stomach slit, her eyes empty—she whispered, "I don't have any spells prepared. I don't have crystals or sachets or potions or *anything*." Her voice broke but she ignored it. She had to keep it together for Gabi, alone down here with a killer. "I only have my wand and raw witchcraft is ... unpredictable. It would take too much from me." *Talking* was taking too much from her—she was winded after half a flight of stairs and a conversation.

What the raw witchcraft would do ... that was the trouble. She didn't *know* what it would do. It could be nothing, or it could turn her heart to glass, her hair to serpents, her soul to ash and glitter. It could erase something Joy desperately needed—her will, her sanity, her ability to consent. It could kill her.

"You shouldn't be here," Peregrine shot at her, sounding a lot like he was contemplating dragging her back up the stairs. Joy daren't look at him; she just bit her lip and kept descending the stairs, ignoring the pull in her tender belly, the burning in her thighs. "You're going to get hurt."

"And Gabi might already *be* hurt."

That was the end of that conversation. Gripping her wand in one hand and Peregrine's elbow in the other, Joy staggered down the last steps. The corridor before them was scattered with pieces of stone and floorboards and drops of blood, but no sachets or vials or her beloved crystals. Accepting the universe wasn't going to reunite her with her prepared spells, Joy gripped Peregrine's arm harder, more out of fear than pain, and they edged down the hallway. Her chest burned with each breath, but she ignored every response of her body to the fear angling through her like a sword. Ignored the fear itself. Gabi—she thought of only Gabi.

"Gods," Peregrine breathed, and Joy twisted to look at him, sucking in a panicked breath of iron and rust. "There are life signs, but they're faint. If Gabi's here, she's in a really bad way."

Joy stumbled forward, sheer desperation powering her now. Any trepidation she'd had vanished, her reservations scattered behind her. She would use raw magic, would allow her witchcraft to interpret her will with no potions or herbs or crystals as a guide. She would pay whatever price it asked of her.

"I can feel it with my magic," Peregrine explained, as if Joy had asked, as if she had room for questions. She breathed hard, narrowing all her energy and attention on physically manifesting her intent, centering her focus on her will and the crystal in her hand. Her arms locked, more braced for pain and impact than a response to the witchcraft heating her insides. She pushed her desire into her witchcraft and down her wand, whispered it, coaxed it, begged it. With relief, she felt it form and begin to rush out of her—and, gritting her teeth, her jaw grinding, she held it in place. *Not yet, not yet.*

"Find her, Peregrine" she said in a hard voice that was barely hers. "Use your magic. Find her." She was panting hard, sweat beading on her forehead. The world narrowed to the battle between her and her witchcraft. Water dripped from a burst pipe running along the floor, soaking into Joy's feet, but she ignored it. Warmth built inside her.

"Peregrine," Joy bit out but—he'd stopped dead and brought Joy to a halt too, his hand clamped around her arm. With so much effort her neck muscles flared and felt like they would snap, Joy looked at him, ground her teeth as she followed his line of sight to the open lift doors at the end of the hall, mere metres away.

The doors were mangled, as if claws and inhuman strength had torn them open, blood smeared in an elongated handprint. Something about the stain reminded her of a mouth full of fangs. And inside the lift... Gods, inside the witch held Gabi against the far wall, claws carving into her chest. Not the way she had attacked Joy earlier, not simply a stab wound in and out. She was holding Gabi there as her nails twisted and tore, not in a straight line like Freya, not throat to navel, but across her collarbone, through the ripped shirt, coat discarded, through flesh and sinew. Blood poured over the witch's hand and for a split second Joy just stared, unable to accept the maw of blood and gore Gabi's chest had become.

And then fire and fury and something Joy didn't have a name for—cold, and pure white, and stark—rushed through her veins. Joy ripped her arm from Peregrine, still frozen and gasping in horror, and she half ran, half stumbled to the lift. As soon as she was close enough to see the swaying strands of Perchta's hair, inhale the disgusting stench oozing from her, Joy ripped the leash off her witchcraft and howled her rage. The power that surged from her, ice cold and burning like holy fire, met her rage and thrived on it, fed it and fed from it until it had grown into something wholly other. Power given form, given feeling and true purpose.

A swell of violet sparks like a wave of water, a storm to kill, to shatter, to devour hit Perchta's back as she stooped over Gabi, her bone fingers dug deep into Gabi's bones. The witchcraft knew what to do and it froze the witch, not like the freezing spell earlier but a true paralysing, a theft of motion and movement and will.

Joy still screamed, a vessel only for fury, as she looked and looked at Gabi. Gabi was unconscious, pinned against the back of the lift by Perchta's clawed hands, pale from blood loss. Black hair had fallen from her ponytail, her shirt ripped, and buttons popped, and her coat puddled on the floor. She looked so unlike Gabi, the neatness and professional mask she prided herself on stolen from her.

Warm blood leaked down Joy's skin, the tentative healing undone, as she hobbled closer, closed the final step between her and the bitch who'd hurt the woman she loved. Here, Joy could see the fragile veins in Gabi's eyes, the flowing blood that began under her collarbone and poured from a vicious wound beneath. The healers had to be able to fix this. They had to.

Joy's voice broke and gave out, her scream dying. She grabbed the witch's hand and ripped it from Gabi's chest, instinctive protective rage crushing her hand around Perch-ta's fingers. The crunch and groan of bone shattering was satisfying as her witchcraft and her wand interpreted her will, breaking every damn bone in Perchta's hand until it hung limp, incapable of hurting anyone else. Gabi slid to the steel floor.

All at once the strength and fury fled Joy and left her gasping, fumbling for the wall of the lift to stay upright as her wounds made themselves known again.

Peregrine exhaled a curse behind her, edging around her slumped body, and Joy lifted her heavy head to apolo-gise, or ask for help, or beg him to get Gabi to the clinic, but his eyes were fixed on her hand, still clenched around Perchta's shattered one. It was blue. Fear skittered through her, rocking her stomach and clenching her throat, as she stared at her own hand. Her fingers, her palm, the back of her hand, all blue. Icy, pale, unnatural blue. Not glowing, not veins of colour, but flat and cold as if her skin colour itself had changed. As if her hand was made of chalcedony or sea glass.

Even in pain, as if guided by something apart from herself, instinct or a guiding presence, Joy lifted her hand and touched Perchta's throat, at the base of her neck. Her hand pulsed, once, a brighter flare of blue, deeper than the cool sky colour of her skin. Joy caught her breath, about to be sick as Perchta's rotted skin changed. Veins went deep blue-black all the way along Perchta's arms and neck, up to her face, and under her clothes, maybe along the rest of her body. Joy stumbled away, that guiding hand releasing her, and vomited.

"What the hell?" Peregrine touched her shoulder, but she recoiled. "Joy, what the hell?"

She just shook her head. She didn't know. She *didn't*

know. A sob wrecked her breathing. A terror so unlike anything she'd ever felt before pushed into every part of her, set her hands shaking, her legs quivering. She was suddenly, abruptly, sure that hurting Perchta had ruined something inside her, altered her forever. And worse, there was no darkening of the veins along her arms, no slowing of her blood flow. The undeniable, always-present signs of raw witchcraft. Without those dark veins ... what was this? Something Perchta had done or something within Joy herself? Every breath was shallower, her head beginning to swim, as she backed away.

Peregrine pushed into the lift and while Perchta was still immobilised, while Joy was staring, stunned and horrified, at the blue skin—of not just the hand that had crushed Perchta's but *both hands*—he scooped Gabi easily into his arms, her head hanging over his arm, hair trailing.

Joy couldn't move, couldn't breathe, as Peregrine carried Gabi—carried his sister—around the paralysed witch and into the tentative safety of the hallway beyond, as he set her down and came back for Joy.

"Joy," Peregrine's voice was gentle. Why? What she had done ... her hands ... what *was* she? Using raw witchcraft was one thing, documented and understood, but Joy had never heard of this. This was ... she was...

"Joy?"

She shook her head, kept shaking it, her hands trembling violently at her sides until her wand was a blur and she almost dropped it. The blood from her reopened stomach wounds had reached her legs, her knees. Was that why she felt weak, dizzy? Or was that ... whatever had been done to her? The blue fingers? She looked at them now and—they were lighter, more like her own porcelain tone, barely an icy hue. What was *happening* to her? Joy stared at her hands, feeling like they'd betrayed her.

Peregrine moved closer, squeezed her shoulder. "Not here. Keep it together until we're out of this place. Wait until—what the hell?"

Joy couldn't take anything else. Movement flashed in the corner of her eye and Joy panicked. Disregarding her injuries and her pain, she scrambled out of the lift. She collapsed a few steps away, breathing fast, her head turned to watch Gabi beside her. She was unconscious on the floor, breathing jaggedly. They needed to get her to Mrs. Stone, to the other healers, but Joy was shaking too hard, and once she'd squeezed her eyes shut, they wouldn't open.

The sounds that met Joy's ears didn't make sense. A woman crying huge, shuddering sobs. And then a familiar voice asking, "Where is it?" Joy locked her body against a shudder. That voice ... Katrina's voice ... Joy had no choice but to open her eyes.

Peregrine had positioned himself in front of her and Gabi, protecting them, but Perchta hadn't moved. She knelt in the open lift, her skin pink again, her hair white and sleek, not cobweb strands. No lethal needle teeth, no blood-streaked claws and elongated fingers, no painfully thin limbs. The tan suit, the blouse, the high blush and pretty features, all of them were back.

Joy stared, her mouth hanging open, as Perchta cried to herself, "Where's my power? Where is it?"

Joy couldn't deal with this. Gabi needed a healer; that was all that mattered. So she got to her feet with Peregrine's help and leaned on him as he once again pulled Gabi into his arms, following him up the staircase and leaving Perchta on her knees in the lift, weeping.

Joy's stomach poured more blood down her front and

her vision swam, dizziness claiming her entirely, but images were playing on a loop in her mind: Perchta's claws deep in Gabi's chest, the wound torn between her breasts, the blood seeping steadily to the ground. Joy gripped Peregrine with white fingers and dragged her legs up two floors, the world swimming, weakness batting her back with every step, her muscles fighting her the whole way. But they reached the ground floor and stumbled through the lobby and staggered between the stone pillars outside.

Joy couldn't believe what she saw through her swimming vision. Tears poured down her face. Healers and medicine were already waiting for them by Town Hall's wide steps, the whole effort organised by a red-faced, furious Paulina, who had not abandoned them but gone to get help. Joy took one look at Mrs. Stone marching right for them, looking as wrecked as Joy but determined and so, so worried. Mrs. Stone's arm settled across Joy's back and Joy sagged, relief and security catching her up in a firm embrace. The wild creature that had driven her to Gabi, to Perchta, now left Joy to face the world alone and she fainted.

Gabi had woken up hours after Perchta forced the sleeping draught down her throat with a massive headache screaming between her eyes and no idea where she was. It had taken a good few minutes to place the open, white room around her as being in the clinic, lights blaring above her and the whole place smelling of disinfectant. At the time she hadn't known how she'd got there, but she'd been told after that Peregrine had gone back for her. Joy had gone back for her. Her dad would have too if he hadn't fallen on the stairs while helping Gus get Victoriya out of Town Hall, his leg giving out. He now had a sprained ankle to go with the previous injury, and a bad mood that would probably take longer to heal despite the long hug Gabi and he had shared.

And Joy... While Gus, Maisie and her dad had gotten Victoriya to her mum, while Eilidh got Salma out, Joy had done something Peregrine had never seen before. That in itself was so rare Gabi had been speechless for minutes. Joy's hands had turned *blue*, from fingertips to the crease of her wrist, full on blue as if she'd been born that sky blue colour.

But when Gabi had crawled out of bed, disobeying orders from three nurses and one disgruntled Peregrine, Joy's hands had been their regular pale colour. She'd looked normal except for the bandages around her stomach and the bruises and cuts on the rest of her. Gabi herself had a scar so bad, so deep and messy that even the advanced healers couldn't erase it. Her arms and the rest of her had healed fine, though, so she tried to be grateful. Even though there was a part of her that had looked in the mirror every morning since and not recognised the body reflected back at her.

Now, five days after she'd gone into Town Hall to confront a murderous witch with a coven and two elves, Gabi sat at Joy's bedside—*her* bedside, technically, since Mrs. Stone had released Joy yesterday. Joy would recover better, process the many potions and healing tonics in her system better, in a more familiar environment. And since the Law House was closer to the clinic, meaning the nurses could make twice daily trips, Joy now slept here, where Gabi could watch over her. Not that she hadn't watched over her vigilantly at the clinic, refusing to be moved and driving the nurses mad when they weren't kept busy and frazzled by Joy's coven. They had come here with Gabi too, the witches, filling the Law House with worry and chatter.

Victoriya had recovered quickly once the full-strength sleeping tonic had worn off, the slice on her arm shallow enough to give the healers no trouble. Gabi could hear her downstairs even now, shouting at Gus and Maisie for something and nothing. The others, Salma, Eilidh ... all fine, to Gabi's immense relief.

"You need to eat something, Gabi."

Gabi lifted her head. Her dad leant against the doorway, an uncompromising look on his face. This was how the last few days had gone. First, he would casually remind her to eat, then he'd start nagging, and finally he'd come and march her into the kitchen where she'd shove down whatever food had been made. It wasn't that she didn't want to eat; she didn't want to leave Joy's side in case she woke up, still terrified. Or in case something happened. Something Gabi shied away from.

"Can't you just bring something up?" she asked on a sigh.

Her dad's footsteps sunk into the thick carpet, his eyes passing over Joy before they settled on Gabi. She wilted under that look, her heart aching so badly she clenched her jaw to keep her expression neutral, which he saw through, of course. He hooked an arm around her neck and drew her against him, hugging her tight, and for a moment Gabi let herself sag against him, let herself be surrounded by that comfort.

"She's going to wake up, Gabi. The healers said she'd be fine."

That wasn't exactly what they'd said. Joy was healed, scarred like Gabi in places but completely healed of her injuries. And unconscious. She'd been that way for five days now, since she'd ... done something to Perchta. Grabbed the witch's wrist with her blue hands and sucked something out of her. The healers said she was in perfect health, externally and internally, but whatever power she had wielded, it could take her body a long, long time to recover from that.

Gabi got to her feet, her knees cracking, but not to follow her dad towards food—to puff up Joy's pillows, tuck the covers tighter around her the way she liked, to smooth a wayward strand of pink hair back from her flushed cheeks. She was breathing steadily but her face was sweaty and red like she had a fever. What if she never woke up? What if she wasn't the same when she did?

"Food," Bo said, and Gabi couldn't argue as he wrapped a solid arm around her waist and steered her to the kitchen.

Eilidh shot to her feet at the sight of Gabi. "How is she?" Five demanding pairs of eyes met Gabi's. She sighed, her shoulders sagging.

"The same," she answered, and took a seat in front of a steaming bowl of Moroccan stew. Infused with herbs and Salma's own blend of spices, it afforded Gabi a glint of comfort, eased a bit of her stress and fear. A different sort of fear now—not urgent and pounding but buried deep and slowly festering like an infection. But the food and Salma's witchcraft helped slightly, and Gabi appreciated it. So, when Salma refilled her bowl when she was done and placed a steaming cup of clear, amber tea in front of her, Gabi finished both of them. She knew Salma was fussing, mothering her the way she did her coven, but it was nice. To have Salma, the rest of the coven, and her dad. In these quiet moments, Gabi felt like she could handle it. What might happen if Joy never woke up. What might happen if she did.

"Thanks," Gabi said, her voice a throaty scratch. She'd wrecked it by shouting at nurses and crying at Joy's bedside until, so hollowed out, she fell asleep. She'd lost track of the number of times she'd told Joy's unconscious body that she loved her, so much it was going to swallow her whole, so much her heart felt like it had been put through a paper shredder and hastily reformed from the scraps.

"Here." Salma pressed a warm thermos of yet more soothing tea into Gabi's hands, her own soft, brown hands folding around Gabi's, another layer of comfort. "For upstairs," she said, and squeezed Gabi's hands before letting go. The others were silent, or at least they would be until Gabi retreated back upstairs and Victoriya and Gus returned to arguing, their own way of dealing with Joy's condition.

The chair scraped as Gabi stood, her hand secured around the thermos, a part of her, the scrap of her that wasn't burdened by fear, touched at Salma's thoughtfulness. "I'll tell you if anything changes," she said, looking at each of them. Gus rumpled and red-eyed, Victoriya absent her usual makeup but scowling and spoiling for a fight, Eilidh stiff-backed by the counter, her whole body frozen as if she could fight off her emotions by staying still, Maisie pacing the floor, her coat ragged and absent its usual gloss, and Salma hovering by the kettle watching Gabi, wringing her hands. Gabi was suddenly so grateful they were here that her eyes stung with tears. Before they could fall, she turned and made herself walk away.

Upstairs, Gabi paused in the doorway to the living room area. The TV was on low, the Food Network as background noise but there was an air of quiet hanging over the room, the kind that pressed into her until it hurt. Peregrine sat on the couch, staring into space, his head bowed, and his broad shoulders hunched inward.

Gabi's gaze went instinctively to the door to her bedroom, the lump in the covers—Joy—just about visible, but instead she crossed the living room to sit on the windowsill, setting the flask of tea beside her as she folded herself up in the window seat. Peregrine was now studiously watching an amateur baker fold egg whites, pretending he hadn't been conscious of Gabi's every movement since she'd paused in the doorway.

Perchta had broken. After Gabi and the others had been taken from the building, Paulina had gathered her whole coven and they'd stormed Town Hall. Between the fifty witches, they'd expected to come out victorious in the fight, but there had *been* no fight. They found Perchta sobbing in the lift by the records room; she hadn't even tried to stop them when they wrenched her to her feet and dragged her upstairs.

She'd been sent to Liverpool, to witches who could better contain her, to cells that had been designed to hold things like her for centuries at a time. According to Gabi's dad, she kept crying about her magic being missing. Gone. Gabi didn't want to think of what—who—had done that. It was better to think about the past few days. *That* at least she could think of and not feel sick with worry.

Which brought them to the lanky, nervous man scrunched up on her couch, who would not be removed from the house for longer than a few minutes at a time. Who even though he had a whole army of brothers to look after, was stubbornly remaining to watch over Gabi.

Her brother.

Gabi had never had friends growing up. She hadn't needed them; she had Peregrine. He'd been the friend she loved most, the big cousin she idolised, and when they got a little older, that childish admiration had turned to solid friendship. And then, somehow, he'd become her best friend. When something went wrong, Gabi went to Peregrine. When her mum died, she ran to him for comfort. Only she wasn't the only one grieving. Not that she'd known, not that he'd deigned to tell her they were much closer related than she'd been told her whole life. She only found out when she'd finally brought herself to read the letter her mum had given her minutes before she died. The letter she hadn't opened until she was fourteen, eight years later, even though Peregrine had read his own letter the day her mum—*their* mum—had passed.

Now, Gabi gnashed her teeth, anger and frustration filling the hole inside her that had opened when she woke in the clinic. They needed to have this conversation, but Gabi would rather focus on the orderly row of terrace houses outside, the flashes of movement behind curtains and the rare kid racing way too fast down the steep road on a BMX.

Eight years. That's how long he'd known they were brother and sister, how long he'd lied to her, kept the most poisonous secret. The worst thing was she hadn't even found out from him in the end. That letter. About her mother's teenage pregnancy, about her father—Gabi's grandfather—pushing the baby onto her older sister, saying Clover was too young, too naïve, to raise a child. About how those siblings had grown up as cousins.

Why couldn't Gabi have read it when her mum gave it to her, and erased that pain all those years later? She could have accepted her brother, learned to think of him as a sibling, not a cousin. She could have gotten over it, and it might not have taken her ten years to speak to him again.

Instead, Gabi had waited too long, and when she'd read it … she ran to Peregrine's tent and exploded. And he hadn't denied it, not their relationship, not the eight years of lying and secrets, the complete and utter betrayal that ripped into Gabi's soul, barely healed after her mother's death, and obliterated what was left of it.

It still hurt. Ten years after she'd found out about his lies, the scope of the secret between them, it still hurt. Maybe more so now. She was capable of bigger pains and larger grudges now she was twenty four instead of fourteen. Then, she'd turned her back on Peregrine, not visiting him at the elven community, staying instead in her box room in the house her dad had moved into when living at her mother's tent had been too painful. She had never been gladder for the brick and mortar house.

A week after she left, Peregrine had sent the first letter. Full of apologies and a desperate plea to talk to him. Gabi had ripped it into pieces. She hadn't read any of the others, even though they came, four or five a year, even now. But she'd kept his number in her phone, and when her dad had texted her Peregrine's new numbers when he changed phones, Gabi had saved those too. She wouldn't let herself question that. He'd hurt her more than she'd ever imagined she could be hurt. Because he wasn't just her cousin but her brother.

Gabi blinked and realised she was crying. But this was better than thinking about Joy never waking up. In a scratchy voice she said, "You carried me out of that building?"

A heavy moment settled between them and then Peregrine said, "I couldn't leave you down there, could I?"

She shrugged. "You could have."

"Joy would have killed me."

Gabi laughed against her own wishes. The idea of Joy, sweet and kind and generally harmless, killing Peregrine, tall and clever and trained for years as an elven warrior, was laughable. Still, Gabi wouldn't have put it past her, not with someone she cared about in danger. She nodded.

"I'm sorry." His voice cracked and Gabi knew he wasn't apologising for anything that had happened in Town Hall. She wouldn't look at him, didn't dare. But his expression must be wretched if he sounded like that. She twisted her fingers together, her eyes on the street outside.

She took a breath and held it until she was steady enough to ask, "Why?"

He released a long breath. "At first? You were just a kid, and it felt weird. You didn't feel like my sister, not like any of my brothers ... so I thought it *couldn't* be true. And you were grieving. You didn't need anything else to deal with."

"And later?" Her eyes would not move from the street outside, her courage spent in the attack three days ago.

She heard the rustle of cotton as he shrugged. "You were my best friend. I thought if I told you, it'd push you away."

Gabi laughed bitterly.

"I know. I did that anyway by not telling you. I know that."

Gabi nodded, was silent for a while. Then she made herself say it, because it needed to be said and he deserved to hear it. "I'm sorry, too. Back there ... when I knew you were hurt, I thought you were dying. I thought you'd die thinking I hate you." She had to stop, to choke down the tears until she could get the rest out. "I don't. I don't think I ever did. I'm just... It *hurts*, Peregrine, that you lied to me for so long. It will always hurt. But I don't hate you, and I'm grateful for you coming with us into Town Hall, and what you did, getting me out and healing Joy. The nurses said you saved her life."

"My healing is shit," he said with a broken laugh. "I doubt I saved her."

Gabi shrugged, because his healing *had* always been shit. Elves specialised in environmental magic, manipulating their surroundings, but back when there'd been more of them—almost two hundred times their current numbers—there had been more kinds of magic, healing among them. Every few generations, a random magic popped up, like it must have done in Peregrine's dad, the old head healer. Gabi hunched over herself; she didn't want to think about that. All roads led back to her mum, who had kept this secret from Gabi and who Gabi wasn't sure she could forgive.

To drag herself from her darkening thoughts she said, "Thank you anyway," and dared to look at him. Relief beat at her when she found his eyes not on her but on the door to her bedroom.

She jolted when his eyes shot to hers and he said, "Joy's awake."

Peregrine's awareness of his environment had always been clearer and stronger than hers; she didn't bother asking if he was sure. She stumbled to her feet, raced across the living room to her bedroom door, and all her breath escaped in relief when Joy croaked, "Gabi?"

Gabi pushed inside, tense and shivery with nerves, but Joy was squinting at the plain blue lamp shade above her; it matched the plain blueness of the rest of the room. Her hair, bubble-gum pink, and the delicate pastels of the crystal ring around her were the only bursts of colour in the room.

Joy said, "I thought you'd have redecorated," and Gabi startled when a laugh tore out of her, a sob trapped inside the sound. Her throat squashed with emotion, her eyes filling with tears. Joy—she was still Joy. She looked the same, sounded the same, wore the same downward quirk of a smile.

Gabi crossed the room in long strides, lowered herself to the bed, and drew Joy into a hug that was probably too tight considering she'd been healing for days. Joy leaned her head on Gabi's shoulder and sighed. And Gabi felt like she had downstairs, with Salma fussing. Everything would be okay

—now Joy was awake, Gabi could handle whatever was thrown at her next.

As long as the future didn't contain gruesome murders, psychotic witches, a whole town turned against them, and invincible evil … everything would be okay.

THANK you for starting a new series with me! Joy's story continues in Coven of Shadows, which will be out soon.